THE DARE ISLAND NOVELS

"If you have not yet visited Virginia Kantra's Dare Island, I enthusiastically encourage you to do so." —The Romance Dish

"A wonderful love story." —Fiction Vixen

"I love this series, and if you're looking for solid romance with a generous helping of steam, Dare Island is a great place to get lost." —The Bookish Babes

"Contemporary romance as warm and gratifying as a perfect day at the beach." —*Kirkus Reviews*

"Filled with tender moments and sexy, sparkling exchanges." —*BookPage*

"Positively sizzles with sexual tension and hums with the rhythm of life . . . I loved it."
—Mariah Stewart, *New York Times* bestselling author of *At the River's Edge*

"Will enthrall the reader and offer lots of satisfaction." —The Romance Reader

"Returning to Dare Island is always a pleasure." —*RT Book Reviews* (4 stars)

"A story as fresh as the Carolina ocean breezes . . . It's always a joy to read Virginia Kantra."
—JoAnn Ross, *New York Times* bestselling author of *You Again*

"Contemporary romance at its most gratifying." —*USA Today*

"Reading this book is like relaxing in a Hatteras hammock, gently swaying . . . Read)

"A fanta . . . Corner

"A sizzl . . . *Weekly*

Carolina Dreaming

VIRGINIA KANTRA

BERKLEY SENSATION, NEW YORK

BERKLEY
SENSATION

An imprint of Penguin Random House LLC
375 Hudson Street, New York, New York 10014

CAROLINA DREAMING

A Berkley Sensation Book / published by arrangement with the author

ISBN: 978-0-425-26970-1

PUBLISHING HISTORY
Berkley Sensation mass-market edition / February 2016

PRINTED IN THE UNITED STATES OF AMERICA

10 9 8 7 6 5 4 3 2 1

Cover art by Tony Mauro.
Cover design by Rita Frangie.

Penguin
Random
House

To Michael

ACKNOWLEDGMENTS

I'm so grateful for the community that surrounds, supports, and loves me—like my own personal Dare Island.

Thanks to Cindy Hwang and the team at Berkley; to Robin Rue and Beth Miller at Writers House; and to artist Tony Mauro and cover designer Rita Frangie for all their good work.

Special thanks to Christian Clinch, Virginia Grisez, and Nancy Northcott for their expert knowledge and patience with my questions; to Laura Florand, Carolyn Martin, and Michael Ritchey for their thoughtful critiques; and to you, my wonderful readers, for returning with me to Dare Island. I hope you enjoy the journey!

One

GABE SHIFTED HIS sea bag on his shoulder, adjusting its weight against the March wind cutting off the ocean. He didn't mind a little wind. Where he'd been, there were no seasons and no privacy, only the stink of metal grease, piss, and violence like the inside of a ship.

Lying in his rack at night, he used to dream of spring. Spring and women and the sea.

When he got out, winter had still lingered in North Dakota in the dirty piles of snow, in the biting cold. But here, the Carolina sun was warm against his face. The long bridge ahead arched like a gull's wing, skimming between sea and sky.

His heart lifted. It had been eleven years since he first crossed this bridge from the marshy inlet over the flashing waters of the sound. Behind him, the highway was littered with fast food chains and beach shops, gas stations and marinas, but this view hadn't changed.

Home is the place where, when you have to go there, they have to take you in.

He'd read that somewhere, Afghanistan, maybe, or jail. His teachers used to complain he wasn't much of a reader, but that line had stuck with him. Maybe because he'd never had a home. There wasn't anybody who felt they had to take him in, no place he belonged.

Except the Marines.

He'd screwed that up. He had screwed up a lot of things.

But one lesson of the Corps stuck with him. When things didn't go as planned, you could either shut down or you could improvise. Adapt. Overcome.

Gabe figured he'd been knocked down as low as he could go. All he needed was a chance to get on his feet again.

A tall white bird stood motionless in the reeds of a sandbar. The water shimmered to the horizon, reflecting back a wide blue sky painted with clouds.

Gabe breathed deep, smelling salt. *Freedom.*

A pickup rumbled by in a rush of grit and exhaust. He turned his face away, pressing closer to the guard rail. Somehow he'd missed the entrance to the walkway bordering the bridge, so he was trapped trudging the traffic lane with no hope for a lift. He guessed not many happy families headed to the beach in March. Not that happy family groups would be picking up hitchhikers anyway.

He smiled wryly. Especially not hitchhikers who looked like him.

Sunburn had replaced his months-old pallor, but he needed a shave and a better wash than he could manage at the sink of some truck stop restroom. He had zigged and zagged eighteen hundred miles cross-country from the North Dakota oil fields to the North Carolina coast in a jagged dotted line that left him hungry and footsore.

When the job went wrong, you went back to the beginning. Like that Inigo guy in Luke's favorite movie, *The Princess Bride*. Gabe and Luke had been boots together. That was Gabe's beginning. Luke would understand.

The bridge crested and rolled smoothly down to the inlet's northern side, a network of sandbars and saltwater channels protected by a man-made wall of rock. Gabe's eye traveled from the beds of rusty pine straw to the municipal sign by the side of the road, its blue and gold lettering standing out boldly against the weathered wood. WELCOME TO DARE ISLAND.

A black-and-white patrol vehicle parked in the shade of the pines.

Gabe's stomach tensed. Nothing to do with him, he told himself. He wasn't breaking any laws, wasn't doing anything wrong. But that didn't stop the sick acceleration of his heart.

A car rattled past on its way to somewhere else.

Gabe tramped along the sandy verge, eyes straight ahead, never glancing at the patrol vehicle's darkened windshield. He wasn't looking for trouble.

As he drew level with the hood, the door swung open. An officer got out, a rangy, rumpled man in his fifties who looked like every Southern lawman in every chain gang movie ever made: graying hair, mirrored glasses, face grooved like a tractor tire.

Gabe stopped, one hand clenching the strap of his duffle. *Is there a problem, officer?*

But he kept his mouth shut. He already knew the officer's answer. *He* was the problem. He'd heard the words on park benches and in public libraries, on street corners and in cafés. *Move along. Your kind's not welcome here.*

He stood and waited, his chest tight.

Southern Lawman jerked his chin toward the posted regulations. "No pedestrians on the bridge."

Gabe could have explained that by the time he figured out he'd missed the only ramp for the pedestrian walkway, he'd been a half mile across the bridge. Instead, since he had shit for brains, he said, "You don't look like a crossing guard."

The officer's expression never changed. "You don't look like an idiot. Why don't you save us both some trouble and turn around now?"

"Can't. Sorry," Gabe said with almost genuine regret. "I'm here to see somebody."

"Is that right." The officer's flat tone made the question into a statement of disbelief.

Gabe nodded, trying to keep his own tone easy despite the tension balling his gut. "Luke Fletcher. We served together." The officer's face could have been carved from stone. But something in his very stillness prompted Gabe to add, "You know him? His folks used to run an inn around here."

Still did, he hoped. He'd been to their place only once, when Luke had dragged him along after their graduation from boot camp. Gabe had never known a family like the Fletchers. Their easy welcome, their wholehearted acceptance of their son's friend, had sucked him in and left him floundering like a swimmer in unfamiliar waters.

For years after that, Mrs. Fletcher had sent Gabe care packages, to Iraq, to Afghanistan. The memory of her kindness made his throat constrict.

Over time, they'd lost touch. Just as well. He didn't like to think of Luke's mom addressing packages care of the Williams County sheriff's department.

The officer pulled a notebook from his pocket. "Name?"

The knot in Gabe's gut tightened. "You charging me?"

"I'm *asking* you. What's your name?"

"Gabe Murphy."

"Where you from, *Mr.* Murphy?" The slight emphasis was worse than a sneer.

The Williams County Jail. "All over," Gabe said evenly. "ID?"

Don't run. Don't lie. Don't make sudden moves. "In my pocket."

The officer nodded, giving him permission to reach for it. H. CLARK read the dull metal name tag below his badge.

Gabe handed over his commercial driver's license. Still valid.

Officer Clark studied it. Studied him. "Be right back," he said, and disappeared into the marked car.

Gabe fixed a bored, I-don't-give-a-shit look on his face, an expression he had perfected by the age of ten. Being called on the carpet was pretty much the same whether you were being harangued by the school principal, some snot-nosed officer, or a jail guard.

Through the windshield, he could see the officer focused on his dashboard—tapping into a laptop, maybe. Gabe waited, sweat collecting in the small of his back, as the cop reached for his radio.

Not guilty. There was no reason for the cops to detain him.

Unless H. Clark was just looking to ruin somebody's day. Which in Gabe's experience, with Gabe's luck, happened all too often.

Returning, the officer handed Gabe his license. No comment. Gabe relaxed a fraction, tucking the card into his wallet.

"Get in back," Clark said.

Shit.

Gabe knew better than to argue. But the word escaped him anyway. "Why?"

"You want to see Luke Fletcher. I can take you to him."

Gabe stuck his thumbs into his belt loops, not moving. *Why?* It was for damn sure the cop hadn't offered out of the goodness of his heart.

Clark scowled. "I don't want you bothering the Fletchers. You got business with Luke, you deal with him."

That made sense. Gabe trusted the man's suspicion more than any kindness. Warily, he climbed into the back of the cop car, stowing his seabag on the seat beside him.

When, ten minutes later, the cop pulled to a stop in front of the squat brick police station, Gabe didn't feel betrayed as much as resigned. An asshole on a power trip didn't give a shit whether you'd actually done whatever it was that was going to earn you a beating. Or detention. Or nine months in jail.

"I thought you were taking me to see Luke Fletcher."

"Yep."

"He in lockup?" Gabe asked, only half joking.

"Worse than that." Clark met his gaze in the rearview mirror. "He's a cop."

Wait. What?

Luke had always been one of the Good Guys, but they'd raised a lot of hell together over the years. Gabe had trouble picturing his old buddy as a police officer.

He slid out of the vehicle, hauled out his duffle. His prison guard look-alike waved him ahead through the station house doors.

And there was Luke, in the flesh, in uniform, and Gabe didn't have to picture anything at all.

"Gabe." Grinning, the tall, blond former Staff Sergeant grabbed Gabe around the neck with one arm. Pounded his back with the other.

Gabe returned his hug. "Luke. You look . . ." *Good*, he decided. The uniform, the life, must suit him. "Very respectable," he said.

"You look like shit," Luke responded frankly. "What brings you to Dare Island?"

Gabe eased back, just a little. "Long story."

"Yeah, I heard some of it," Luke said.

The radio call, Gabe thought. He cleared his throat, aware of Clark and some lady behind a desk listening in. "When did you leave the Corps?"

Luke's blue eyes narrowed at the change of subject, but he answered readily enough. "Eight months ago. I'm married now. With a little girl."

"Congrats, bro. That's . . ." Weird. Luke, a cop. Luke, a dad. "That's great. I didn't know you had a baby."

"Neither did I."

Gabe frowned. "How old is she?"

"Almost twelve."

"No shit." There had been a high school girlfriend, Gabe remembered. Luke had talked about her some, back in their boot camp days. She'd dumped Luke's ass when he joined up, but obviously things had changed. "So you and . . ." *What was her name? Debbie?* "Diane got married?"

"Dawn." Luke shook his head. "Long story. I'll fill you in over coffee, and you can tell me what you're doing here."

The middle-aged woman behind the desk—dark hair, dark eyes, bright coral lipstick—swiveled in her chair. "We have a call. An animal complaint on Shoreline Drive. Sounds like the Crowleys' dog got loose again."

Luke nodded. "I'll take care of it on my way back."

"You going to Jane's?" Clark asked.

"That's the plan," Luke said easily. "I'll tell her you said hi."

"Why? I'll see her myself tonight. But you . . ." His fierce gray gaze speared Gabe. "You stay away from her."

"Maybe I would if I knew who you were talking about."

"Jane," Clark said. "My daughter."

JANE CLARK READ over the builder's proposal for the expanded enclosed patio at Jane's Sweet Tea House, trying not to think of all the things that could go wrong.

"We don't have to do this now," said Sam Grady, the builder. "We can schedule the work for the fall, when times aren't so lean."

He meant to be kind.

But Jane shook her head. "I was hoping to get the work done before the tourist season starts. There's a new coffee shop opening up right on the harbor, did you hear? I can't afford to lose half my summer business to the competition."

"Yeah, I heard." His gaze met hers. "It's a Grady property."

The Grady family owned, managed, or developed half the island, including Jane's bakery. But the news still tripped her up, a short, sharp pain, like jamming her toe on the wheeled bakery rack. "Oh."

"You don't have anything to worry about." Sam flashed her the Grady grin, white teeth and charm. "It's a coffee shop, not a bakery. Beverages, smoothies, maybe ice cream. Nothing like what you can offer here."

"You don't know that," Jane said.

"Actually, I've seen the business plan."

"When? How?"

Another quick, apologetic glance. "My company's doing the upfit on the building."

Jane sucked in her breath. O-kay. Sam had a business to run, a payroll to meet. She didn't expect him to turn down work on her account. But . . . he was her landlord. Engaged to marry her friend. His taking a job with her competition felt oddly like betrayal.

"Who signed the lease?"

"Ashley Ingram," Sam answered promptly. "Her parents cosigned."

"Ashley?" Another mental stumble. "Blond, sort of curly hair, twenty-ish?"

"Yeah. Have you met?"

Jane twisted her braid around her finger tightly enough to turn the tip of her finger blue. "I may have seen her around."

A blond, curly-haired twentysomething named Ashley had been sitting with her laptop in Jane's place for the better part of a week. Jane had figured the girl was just another customer taking advantage of the bakery's free Wi-Fi. But she could have been taking notes. On Jane's menu, on her hours, on her prices . . .

Swallowing, Jane looked again at the estimate. If her decrepit delivery van lasted another season . . . If the dishwasher didn't break . . . As long as seven-year-old Aidan didn't require anything outrageous like stitches or new shoes or regular appointments with a counselor . . .

She could afford to do this. She couldn't afford *not* to.

"How soon can you start?"

"I'll have to work you in. We were already slammed before the last storm hit, and now between repairs and this upfit . . ." Sam looked at her face and stopped. "Fortunately, it's not a big job. A small crew could knock it out in a week. Two, tops, depending on the weather. As long as you don't mind being flexible about the schedule, I can be flexible about costs."

"Thanks, Sam. But you're already giving me a break on the quote. I don't need charity."

"It's not charity. Let me work it out with the rental side. We can fix it so you're paying on an installment plan. Add a little to the rent every month."

The rush of relief left her almost light-headed. "That would be great. Here." She thrust a pink-and-white bakery box at him.

His brows rose in surprise. "What's this?"

"Cupcakes. To say thank you."

"You didn't need to do that."

She smiled, secure again. "Think of it as the first install-ment. Cappuccino cream for Meg and brown butter banana rum for you."

"Can't say no to that. Thanks, Jane."

She followed him to the bakery door, watching as he strolled down the steps and away, hard-working, handsome, successful Sam Grady. A genuinely nice guy, six years ahead of her in school and forever out of reach.

Not her type, she would have said back then, when she was young and stupid and her type meant pretty much any guy her father disapproved of who showed her a little attention.

As Sam reached the end of the walk, a police car pulled up behind his truck. Sam stopped as the driver's side door opened and Luke Fletcher got out. The two men greeted each other.

They made quite a picture, Jane admitted—Sam, lean and elegant, with his unruly dark hair and killer smile, Luke, blond and broad-shouldered in his police uniform.

Not that she was looking. Much. Luke was recently mar-ried to a lawyer from Beaufort. Jane had designed their wedding cake. Sam was engaged to Luke's sister, Meg. Even if Jane had had time for romance, she didn't poach.

Still, she wasn't immune to a little flutter of female appre-ciation.

But it was the third man, getting out of the back of the police vehicle, who made her catch her breath.

Travis.

Her heart squeezed and then stopped.

She forced herself to breathe. Not Travis. Her ex wouldn't be out of prison for at least another month.

But the resemblance was strong enough to make her palms grow damp. Long, rangy build, torn jeans, sun-streaked hair hanging around a stubbled face. Both the hair and his shirt needed washing.

Luke introduced the stranger to Sam. She studied him through the glass door as the three men stood talking, noting subtle differences. The stranger was taller than Travis, or maybe he simply stood straighter. His skin was sunburned, his eyes darker.

But he was definitely the same type. Her type.

Jane shivered deep inside.

Her type left bruises.

Two

THE AIR WAS thick with warmth and the smells of baking, cinnamon and vanilla, wrapping Gabe in a blanket of comfort. He curled his hands around his coffee mug, forcing himself not to snatch the other half of his All Berry Muffin and wolf it down like a starving dog with a steak.

You didn't get muffins like that in jail.

His gaze slipped to the blonde behind the counter, with the big gray eyes and gawk-worthy rack and skin like cream. There were a lot of things he didn't get in jail.

He took a sip of coffee, searing his tongue. *The blonde is not on the menu, dickhead.* He had enough on his plate without getting involved with some redneck lawman's pretty daughter.

". . . surprised you got out," Luke was saying on the other side of the table. "I always figured you'd do twenty years in the Corps."

So had Gabe. After the clusterfuck of his childhood, being a Marine was all he'd ever wanted. All he had.

"The Corps had other ideas," he said. Another bitter swallow.

"You're a good Marine," Luke said.

"A good combat Marine. I sucked at taking orders, and you know it. You cleaned up my shit often enough. No way they were keeping me around in this drawdown."

"What have you been doing?"

"Nine months in county jail," Gabe said, straight-faced.

Luke's eyes narrowed. "Before that."

"Driving rigs for a fracking operation in North Dakota."

"Decent job."

"Good money," Gabe said. That's what had drawn him in the first place. After six tours in the sandbox, he was used to cold winters and rough conditions, the constant company of men, the heavy drinking, the threat of violence that hung over the housing camps like the gray, overcast sky.

"Work dry up?" Luke asked.

Gabe shook his head. He could have gotten his old job back. Or one like it. A man who couldn't find work anywhere else could always get a job in the fracking fields, in the boom-towns fueled by testosterone and the promise of easy money. Half the assholes he worked with had done time.

But the other oil workers didn't trust him anymore. The locals didn't want him. He was tired of simply existing, sick of the life he had led since leaving the Corps. Scared of the man he might become if he stayed.

He looked down at his scarred hands, his thick wrists sticking from the frayed cuffs of his fatigue jacket.

His father's hands.

The thought made him cold inside.

It didn't matter where he'd been, Gabe reminded himself. He had to focus on where he was going. Even if he had to crawl to get there.

"So, what brings you here?" Luke asked.

When the job goes wrong, go back to the beginning.

Gabe shrugged. "Needed a change, I guess."

"There aren't a lot of jobs around," Luke said frankly.

"Dare Island's no boomtown, especially in the off-season. But you can stay with us until you find your feet."

"Thanks, pal." Gabe swallowed regret. "But I don't think so."

"Why not?"

Wasn't it obvious?

He glanced again at the blonde behind the counter. Luke had introduced them when they walked in. Jane Clark, the deputy's daughter, the one Gabe was supposed to stay away from. The pretty baker had stared at him as if she'd seen a ghost, her eyes wide in her smooth-as-milk face.

Her daddy must have called ahead to warn her.

Gabe had practice not caring about other people's opinions. His parents, his teachers, even a couple of his commanding officers had written him off a long time ago. So he didn't give a crap about some Southern lawman's opinion. He didn't even care so much about the blonde. But her reaction reminded him that there were plenty of people who would be equally suspicious of a down-on-his-luck drifter, who would be only too eager to send him on his way.

Not Luke. But . . . Gabe surveyed his former brother-in-arms, the sharp new uniform, the shiny gold ring on his finger.

"You have a wife now," Gabe said. "And a twelve-year-old daughter."

"Taylor." Luke grinned. "You worried she's going to braid your hair while you're sleeping?"

Gabe didn't smile back. "It's not your kid I'm worried about. How's your wife going to feel about you giving couch space to a transient with a record?"

Gabe almost missed it, that barely perceptible hesitation Luke covered with another smile. They'd played poker together for too damn many years. He knew all Luke's tells. You couldn't throw that kind of history away. They shared a past.

But not a future. Luke had a good thing going here. Gabe wasn't screwing that up for him.

"Kate's fair," Luke said. "She won't judge without all the facts."

"You said in the car she's a lawyer."

Luke nodded with obvious pride. "Family lawyer. That's how we met. She contacted me in Afghanistan when Dawn died and left me guardianship of Taylor."

"So she does wills and stuff."

"Wills, custody agreements, restraining orders. Kate does a lot of work with abuse victims."

A lawyer and a cop. With a kid.

Gabe grunted, turning his mug around in his hands, trying for once to think before he spoke. "No matter how fair-minded she is, I don't see a woman whose job is protecting women and children welcoming a killer under her roof."

"She's married to a Marine," Luke said quietly.

Gabe looked up. Their gazes locked.

There were things they had seen and done in Afghanistan that they didn't talk about. That didn't mean they didn't think about them. Dream about them.

Luke had joined the Marines to follow in his father's footsteps, to be the man his father was. Gabe had joined up to get as far away from his father and his father's example as the Corps would take him. But in Afghanistan, the reasons didn't matter. They fought for the same cause. Not to save the world, but to save their lives and the lives of the guys serving next to them. *Kill or die.*

"That's different," Gabe said. "That was war."

Luke lifted an eyebrow. "Justified killing."

"Yeah."

"Isn't that what the jury decided in your case? You were acquitted. I saw the verdict. Not guilty on all counts."

"That doesn't change what happened. A man died. I killed him."

"Is that what you told the arresting officers?"

Gabe's jaw set. "I screw up, I take responsibility."

"Jesus, Gabe," Luke said with exasperated affection. "I

swear, if somebody wanted to beat you, you'd hand them the stick."

Gabe shrugged. He never had been any damn good at groveling to authority.

"So, what happened?" Luke asked.

"He swung first."

Luke nodded, satisfied. "Self-defense."

Gabe took a swig of coffee. "Something like that." Self-defense, defense of others—his lawyer had explained that they were the same.

If Gabe had been a local boy, particularly with his service record, the case against him might never have been filed. But the tiny North Dakota town where he had been charged was reeling under an influx of oil workers and crime. The district attorney was up for reelection and determined to make a name for himself. Hell-bent on making an example out of somebody. He had even turned Gabe's military service against him, invoking the civilians' fear of PTSD.

Gabe was a flight risk, the DA had argued. A transient. A troublemaker. And because of that, Gabe had been locked up awaiting trial through continuance after continuance.

"Then we're good," Luke said.

Gabe shook his head. "Best if I'm on my own right now," he said stubbornly.

"Best for who, pal?"

For you, idiot, Gabe thought. He clamped his mouth shut.

"Fine." Luke exhaled. "There's a fishermen's motel down by the pier. Nothing fancy, but they ought to have a vacancy this time of year."

Gabe didn't care about fancy. Even before he'd been extended the hospitality of the Williams County Jail, he and Luke had slept on rocks and under tanks and side by side in a crowded hooch where you had to layer on every stitch you owned to keep from freezing in your cot at night. When he was working the oil fields, he had stayed in a "man camp," where they bunked dormitory style, six to a trailer. Gabe would have been grateful for anyplace that had hot water and a mattress. But paying for a lawyer from one county over had taken almost every cent he had. He didn't have money to waste on a motel room until he got a job.

"I'll think about it," he said.

"If you need me to spot you a couple nights, just until you find something . . ."

Gabe's jaw set. "I'm good."

Luke frowned. "I'm on duty tonight. If you just need a place to crash, the holding cells are usually empty."

God, he was tempted. But he'd be damned before he'd sleep behind bars again.

Especially with his old buddy on the other side. They were brothers, but no longer equals. The realization chafed.

"More coffee?" The owner, Jane, stood by their table, bringing with her a pot of coffee and the scent of cinnamon.

Gabe nodded. "Thanks."

She avoided his eye as she refilled his cup. He wondered how much she'd overheard.

Luke's radio crackled. "Dare Island to Fletcher," said a woman's voice. "Please respond."

Luke touched the mic clipped to his shirt. "Fletcher."

"Luke, we have a 10-50 with injuries, possible fatality, at the corner of Beacon and Long. Chief's on his way. Fire department on scene."

Luke was already standing, reaching for his pocket. "On route. Code 3. I've gotta go," he said to Gabe. "Accident by the bridge."

"I can help." He had trained as a combat lifesaver. In a firefight, he could handle anything from a blocked airway to an open chest wound.

Luke shook his head. "EMTs already on the scene." He hesitated a moment. "You okay here?"

"My seabag's in your car."

"Right." Luke dropped some bills on the table. "Let's go."

They moved with purpose toward the door. The buzz of adrenaline, the relief of action . . . It was like old times again, grabbing their gear, saddling up for a mission, riding to the rescue. *Game on.*

Except there was nothing, this time, that Gabe could do to help.

Luke tossed Gabe his bag. "Dinner tomorrow. My place."

"Yeah, yeah, go."

The door of the patrol car slammed. The siren wailed to life. Luke pulled out, tires crunching, blue lights flashing.

Gabe stood alone in the parking lot, his heart rate slowly dropping, watching those lights disappear in the distance, leaving him behind.

Not like old times.

Suck it up, buttercup.

He shouldered his bag and trudged inside.

Jane Clark was leaning over, wiping down their vacated table, her thick blond braid falling over her shoulder like some princess in a fairy tale. Or the Swiss Miss on a cocoa package, something tasty and wholesome. His stomach rumbled. He saw, with regret, that his half muffin was already cleared away.

She looked up at his entrance, her shoulders instinctively rounding, protecting her chest, like a woman who had learned to fend off the wrong kind of attention from the wrong sort of guy.

Not another soul in the place. No wonder she was wary.

He stopped by the door, giving her a moment to recover.

She straightened, wiping her hands on her big white kitchen apron. "Did you need something?"

He needed a lot of things—a meal, a shower, a bed. But his dwindling roll of bills had to last until he found a job. His gaze dropped to the Wonder Rack before he fixed his eyes firmly on her face.

There was a time he could have talked any woman into taking him home for an hour or the night. But her body language made it clear she wasn't that kind of woman. Or maybe he was trying hard not to be that guy anymore.

He cleared his throat. "How late are you open?"

"Until four. It's the off-season," she added, as if the early hours required an explanation.

It was almost four now. The public restrooms would be locked until May, the local businesses shuttered by five. "Mind if I use your restroom before you close?"

"Go right ahead."

He washed in the sink and then did his best to mop the floor with paper towels.

When he came out of the restroom, Jane was behind the counter. She saw him and closed the cash drawer of the antique register. *Ping.*

"I was arrested for murder," he drawled. "Not robbery."

Her face flushed.

He was such a dickhead. Nice to know he was still proving the old man right: *Open mouth, make trouble.* And his teachers: *You'll never learn.*

He waited for her to call her dad on him, but she just gave him a long, dry look. "Is that supposed to be funny? Or reassuring?"

He found himself grinning. "Maybe both?"

"Maybe your delivery needs work," she suggested.

His grin broadened. "Yes, ma'am."

She looked away, but not before he saw a smile tug the corners of her mouth.

She followed him to the door. The trees outside obscured the view from the street. The gravel parking lot was empty.

Gabe frowned. Dare Island was a long way from the roughneck boomtowns of North Dakota. But she was here all alone, with Luke and the entire police force tied up at some accident by the bridge.

He turned. She stood very close. Not touching, but he was aware of how soft she was, how round and plump and female. Vulnerable. "Make sure you lock up behind me."

She gave him an odd look. Because, yeah, from her perspective, the biggest threat on this quiet island was him.

She didn't say anything, though, just handed him a white bakery bag.

"What's this?"

"Coffee and a sandwich. Be careful it doesn't spill. I put the coffee in a thermos cup, but, well . . ." She shrugged. "You never know."

You never did. He'd certainly never expected this. He had figured she would rush him on his way, not make him a sandwich.

"Let me pay you." He might not want to throw money away on a motel room, but he had enough cash and pride left to pay for a damn sandwich.

"Luke already did."

Gabe remembered the bills Luke had left on the table. "That was your tip."

Her flush deepened. She had the prettiest skin, fine-pored and smooth, the color surging below the surface. "Owners don't accept tips."

He wouldn't know. Almost every damn thing he possessed fit into his seabag.

He searched for a way to keep the conversation going. Not hitting on her, just . . . not leaving yet. "This is your place?"

"Yes." Not encouraging.

"It's nice." *Nice. Jesus. Way to dazzle her with compliments, dude.* He looked around at the hand-painted tables and mismatched chairs, seeking another word. "Cozy."

"Thanks." One syllable.

He tried again, remembering what Luke had said about the island in the off-season. "Must be tough this time of year. You ever think about moving?"

"No. My family's here."

Four whole words. Jackpot. Gabe looked at her left hand, but he didn't see a wedding band. So the family she was talking about must be the hard-ass who drove him to the station. Officer H. Clark. Her father.

You stay away from her.

There was a time when Gabe would have taken those words as a challenge. Never mind that she was the prettiest thing he'd seen in a long time, that her skin was like milk and her eyes were like fog and she smelled like freshly baked cookies. He would have made a play for her just to piss off her old man.

She stood there, holding out the paper sack, watching him with a pleat between her eyebrows.

He was an asshole.

She deserved better.

Besides, Clark wasn't simply Jane's father. He worked with Luke. And Gabe was not fucking things up for his buddy on or off the job.

He clenched his teeth, locking in all the things he shouldn't say, and took the bag. "Thanks for the coffee."

JANE THUMPED HER forehead on the inside of the door as if she could knock some sense into it.

DON'T FEED THE STRAYS.

The warning was tacked up outside every restaurant and in half the tourist shops on the island.

It only encourages them, Jane's old boss, the chef at the Brunswick, had explained the first time he caught her slipping scraps out the back door to the kittens playing just beyond the reach of the lights.

You're supporting the feral population, scolded Carol Oates, who ran the island's trap-neuter-return program.

In her head, Jane knew they were right. So she let Carol set humane traps in the bushes behind the bakery. She placed her pans full of cat food away from the kitchen door, on the other side of the carport. She took precautions.

But how could she let them go hungry when it was in her power to feed them?

Or Gabe, either.

She walked through the empty bakery by the soft glow of the display cases.

When he stood straight-shouldered in her shop, so

stubbornly refusing to give in to the battering the world was giving him, and looked around her shop with that light of appreciation in his eyes, with that *hunger* . . .

Well, how could she turn him away unsatisfied?

Feeding people was what she did. Who she was. That didn't mean she had to be stupid about it.

She armed the bakery's security alarm, dimmed the shop lights, and shut the back door.

Make sure you lock up behind me. The memory of Gabe's deep-timbred voice whispered over her skin.

She didn't need his warning. She'd had the security system installed six months ago, after her ex showed up again and vandalized the bakery's HVAC unit. Not that the setup had prevented Travis from making threats. Demanding money. Walking through her bakery door as if he owned the place and assaulting one of her employees.

Her hand tightened on her keys.

All the safety precautions in the world couldn't make up for her stupidity in taking up with Travis in the first place.

But she was no longer that naïve girl, desperate for love and flattered by attention from a dangerous stranger.

Jane crunched over the oyster-shell drive to her car. She had learned from her mistakes. She lived with the consequences every day. And if she ever forgot, her father was there to remind her. Gabe Murphy, with his sun-streaked hair and strong, muscled arms, was a mistake she simply couldn't allow herself to make.

She drove down Main and along School House Road, past shingled houses huddled under the trees, a playground, one ball field, two graveyards. The moss-covered tombstones had the same names as the rural mailboxes by the side of the road: Doyle. Fletcher. Nelson. Clark.

Home.

Jane pulled into the driveway of a faded blue two-story bungalow, careful not to block her father's patrol car.

"Hey, Daddy," she called as she came into the kitchen

carrying a bakery bag of essentials, milk and fresh snicker-doodles. The cookies were a bribe, a thanks, a guilt offering. "Aidan? I'm home."

No reply. But she could hear the television from the other room, Hank watching ESPN, the way he had every night as far back as she could remember. When Jane was a little girl, nine or eleven, even thirteen, she used to sit with him sometimes, hoping he would look over and see her. Talk to her.

Of course he never did. Talking wasn't their thing.

She slid the milk into the fridge and took out a package of chicken thighs.

"Aidan? Dad?" She poked her head into the living room. "Hi."

Hank nodded without taking his eyes off the TV. Seven-year-old Aidan hunched over a sprinkling of Legos on the coffee table, his straight brown hair flopping over his face, into his eyes. His shoulder blades stuck out from his back like the stumps of wings. At her greeting, he twitched one shoulder in acknowledgment or dismissal.

"How was your day?" Jane asked.

"Okay," Aidan mumbled.

Just like his grandfather.

Jane had read all the books the school counselor gave her. She knew she should be grateful that her son had a positive male role model in his life. She *was* grateful that her dad was around to fill in around her bakery hours, to see Aidan off to school every morning, to be home on the nights Jane had to close.

But Aidan was only seven. Young enough to still need hugs and bedtime stories. Too young for his little-boy sweetness to be lost, for him to go all strong-and-silent on her all the time.

Jane stooped, brushing the hair off his forehead to kiss him.

Aidan flinched.

She drew back, narrowing her eyes. His cheekbone was red and puffy. She ran her fingers down the side of his jaw, tipping his face to the light. His lip was swollen, split and bloody.

Her stomach hollowed. "Aidan! What happened?"

His shoulders rounded as if he could draw his head in like a turtle.

"Who did this?" she asked.

Another shrug.

"Did you get in a fight? Did somebody pick on you?"

He shook his head.

"Aidan . . ."

He tugged his chin away, his gaze dropping. "I'm fine."

"Did it happen at school?" Children could be suspended for fighting at school. Even teasing or bullying earned a visit to the principal's office. Jane looked at Hank. "Did you talk to his teacher?"

"Wasn't at school," Hank said. "I sent him out to play, and he came home with a busted lip."

Her heart squeezed. "You should have called me."

"What for?"

"I could have done something."

"I put frozen peas on it," Hank said.

"That's great, Dad." She regarded Aidan's small, pinched face, his broken lip. She could tell by the look on his face that she wasn't getting anything more out of him now. So she comforted him the only way she could, the only way he would allow. "I brought home snickerdoodles." Cookies made everything better. "Go wash your hands and you can have one."

Aidan looked up, a glint in his eyes. "Before dinner?"

Jane fidgeted with the end of her braid. The hardest part of being a single parent was making decisions all the time, all by yourself, always with the awareness that you were potentially screwing up. "I don't see how it can hurt. Just this once."

He smiled, a quick, fugitive smile, and then winced because of his split lip. "Cool."

She waited until her son was out of earshot in the kitchen before she turned to Hank. "Did he tell you what happened?"

"He got into a fight. That's what boys do."

"He's bleeding."

Hank's face settled into the same stubborn, uncommunicative lines as Aidan's. "What do you want me to do? Go down to the playground and make arrests?"

"Nnoo," she said uncertainly, thinking, *Maybe*. "He's only seven."

"You baby him."

She wanted to. Needed to. She wanted to cocoon him in protection, to swaddle him with all the mothering she'd lacked. To give him not only cookies and hugs, but that deep-in-the-bone certainty that he was someone special, that he was loved, that he was deserving of love.

Because she knew what it felt like to grow up without those things. How part of you was always unsure, always doubting, always vulnerable to the wrong person who paid you a little attention.

Because if your own mother walked out on you, if she couldn't love you, you learned to accept whatever you got. You started to believe that's all you deserved, scraps of affection.

Or worse.

She swallowed the ache in her throat. "I just want to know that he's all right."

Hank reached out, almost as if he might pat her shoulder, before his hand dropped awkwardly. "Boys don't tell their mothers everything."

"Maybe he should talk to somebody."

Hank grunted. "Who?"

"I don't know. A counselor at school. Lauren."

Lauren Patterson, with her piercings and tattoos, looked more like an indie musician than a bestselling author. Or a school psychologist. But after working briefly at the bakery last summer, Lauren was back on the island, newly engaged to the chief of police and apparently happy as a counselor at Aidan's school. Jane had always found her easy to talk to.

Hank scowled. "The boy doesn't need to snitch on every playground fight to Jack Rossi's fiancée."

"It's not snitching to report a bully, Dad. Anyway, anything Aidan would say to a counselor is confidential. Lauren's not going to call the cops."

Even if she was sleeping with one.

"You're making a mountain out of a molehill. Boy's got to learn to defend himself," Hank said. "Let him handle his own problems."

Jane sighed. "It's not just the fight, Dad." She hesitated. "He still hasn't processed what happened with Travis."

Hank snorted. "Processed?"

"Dad. You know what I mean."

Hank's face set like a mule's. "That was seven months ago. He's fine."

"Fine" was one of those words they used to fill the spaces of the things they didn't talk about, a Band-Aid word to cover the anger and fear, the silence and hurt.

Aidan was *fine* growing up without a father. *Fine*, with a father whose only interest in obtaining custody was claiming child support. *Fine*, with that father in jail.

"That bum come into the bakery this afternoon?" Hank asked.

The question sounded like a change of subject. But it wasn't, Jane knew. This was why they didn't talk. Every topic led back to her lack of judgment, her failure to listen to Hank, her terrible choices in men.

"What bum?" she said, knowing she was being evasive. Also cowardly.

"Murphy. Inmate from North Dakota. Killed some guy in a bar fight."

"He was acquitted, Dad." She had overhead that much.

"That just means there wasn't enough evidence to put him away," Hank said with the cynicism of almost forty years in law enforcement.

"Luke seems to trust him."

"Because they served together. He could've changed. And if he wasn't changed before he was locked up, he is now. Nine months in jail? Guy's a hardened criminal by now."

"Since I didn't know him before—and I don't know him now—I couldn't say."

"He planning on sticking around?"

If you need me to spot you a couple nights, Luke had said, *just until you find something . . .*

"How would I know? He didn't talk to me," Jane said, her voice even. "Ask Luke."

Hank's scowl deepened, his gaze still fixed on the TV. "Guy like that . . . he's trouble. He bothers you, you let me know."

Under his gruff tone, she heard his affection and his fear. She leaned over his recliner to kiss his rough cheek, surprising them both. He smelled of bay rum and tobacco, safe and familiar.

"I'm fine, Daddy." She had Aidan to think of now. She couldn't let herself be anything but fine.

She thought of the stranger, Gabe Murphy, fresh out of jail for killing a man, and of her ex, Travis, doing time for assault. And she wished with all her heart that just once she could be attracted to a good man, a gentle man, a guy who was no danger to her heart or her bones, a man who didn't leave scars.

But then she wouldn't have had Aidan.

And Aidan was all that mattered.

Three

HE HAD COMPANY.

Gabe's senses, honed by nine months in a cellblock and six tours in the sandbox, went on alert. He raised his head from the sandwich in his hands, scanning the perimeter of his campsite.

He'd considered spending the night under one of the big empty houses on stilts that stood along the beach. The ocean-front rentals provided benches, shelter, even outdoor showers, some of them. But the police were paid to patrol and protect private property. Gabe could tolerate being moved along, but he didn't want to give that son-of-a-bitch Clark an excuse to arrest him. Things with Luke were awkward enough already.

So he'd made camp instead under a dense thicket at the edge of a trailer park. PARADISE SHOALS, according to the sign.

Gabe surveyed the junkyard cars, held together with hope and Bondo, and the mildewed plastic garden furniture under the trees. *Paradise, my ass.* But at least no anxious home-owners or merchants were likely to see him and call the cops.

The bushes rustled.

His muscles bunched. Silently, he set down the sandwich, prepared for action.

A blunt black nose poked through the bushes.

Not a terrorist looking for an ambush. Not a prisoner seeking out a victim.

A dog.

A big dog. Gabe eyed it warily as its body followed its nose out of the shadows: broad head, heavy shoulders, dirty tail close to the ground. Cautiously, it eyed him back before fixing its gaze on his sandwich.

"Oh, hell, no," Gabe said.

Probably belonged to one of the trailers. It looked like a trailer park dog, a lean, mean, scruffy bastard. Some kind of pit bull–shepherd mix, maybe, smart and aggressive.

Except it hadn't growled at him. Or barked.

Its black-and-tan coat was gray with grime. Its shoulders stuck up, its belly caved in. No collar.

"Go home," Gabe said.

The dog stared at him, nose quivering at the scent of ham sandwich. It had cartoon-dog eyes, big and brown, with tan patches like eyebrows, giving its face a hopeful, quizzical expression.

"Seriously. Go away. I don't have anything for you."

The dog sat, watching him. Its tail brushed the ground slowly, sweeping pine needles from side to side.

Gabe had never had a pet growing up. Even if animals had been allowed in their apartment, his home life wasn't fit for a dog. But he'd seen plenty of strays before, abandoned along the highway or traveling in feral packs in Helmand Province. There were always dogs hanging around the forward operating base, adopted by successive combat rotations of Marines. And Gabe had always fed them, even when the brass cracked down and ordered him not to.

Shit. "Fine."

His stomach growled as he pulled a piece of ham from his sandwich and tossed it to the dog.

The dog caught the meat with a neat snap of its massive jaws and then settled back on its haunches, those brown, expectant eyes on Gabe.

He shook his head. "That's it."

The cute blonde had packed the sandwich for him, not some dog. He was hungry, damn it.

The dog cocked its head, trying to understand. Because, shit, it was probably hungry, too, and it wasn't whining.

Gabe hefted the paper sack. When he'd opened it, he'd discovered the sandwich, thick with ham, and not one but two giant chocolate chip cookies. His throat tightened. He didn't have words to describe what that meant to him, that the coffee stayed hot until he was ready to drink it, that he had a second cookie to eat whenever he felt like it. The little blonde's kindness got under his skin, burrowing deeper, toward his heart.

The dog swallowed and watched him, panting gently.

"Stupid mutt," Gabe said, and put half the sandwich on the ground.

He watched the dog bolt the food, trying to ignore the satisfied feeling around his heart.

"But no cookies," he said firmly.

One of his buddies—Luke, probably—had told him chocolate was bad for dogs.

GABE HAD LEARNED to sleep lightly in jail. Sleeping outdoors wasn't much better. If the sun didn't wake you, the bugs would. Or the cold. Or the rain.

But when he woke the next morning he was warmer than usual. Also covered in dog hair.

"Fleas, too, probably," he told the dog as he shook out his bedroll.

The dog yawned, unconcerned.

Dew silvered the dark bushes. The air smelled of earth and sea, of rotting marsh and sprouting leaves. Gabe took a deep breath, filling his lungs with the smell of spring.

And bacon. Somebody in the trailer park cooking breakfast.

Gabe's stomach growled.

The dog sniffed at the bushes and lifted a leg before trotting back to sit at Gabe's feet.

"Sorry, pal. I got nothing."

God, he was hungry. Served him right for feeding half his dinner to a dog.

The dog cocked its cement-block head. Looking for another handout, probably.

Gabe scratched behind its battered ears. "You don't want to stick with me. Go bother the family with the bacon."

The mutt didn't move.

Gabe removed his fingers from the warmth of its thick ruff. "Go on. Get out of here. Find somebody who can take care of you. Get."

Those big, brown, Disney-dog eyes regarded him reproachfully from its ugly mug before the dog heaved itself to its feet and wandered off through the trees.

Gabe set his jaw against the urge to call it back. It was for the best, he told himself. For the dog's own good. He had to get his own life in order. He couldn't take responsibility for a dog.

He shouldered his pack. The street had no sidewalk, only a grassy verge spilling sand onto the asphalt. Above the peaked roofs, the sky was tinged with pink and gold. The sea, caught in glimpses between the houses and the trees, was the color of the sky.

His spirits lifted, an unexpected, welcome rush. He liked this place, the smell of salt, the birds' early-morning racket. Maybe his instincts and his memories had been right after all. *Go back to the beginning.* Not all the way back to his crappy childhood, but here, where he'd first experienced what a family could be, where he'd caught a glimpse of what his future could look like.

He lengthened his stride purposefully. He didn't need to grab on to Luke like a baby clutching the hand of the nearest adult. He could walk on his own. Make a fresh start. Find work somewhere, someplace warm, within sight and smell of the sea. He'd heard they were hiring construction workers down in Florida.

The bakery's lights glowed in welcome. OPEN, proclaimed the neon sign in the window. But he saw only two vehicles in the parking lot, an old sedan with North Carolina plates—*Jane's?*—and a white, even older-model van like a painter's van with a vent on top. JANE'S SWEET TEA HOUSE, read a small magnetic sign on the side. Both Jane's, then. She must be alone inside.

He could see her through the plate glass window, her hair as yellow as butter under the light as she filled the sleek display cases with pastries. Beneath the square white apron she looked pink and round and soft.

Hunger hit him, sharp as a cramp.

She was so pretty. Kind, too, despite her caution. Gabe saw her kindness as a strength.

His mom had not been strong. Peggy Murphy had been too busy placating her husband to have much attention left over for their son. Everything she did was with an eye on big Scott Murphy's moods, on his fists. Tess Fletcher had always been kind to Luke's friends, but Gabe had known he wasn't really entitled to her affection. It was borrowed, secondhand, like the clothes he'd worn to school.

His entire life, he had craved someone of his own who would care for him, who would pack him cookies or fuss over whether he stayed warm, who would do the small favors a woman does for the people she loves.

He wanted to thank Jane for the cookies and the thermos.

But he didn't want her looking at him the way she had last night, startled and wary, like he was some creepy thug in a dark alley. Yeah, okay, he wasn't the Marine he had been. But he had never hurt a woman in his life.

See? he told the gibing voice in his head. Not his pop, after all.

Fishing the thermos from his pack, he set it on a table near the door.

32   VIRGINIA KANTRA

She had a nice setup here, he thought, looking around. Picnic tables and big wooden chairs scattered over the short, tough grass. Some kind of purple flower, flat-faced and bright, bloomed in planters by the porch, and daffodils—he recognized the sharp spears and yellow trumpets—pushed up under the trees.

So, yeah, okay, the place could use some work. Minor repairs to the porch and furniture, some paint, some stain. Not that he was criticizing. He was looking a little weather-worn himself. But it wouldn't take much to put the yard in order, just a rake and some time.

He spotted the rake, leaning up against the cedar shake siding. And God knew he had the time.

Maybe he'd found a way to thank her after all.

JANE ARRANGED THE glistening pastries in the bakery case, rows of cheese Danish and chocolate brioche, cinnamon buns and lemon-glazed scones, muffins studded with chocolate chips and bursting with berries.

She loved baking, all the scents and textures. The smell of vanilla, the squish of dough between her fingers, satisfied something deep inside her. She loved the way you could take a few simple fixings, flour, sugar, butter, and make something satisfying and sustaining—a wedding cake, a loaf of bread, a life.

Who would have guessed that after Travis left her ~~broken~~ flat, she would turn her line cook experience and a few community college classes in cake decorating and small business management into running her own bakery?

In her kitchen, she was in control. She could trust her taste and her judgment. When she was baking, she had the confidence to be creative, to take risks, to add chilis to chocolate in a cupcake or combine lemon and thyme in a scone. As long as she kept the right balance of ingredients, everything would turn out fine.

Because baking never let you down. Even if you screwed up, you could always throw everything out and start again.

Unlike life.

The silver bells over the door chimed, signaling her first morning customer.

Lauren Patterson entered the bakery, her dark hair bundled in a messy knot, a silver cuff twining around one ear. "God, it smells good in here. I'll take one of everything."

Jane smiled and pulled out a bakery box. "Do you have a staff meeting or are you just really hungry?"

Lauren laughed. "I thought I'd sprinkle muffins around the faculty break room. Buy a little goodwill."

"In that case, I'd get a dozen blueberry mini muffins, a dozen caramel mocha mini cupcakes, and a half-dozen brownies."

"Brownies? At seven in the morning?"

"Everybody loves chocolate," Jane said.

"So true. Oh, maybe one of those big cheese Danish for Lois Howell?"

School boards and principals came and went, but Lois Howell, the raspy-voiced, orange-haired school secretary, had run the place since before Jane was born.

"How about a red velvet cupcake?" Jane suggested. "Those are her favorite."

"Perfect. Thanks. She's been filling me in on everything I need to know about the island families." Lauren smiled lopsidedly. "Which is pretty much everything."

Uh-oh. Jane's gaze flickered to Lauren's face, trying to see beyond the bright tone, the crooked smile. Lauren was always so outgoing, so optimistic. She was two years older than Jane, but her cheerful energy always made Jane feel ancient—or at least very, very tired. It was hard to imagine Lauren needing Jane's reassurance.

But then, Jane couldn't imagine doing what Lauren had done, leaving everything safe and familiar behind to make a new life among strangers. That kind of courage deserved a deeper response than a cookie.

"You'll catch on quick enough," she said reassuringly. "Everybody talks to everybody here."

"Within limits. I'm still a dingbatter." *Dingbatter* being the downeasterners' term for Yankees, vacationers, or anyone from Away.

"They'll come around. The kids like you." Aidan liked her. She really should talk to Lauren about Aidan.

Lauren's face lit up. "I love working with the kids. One of the things that's so great in a community like this is the age range of the students I see. I'm dealing with everything from gum in girls' hair to college applications."

"What about fighting?" Jane asked.

Lauren grinned. "You mean developing communication and conflict resolution skills? Yeah, we see some of that."

Her look, her tone, invited Jane to smile back. But the image of Aidan's bloody lip, the defensive hunch of his shoulders, got in the way.

Lauren's eyes narrowed. "Why do you ask? Is Aidan having a problem at school?"

Jane hesitated, her father's voice rumbling in her head. *You're making a mountain out of a molehill. Let him handle his own problems.* "Maybe . . . after school, I think? He came home from the playground with a split lip. My dad says all boys fight. But . . ."

Don't hit, she'd told Aidan from the time he was very young. *We don't hit in this family.*

And tried to forget the time when that hadn't been true, when Aidan's father had hit her. Hurt her.

I'm sorry, Travis always said afterward. At least, he'd said it at the beginning. *God, I'm so sorry, Janey.*

"What did he say?"

Jane blinked. *Aidan.* They were talking about her son. "Nothing."

Not after supper and not at bedtime. When she went to kiss him goodnight, Aidan had turned his face to the wall covered in dinosaur posters, his shoulder rising like a gate to shut her out.

"Have you talked to his teacher?" Lauren asked.

Jane shook her head. "He's never been in a fight before. It just happened yesterday. I don't even know if it happened on school grounds. If it's even school business. If they'd care. I don't want to get him into trouble."

She winced at the familiar litany of rationalizations.

The first time Travis gripped her arm, leaving a circlet of purple bruises like a tribal tattoo, she'd convinced herself— or had he convinced her?—that talking would only make things worse. The justifications rushed back, crowding her throat, choking her. *He's never done it before, he didn't mean it, if only he wasn't frustrated, drunk, jealous, angry, disgusted with himself, with his life, with her . . .*

The excuses piled up and up, like a wall between everybody else and her secret, leaving her cowering behind it, alone with her pain and humiliation.

"Would you like me to chat with his teacher? Sylvie Cunningham, right?" Lauren asked. "I could ask if she's noticed anything in class."

The relief that rushed over Jane felt shameful. Aidan was her son, her responsibility. But she honestly didn't know what to do. "Would you?" she asked hopefully.

"Sure."

"You don't mind getting involved?"

Lauren's lips quirked. "That's why I became a counselor. Because I like meddling."

"Because you care," Jane said. "Islanders are used to handling things themselves. But if you give them time to get to know you, they'll come around."

"That's what Jack says." Lauren's voice, her whole face, softened when she said her fiancé's name.

"Well, he would know," Jane said, tucking a red velvet cupcake into the box. "He hasn't been here that long himself. But everybody trusts him."

Lauren beamed. "They do, don't they?"

Jane nodded. "He's a good police chief."

"He's a good guy," Lauren said.

He was. It was hard not to feel a little jealous. Not over Jack, exactly. Though there was a time, right after he'd moved here, when Jane had thought . . .

But beyond one kiss at a wedding two years ago, they had never . . . She would never . . .

Anyway, she probably bored him silly.

Besides, Jack was too dark, too cool, too controlled for her liking. She was drawn to sulky rebels with bad-boy stubble and sun-streaked shaggy hair and muscles like rope.

An image of Gabe Murphy slid into her mind, tall and blond with eyes that weren't green or brown or gold but some intriguing combination of all three.

No, she told herself firmly, and shut the bakery box. "I think you two are good together," she said.

"Thanks. So." Lauren gave her a bright look and swiped a cookie sample from the plate by the register. "How's your love life these days?"

Jane smiled faintly. "Is this another example of you getting involved?"

Lauren pressed a hand to her heart. "Only because I care."

Jane shook her head and rang up her order. With the friends and family discount, because, well, Lauren *did* care. "I don't have a love life. I don't have time."

Lauren nibbled another sample. "That's an excuse."

Maybe.

"Don't you want a relationship?" Lauren continued.

"I have relationships. I have Aidan. My dad. My friends. You." If she let herself want other things, where would she be? Making the same old terrible mistakes. She could raise her son, she could run her business, she could manage her life on her own.

"What about sex? You must miss sex."

"I barely remember it," Jane said.

Probably just as well.

She'd loved sex once—the flush of attraction, the feeling

of closeness, the thrill of the forbidden. But somewhere along the way, sex had gradually become a chore.

Travis had barely seemed to notice when she wasn't in the mood anymore. Or maybe by that point he hadn't cared. He certainly hadn't bothered to hide his disgust that the eager, curvy nineteen-year-old he'd married was now tired and bloated all the time. *Jesus, Janey, you really let yourself go*, he'd say, reaching for her.

Her shoulders rounded, remembering.

Lauren's eyes narrowed. "Jane, did Travis ever hurt you—abuse you—that way?"

Jane blinked. Despite all the books Lauren pressed on her, she'd never identified what Travis did to her as abuse. As—what did they call it?—marital rape.

It was just something necessary and unpleasant to get through, like scrubbing behind the toilet in the bathroom. Something she needed to do to keep the household running. Even when you were exhausted from work, or heavy with pregnancy, you still had to get down on your knees.

"No," she said. *Not really.*

"Because if you ever want to talk about it . . ."

Ha. "It's not an issue."

"But it could be," Lauren said.

Jane shook her head. "It's not like there's a line of available single men knocking at my door." Or her father's door, since she lived with him and her seven-year-old son. Which made the possibility of her ever having sex again in this lifetime even more remote. "If my dad doesn't scare them off, then Aidan does. Most men who want to get married aren't looking for a package deal."

Lauren made a humming sound. "You know, not every relationship has to lead to love and commitment. Sometimes sex is all about the chemistry."

That's how Lauren's relationship with Jack had started, Jane remembered. A rebound relationship for him, a summer fling for her. She glanced at Lauren's shiny new engagement ring and smiled. "How's that working out for you?"

Lauren laughed. "Okay, sometimes chemistry can turn into something more. Which proves you should be open to possibilities."

Jane rolled her eyes. "What possibilities? We live in a fishing village with a year-round population of one thousand eight hundred and some. The good guys, guys like the Fletchers or Sam Grady, are all taken. Or they move away."

Lauren nibbled on another sample. "There's your old boss at the restaurant. Adam? He's hot."

"Do you know what the divorce rate is among chefs?"

"Okay, what about Nick at the firehouse? I've seen him in the weight room. Nice pecs."

"I'm not going out with a guy who looks better in a wet T-shirt than I do. Besides, he's five years younger than me."

"I'm six years younger than Jack."

"That's different."

"Ah ah." Lauren waggled a finger. "Let's not fall into traditional gender stereotypes."

Jane bent her head, carefully counting out change. She knew all about stereotypes. By now she should be used to being dismissed on account of her appearance. Even her friends sometimes looked at her and saw . . . What? Baker Barbie. As if because she spoke with a drawl and spent her time baking cookies, because she had blond hair and big boobs and kept house for her father, she must be some kind of weird throwback to the 50s.

"Stereotypes don't have anything to do with it," she said mildly. "You and Jack met as adults. I used to babysit Nick."

Lauren grimaced. "Okay, I can see that might be a problem."

Jane smiled. "Face it, if the love of my life was living on the island, I'd have found him by now."

"What about that guy I saw when I came in?"

Jane closed the cash drawer with a ping. "What guy?"

"Outside. With the rake? I thought maybe you'd hired some help."

Jane's brows puckered. She glanced toward the wide front window. "No, I . . ."

Something moved in the yard. A man. The sun glinted off the blond streaks in his hair, slid over his long, lean, muscled arms. He was holding a rake. Her rake.

"What is it?" Lauren asked at her elbow. "Who is it? Do you want me to call Jack?"

"I don't . . . No." Jane drew an unsteady breath. "It's Luke's friend. Gabe something? He was in the shop yesterday with Luke."

"Ah," Lauren said in her therapist's voice. Withholding judgment.

Did she know about him?

Of course she did, Jane answered her own question. This was Dare Island. Even if Lauren wasn't fully tuned in to the island grapevine yet, she was engaged to the chief of police.

"What's he doing here?" Lauren asked.

Jane's heart hammered. Really, she had terrible taste in men. "I have no idea. I didn't invite him."

No, you just fed him, her conscience mocked. *Don't you ever learn? You don't get rid of strays by feeding them.*

Lauren's dark eyes regarded her thoughtfully. "You know, sometimes people can do bad things for good reasons."

"You mean me," Jane said flatly.

"Actually, I was talking about Gabe Murphy. Jack says he was charged with killing a man in a bar fight. I Googled him. According to the local paper, some oil workers attacked a local waitress and he intervened."

He'd been careful not to crowd her, Jane remembered. *Make sure you lock up behind me.*

She moistened her lips. "Are you saying he's innocent?"

Lauren might feel that way. She was pen pals or something, wasn't she, with a guy in prison? Living proof, if Jane was looking for it, that one experience of violence didn't have to leave you scarred for life.

On the other hand, nobody blamed Lauren for anything

worse than being in the wrong place at the wrong time. Lauren seemed to bring out the best in people.

Unlike Jane, who attracted the worst.

"Not guilty," Lauren said. "Not the same. I mean, it's good that he saved that woman. But he still killed a man. Maybe he could have handled the situation differently. I don't know him well enough to say. But I know you." Her gaze met Jane's. "I care about you."

Jane flushed, hearing the worry—and the warning—in Lauren's voice. She didn't know Gabe, either.

Living with Travis had systematically eroded her faith in her own judgment. But she wasn't stupid. You didn't have to be a psychologist to understand that a woman who had been beaten and broken should stay far away from a man who solved problems with his fists.

Four

THE SUN SANK into Gabe, warming his muscles. The steady, repetitive scrape of the rake loosened the knots in his shoulders.

After his first continuance, his jail guards had decided he wasn't a violent threat and put him to work in the sunless kitchens. Gabe had been grateful to get out of his cell. But he had hated the stink of the rising steam, the smells of rancid grease and garbage and the chemicals used to clean the cooking pots.

He lifted his head, breathing in the scent of pines and sea, a whiff of baking bread. A bird piped from the trees.

Since leaving Detroit for Parris Island, he had never lived in any one spot long enough to develop an attachment to a place. But he liked it here. It would have been nice, this time, to stay. To have a reason to stay.

But not if his being here fucked things up for Luke.

Florida, that was the plan.

An early morning jogger crunched up the drive, huffing

a greeting. "How's it going?" The masculine equivalent of have-a-nice-day, no response required.

Gabe nodded without speaking.

A pretty brunette came out of the bakery carrying a big pastry box. He'd noticed her going in. Hard not to, with those piercings. She gave him a long look and a quick smile as she passed. "Good morning."

"Morning," Gabe said carefully.

He wasn't used to all this friendliness from strangers. He'd been living on the street, in the shadows, where passersby averted their gaze, where no one noticed him but the cops.

A few more customers came and went, an old man with a much younger one, a couple of moms with strollers, an older woman with a laptop. Coming or going, they all said hi. It was weird. In a good way. Gabe finished with the front yard and moved around back.

"What do you think you're doing?" A woman's voice, torn between amusement and annoyance. "Get away from there."

Now *that* was more what he was used to.

He turned.

Jane Clark stood framed by the kitchen door, her hands on her curvy hips under a wide, white apron, her blond hair slipping its braid. Like the St. Pauli Girl on a long-neck bottle of beer. His throat went dry. A surge of lust tightened his stomach muscles.

But she wasn't talking to him.

"That food is for the cats," she told the dog gobbling kibble from a metal pan a few yards away.

The big, dirty, familiar-looking dog.

Gabe's mouth relaxed. "Guess he didn't read the sign."

At the sound of his voice, the dog raised its head. Abandoning the food, it bounded over and flopped onto its back, waggling its privates in the air. *Dumb mutt.*

He hunkered down to rub its belly.

"Is that your dog?" Jane asked. Unlike the dog, she didn't appear especially overjoyed to see him.

"Nope." Gabe gave the mutt a final scratch and straightened. The dog scrambled up, trying to lick his face.

"Down," Gabe ordered.

Its butt dropped. Huh. That was a surprise.

A corner of Jane's mouth tucked in. "Are you sure?"

Her smile softened her severe expression, making her look approachable. Touchable. She really should stop doing that. Smiling at him. Feeding him. Because every time she did, she only made him hungry for more.

Her mouth compressed. Frowning again.

What? he thought.

Oh, right. She had asked him a question. About the dog. They were talking about the dog that was now pressing against his leg.

He scratched its head so he wouldn't reach out and pet her instead. "It's a stray," he said. "It only likes me because I fed it."

"You fed it." He couldn't read the tone of her voice. Another question?

"Stupid bastard ate half my sandwich."

She was looking at him oddly. Because, yeah, what kind of idiot fed his dinner to a dog? She was probably insulted he'd wasted her handout.

He didn't want her thinking he didn't appreciate her generosity, so he said, "It was a really good sandwich. The cookies, too. Thanks."

She stared at him a moment longer, as if she expected him to jump on her like the stupid dog. Lick her face. Hump her leg.

Gabe clamped his jaw against disappointment. Right. What did he expect? That she was going to invite him in for a cup of coffee?

She crossed her arms over her mighty rack. "What are you doing here?"

I wanted to see you again. But he wasn't admitting that. Not even to himself.

He rested a forearm on the rake, trying to look as

nonthreatening as possible. "Just passing through." She continued to regard him doubtfully. "Luke Fletcher can vouch for me. I'm having dinner at his place tonight."

JANE CROSSED HER arms a little tighter over her wildly beating heart. She appreciated his attempt at reassurance. But she wasn't that easily frightened. Or that dumb.

He needed to go.

"I don't mean here on Dare Island. I meant . . ." She flapped her hand. "Here." *At my bakery. In my space.*

He glanced around the yard, making her see everything he had done with fresh eyes. A winter's worth of debris had been raked away from the foundation, the leaves neatly piled, the trash bagged.

Her cheeks ignited. She bit back the urge to apologize.

"I thought . . ." he said slowly. He shook his head. "I brought back your thermos."

He . . . Well. Wow. She wasn't expecting that. "You didn't have to do that."

He shrugged. "It's out front. On one of the tables."

"You can keep it."

His jaw set. "I don't take charity. And I pay my debts."

Oh. Understanding surged inside her, a liquid tug at her heart and her knees.

Oh, crap. She'd misjudged him.

When she was starting over, it had been so hard for her to ask for her father's help. To accept anyone's help, especially when it meant admitting her own mistakes. Even yesterday, with Sam, she had balked at accepting charity.

Sometimes, when you didn't have much else, all you had to hold on to was your pride.

And sometimes that was just foolishness.

"Well . . ." She twisted her hands in her apron, embarrassed by her own bias. "Thank you."

Gabe nodded shortly.

She stood there a moment, her heart knocking at her ribs,

before she ducked her head awkwardly in reply and retreated to her kitchen.

Running away.

Crap. She leaned against the stainless steel counter, pressing her hands to her hot face. What was the matter with her?

Gabe Murphy hadn't been anything but helpful and respectful. Yes, he did bear a distressing resemblance to Travis. On the other hand, she couldn't imagine Travis doing yard work. Or feeding a stray. Or wasting time or energy on anyone but himself.

So her discomfort around Gabe wasn't his problem. It was hers.

The oven timer went off. Jane bent to pull out a half sheet of strata, her mind churning like a blender. Was she really still so controlled by her ex, by her past, that she couldn't recognize the goodness in a fellow human being? That she would let her fear dictate how she treated a stranger?

She set the baking sheet on the counter, her cheeks still flushed from the heat of the oven. Being smart was not the same as being afraid. Being strong didn't mean she had to be unkind.

She cut a slab of strata and nestled it in a take-out tray. When she looked outside again, the backyard was clear of leaves.

And Gabe was gone.

She hurried through the rows of tables to the front door, noting in passing that the sugar dispenser needed refilling and the crumbs around the highchair in the corner, where the moms were having coffee, needed to be swept. But those things could wait.

She burst onto the porch.

The rake was propped neatly in its customary place against the outside wall. And Gabe . . .

"There you are," she said. Her voice was too loud. She clutched the cardboard tray a little tighter. "I was afraid you'd left."

He straightened, his seabag at his feet, as she came down two shallow steps to the yard. Watching her with the same alert look, the same stiffened posture as the dog. As if he were just waiting for a scrap of encouragement or a sign of weakness to pounce.

"Just finished up."

"You didn't have to do that," she protested.

"Yeah." A long look. "I did."

She swallowed and glanced away. "You did a lot of work this morning. You must have worked up an appetite."

"Some," he admitted.

Her gaze met his. His eyes were the color of the sun striking through the trees, brown and green and gold. He smelled of sun and leaves and potent male, a vaguely erotic combination. Her breath went short. But he didn't touch her. Didn't make any gesture toward her at all.

Why did that make her want so desperately to be touched, to wonder how it would feel?

"I brought you something," she said.

His gaze dropped briefly to the tray before focusing on her face. "You fed me already."

"A sandwich. Yesterday. Which you gave to the dog."

"Only half," he said.

He sounded defensive, grumpy, like Aidan did sometimes when he kissed her goodnight, as if his sweetness were something to be ashamed of.

She took a cautious step closer.

"I won't bite," he said. "Unless you want me to."

Her gaze flew to his face. His tone was mocking, challenging, almost, but those eyes . . . His eyes were kind. His jaw was hard and stubbled, his lower lip full and soft. Vulnerable. The contrasts of him intrigued her. She wanted to test his textures with the tips of her fingers, wanted to . . .

Oh, no. Nope. Not going there.

Her cheeks burned. She couldn't think of a thing to say. Boys had been teasing her since she developed boobs in seventh grade. Because of her father, it never went beyond teasing. But she sucked at snappy comebacks. She wouldn't think of a good putdown until three days from now when she was kneading dough or folding socks. And yet . . .

She held his gaze, and something ignited inside her like a spark. "Bite this," she said and set down the tray.

Laughter leaped in his eyes, warming them, warming her. "What is it?"

"Strata. Basically a breakfast bread pudding with sausage and Gruyère."

He picked it up, poking at it with the plastic fork. "Never had it before." His mouth quirked. "Never even heard of it before."

Her own smile escaped. "You mean they didn't serve strata in . . ." Her breath caught.

In jail. The unspoken words pulsed in the silence.

"In the Marines?" she finished in a weak voice.

"No, ma'am," he said quietly. Evenly. "They sure didn't."

He ate. The dog wriggled closer, its eyes fixed on every forkful that went into his mouth.

Tentatively, she reached out to pet it. The dog shied away, moving closer to Gabe.

"He doesn't like me," she said, oddly hurt by the stray's rejection.

Gabe glanced up. "Are you kidding? You're the giver of the goodies. The mutt likes you fine. It's head shy, that's all."

"Head shy?"

"Flinches when you go for its head," Gabe explained. "It's used to being chased off. It expects you're going to hit it. Probably been abused, poor bastard."

Her breath caught. *He doesn't mean anything by it*, she told herself. *He doesn't know anything about me.*

The dog nudged against Gabe's leg. He ruffled the fur at its neck. She watched his hands, strong and long and lean, as he dug in. The dog pressed closer, panting slightly, its eyes half closed in ecstasy.

An inconvenient sizzle kindled in the pit of her stomach, in the tips of her fingers.

"He lets *you* pet him," Jane said. Good heavens, she sounded as sulky as Aidan.

"He trusts me."

Her heart beat faster. "Why?" *Why should he? Why should I?*

"I'm kind to animals. Plus . . ." Gabe met her gaze, that half smirk tugging the corner of his mouth. "We slept together. It makes a bond."

That was true.

If Travis hadn't been the first boy she'd ever slept with, would she have loved him? Stayed with him? At nineteen, she'd believed that her skipping heart and sweaty palms were the signs of some deep, eternal love. That being close to someone, that feeling desired, were worth risking everything for.

She knew better now.

"I need to get back to work. You can, um, just throw out the tray when you're done."

Gabe watched her closely, the smirk fading. "Sure. You do what you have to do."

I always do, she thought bleakly.

She turned and marched inside, leaving the danger outside. Putting temptation behind her.

Five

HENRY LEE CLARK propped his feet on his desk, leaning back in his swivel chair. The sight of his size twelves on the furniture usually got a rise out of Marta Lopez, the police department's administrative assistant. But today she ignored him, her bright coral nails tapping briskly on her computer keyboard.

Damn it.

Luke Fletcher was out on patrol, Jack Rossi behind the closed door with its cheap metal POLICE CHIEF sign. Hank wanted to annoy *somebody*.

Being at work usually relaxed him—the familiar file cabinets, the wanted posters, the rack of locked-up rifles in the gun closet, even the smell of coffee sitting until it turned to sludge. He'd always been more comfortable with men than women, always better suited to the job than things at home. Which was why—even after his retirement from the county sheriff's office, even after he'd supported the hiring of outsider Jack Rossi as Dare Island's police chief—Hank had hired on as backup relief officer. Let the younger man worry about writing grants and kissing the town council's asses. As long as Hank could report to work every day, he wasn't dead yet.

Most of the calls that came in were parking or noise complaints, reports of vandalism and petty theft, a little drugs, an occasional domestic, negotiating disputes between neighbors. Not even much of that in the off-season. Islanders were an independent lot, used to settling their own problems. After years of big busts, gang-related crime, and high-speed car chases, working for a small police department sometimes made Hank feel like a meter maid with a gun.

And that suited him, too. He was fifty-goddamn-nine years old. Too old for excitement. Or a change.

But today he couldn't get comfortable in his chair or in his skin.

Hank dropped his feet, prowling restlessly between the three desks to the coffeepot.

"You don't need more coffee," Marta said without pausing a beat in her typing. "You're like a long-tailed cat in a room full of rocking chairs as it is."

He set down his mug, happy to have someone to vent his frustrations on. "It's that Murphy fellow. I don't like having some transient on the island, sponging off the Fletchers."

"The Fletchers are very capable of looking after themselves. You worry too much. And you drink too much coffee. No wonder your blood pressure is so high."

"What are you, my mother?"

"I have four boys already. I don't need another one."

"Wife, then."

Their eyes met. For no reason at all, Hank's heart started pounding.

"If I were your wife, you would take better care of yourself."

"Or kill myself."

Marta pursed bright lips. "Either way, your blood pressure wouldn't be a problem anymore."

A laugh escaped him. Hank did his best to turn it into a cough.

Marta turned slightly from her computer screen. "Tell me what is bothering you."

"Gary Wilson took his grandson Ethan fishing this morning. He saw that Murphy fellow at Jane's."

"And this worries you because . . . ?"

"He was raking her yard," Hank growled.

Marta raised dark, arched brows. "I am sure her grass will recover."

"People are talking."

"People always talk. He's new in town. And handsome."

"He's a jailbird."

"He's a friend of Luke's."

"Then what's he doing hanging around my daughter?"

"I don't know. But I do know if you go over there and protest, Jane will think you do not trust her judgment."

Hank scowled. "So now you're an expert on what my daughter is thinking."

"Of course not. She is your daughter. But I am a woman. It is what any woman would think."

He knew Marta was a woman, damn it. He'd been made aware of it every day since Jack hired her, her perfume and her earrings and the way she crossed and uncrossed her legs when she got out of her damn chair.

When Hank started with the sheriff's department almost forty years ago, law enforcement was all male and almost all-white. Marta stirred things up, stirred him up, in ways he didn't like to acknowledge. Even to himself.

"Well, I know how guys think," Hank said. "And I'm telling you, this Murphy bum is after more than Jane's cupcakes."

"And what makes you think she will give it to him?"

"She did before."

Marta's dark brows drew together. "They knew each other before?"

"No, damn it. She hooked up with some loser before."

And he hadn't stopped her.

The guilt of that would be with him always. His baby girl still hadn't recovered.

Hank had known that Travis was trouble. He'd warned her. But all his warning had done was gloss the bastard with the shine of forbidden fruit.

Maybe Jane would have listened to a mother's advice. But Hank couldn't be her mother. And when it counted, he hadn't been the father she deserved, either. A father's job was to protect.

Old, impotent fury stirred. He should have killed the son of a bitch when he had the chance.

The chief's door opened and Jack came out. "If you two are done bickering like an old married couple, I could use those reports. I'm going out to check on Dora Abrams."

Dora Abrams was eighty-four years old and called in for everything from suspicious noises to a stopped-up toilet.

"I'll take it," Hank said. "Her house is on my way anyway. Aidan will be home from school in forty minutes."

Marta smiled at him. "You're a good grandfather."

He didn't deserve her praise. "Boys are easy."

Her smile broadened. "You say that because you have only raised a girl. Wait until he gets older."

"THAT'S FORTY-NINE DOLLARS a night," said the clerk at the Fishermen's Motel, middle-aged and wiry, sporting a paunch and a walrus mustache. He looked past Gabe toward the parking lot. "That your dog?"

Gabe glanced over his shoulder. The mutt sat panting gently in the sunshine on the other side of the glass door. "Is that a problem?"

"I'll need a ten-dollar damage deposit a day. Nonrefundable," he added before Gabe could speak.

"He's not my dog," Gabe said.

"Whatever, buddy. Fifty-nine dollars. Unless you want

me to call the cops to get him. I don't allow strays on my property."

He paid. It was easier than explaining to Luke or that hard-ass Clark what he was doing with a dog.

There was a rack of fly-specked postcards standing on the counter—grass waving on the dunes, the fishing pier—and he bought one of those, too. As long as he was here, he might as well follow routine. "You got a washing machine in the building?"

"End of the hall. You'll need quarters."

"You make change?"

"Sure."

Gabe stopped by the laundry room on his way down the hall, tossing a load of clothes into a washer, using leftover laundry soap from the shelf above. He grabbed a half-empty bottle of detergent to take to his room. The Fishermen's Motel didn't seem like the kind of place that provided complimentary toiletries.

The dog sniffed the edges of the motel room door before slinking inside.

Gabe dumped his seabag on the quilted bedspread and looked around at the paneled walls and dirty blue carpet, the faded poster of the harbor over the TV.

He grinned. Compared to some of the places he had slept on deployment, and some of the places he had slept since, the Fishermen's Motel was the fucking Baghdad royal palace.

He turned on the hot water in the tiny bathroom, regarding his reflection in the spotted mirror over the sink.

He wasn't meeting Luke's wife and daughter looking like a homeless drifter. Too late for a haircut. But he could shave.

When he got in the shower, the dog, who had been padding around investigating the carpet smells, stuck its nose past the curtain and whined.

"Oh, hell, no," Gabe said.

The mutt dropped its head, staring up at him with those hopeful cartoon eyes, its tail waving slowly back and forth.

Gabe sighed. He hadn't caught fleas last night. That didn't mean he'd get lucky two nights in a row. Anyway, the beast was filthy. He couldn't keep it in his motel room in its current condition, nonrefundable damage deposit or not.

"Fine." He pushed back the shower curtain. "But remember, you asked for this."

Catching the dog under the elbows, he dragged it under the water with him.

"YOU'RE ASKING FOR trouble," Hank said to Jane when she got home that night. "Letting that no-account jailbird hang around your shop."

Jane looked around automatically for Aidan, who was doing his homework at the kitchen table. "Dad, can we not use that word, please?" she asked in a lowered voice.

Hank's bushy eyebrows shot down. "Are you defending him now, too?"

Too? Who was defending Gabe to her father? Not that it mattered to Jane.

"No, I'm trying to protect . . ." Her gaze went to her son. *Aidan.*

She had talked to him, tried to talk to him, about his father in prison.

It's a place where grownups go when they break the rules, she had explained to his down-bent head.

Lauren and all the books had advised her to be honest, to talk to him about his feelings.

You know you're safe now, don't you, Boo? His baby name, shortened from Pooh Bear. *I talked to a lawyer to make sure he can never try to see you, never try to take you away, again.*

Aidan had looked up at that, his eyes gleaming through his lashes. *He never tried to see me before.*

It was true. Travis had left them before Aidan's first birthday. Until eight months ago, Aidan had had no contact with his father.

Now Aidan slid out of his seat, his straight brown bangs hiding his expression. "I'm done with my homework. Can I go to Christopher's house to play Legos?"

She rubbed his arm gently, as if she could smooth away some invisible hurt. "Why don't you invite Christopher to come here?"

"But, Mom, he has the new Avengers set."

Jane regarded her son's split lip. His mouth was still swollen from yesterday's fight, but his aggrieved tone sounded reassuringly normal. She didn't want to let Aidan out of her sight. But he needed friends, and the Pooles lived right down the street. Gail Poole was a math teacher at the high school. Nothing bad would happen under her supervision.

"Okay," Jane said as cheerfully as she could. "We're having dinner in an hour. Be home by six thirty."

Aidan ran for the door.

"And watch out for cars!" she called after him.

The screen door banged shut.

"You want to protect him, you'll keep away from that Murphy fellow." Hank's craggy face was fierce, his tone gruff.

In his own way, he worried about her as much as she worried about Aidan.

She smiled at him affectionately. "I wasn't planning on bringing him home for supper, Daddy."

Although I did make him breakfast. Okay, not a thought she could share with her father.

Hank grunted. "Gary Wilson saw him raking your yard."

Jane resisted rolling her eyes. She should have known the island gossips would pass along that little detail. "I gave him a sandwich. He wanted to pay me back. I thought it was actually pretty nice of him. Helpful." *Responsible.*

"That's what he wants you to think. Back when I was with the sheriff's department, there was a guy in this neighborhood went around knocking on doors asking for yard work. Some fool woman says yes and convinces all her neighbors he's really a good guy down on his luck, just needs a chance." Hank stuck his thumbs into his belt loops. "Course it was all a scam so he could case out the neighborhood. Six weeks later, all their houses are broken into and Mr. Helpful is gone. Along with their TVs, laptops, power tools, and anything else he could get his hands on."

Jane knew her dad was only trying to look out for her. But his almost forty years in law enforcement had given him a pretty cynical view of human nature.

Jane had fed Gabe as a kindness. Paying it forward, because she had needed kindness in the past, too, and because he had been kind to that dog.

Not because she was softhearted or softheaded or because she was letting herself be taken advantage of by some hot drifter with hard muscles. Nope. Not this time. Never again.

"I don't think Gabe Murphy was casing out the bakery, Dad."

I was arrested for murder, he'd said. *Not robbery.*

Hank scowled at her as if she had no more sense now than she had at nineteen. "You have no idea what he's capable of. He could get violent again. You really want to take that chance?"

Jane pressed her lips together.

She wasn't an innocent anymore. She had learned to run her business through trial and error, to move past her mistakes and trust her own judgment.

But . . . Misgiving seeped into her stomach. Wasn't it safer, where Gabe was concerned, to listen to her father the cop?

She could take a risk for herself. But not for her bakery. And certainly not for Aidan.

"I have a security system," she reminded her father. "Anyway, it doesn't matter. He's just passing through. He'll be leaving soon."

"Not soon enough," Hank said.

She thought of Gabe's eyes, his arms, his grin, and her heart gave a little kick against her ribs. "No," she agreed. "Not nearly soon enough."

Six

THE PEAKED ROOF of the Pirates' Rest, rising through the trees, felt weirdly familiar.

Gabe had visited the Fletcher family's bed-and-breakfast only once, eleven years ago. But that roofline was etched in his memory, embedded in his brain.

Back in Afghanistan, everybody who had anybody got emails. Digital pictures from home. Mrs. Fletcher sent Luke actual photographs, tucked into care packages of socks and eye drops, baby wipes and hard candy, slid into envelopes along with the latest family news. Maybe because Luke's dad had served in Nam and Beirut, and Mrs. Fletcher had never adjusted to communication in today's Marine Corps. Or maybe because she knew, with a military wife's under-standing or a mother's instinct, that sometimes a guy needed a tangible reminder of home. Something to hold on to.

Somewhere Gabe had hit on the idea of sending his own postcards, palm trees and temples, *Greetings from Iraq*. He never knew what to say. His own mother never wrote back.

But the very act of sending them reminded him there was a world beyond the sandbox. Something worth fighting for.

There was this one picture Luke had taped to his locker—parents, Tess and Tom; older brother, Matt, with Matt's teenage son, Josh; and their sister, Meg—all framed by the sheltering eaves and solid columns of the porch. The freaking perfect American family. Not Gabe's family. But he used to sneak looks at them, the way they leaned into one another, casually touching, smiling and squinting in the sun, and think that would really be something to come home to.

Maybe that's why he found himself standing at the back gate, the entrance he'd used with Luke all those years ago as if he were family.

The prodigal son returns. He wondered if they'd killed the fatted calf for him or if he'd be eating with the pigs tonight.

He never even thought to ask Luke if he still lived here. Too late now.

A dog barked from one of the guest cottages. Gabe put his hand on the gate and swung it wide as the cottage door opened and Luke came out.

He grabbed Gabe in a one-armed hug as if they hadn't seen each other just yesterday. He pounded Gabe's shoulder and released him, fixing him with that uncomfortably penetrating gaze. "You look . . ."

Gabe smiled wryly. "Presentable?" he suggested.

The shower and change of clothes had restored him, on the outside at least, to a semblance of the Marine Luke used to know. As if Gabe had scraped off three bad years along with the bristles and grime, leaving him without his layer of protective camouflage. Clean, but also raw and vulnerable.

Luke grinned. "I was going to say 'less like roadkill.' Come inside."

Gabe glanced at the small yellow cottage. "You live here now?"

Luke gestured for him to go ahead. "Good for Taylor to have her grandparents around."

"And the rent money probably comes in handy for your parents in the off-season," Gabe said.

Luke smiled and shrugged, confirming his guess. "Come meet the family."

A fluffy white cat regarded Gabe balefully from the arm of the sofa before jumping down and running off. A long-legged, long-haired child sprawled on the braided rug in front of the television.

"Jesus," Gabe said. "She looks just like you."

Clear blue eyes—Luke's eyes—met his gaze. "Except I'm twelve," she pointed out. "And a girl."

And a handful. Gabe swallowed a grin.

"My daughter, Taylor. Gabe Murphy. And this," Luke said, sliding his arm around the waist of the woman next to him, "is Kate."

Luke's wife was beautiful, with warm coppery hair and the same cool, assessing eyes as the cat. "Gabe." Her smile was polite, her handshake smooth and firm. "Thank you for coming."

Gabe didn't blame her for the guarded look. He was used to people looking at him like he was a bomb waiting to go off. Plenty of vets struggled to adjust to civilian life. And plenty of civilians didn't wait for a formal diagnosis of PTSD to make a judgment.

Kate was a lawyer. She probably saw all kinds of cases of alcoholism, anger management, abuse. Given what Luke had probably told her about him, it was no wonder all she saw when she looked at him was a rap sheet and a problem.

"Thanks for having me," he said. "Can I do anything? Give you a hand, maybe, in the kitchen?"

"Actually, there's been a change in plan," Luke said.

Right. Gabe looked at the wife. This is where Luke told him they were going out for dinner, just the two of them, away from his wife and daughter.

"Sure," he said easily. He nodded to Kate and Taylor. "Nice meeting you."

Luke frowned. "They're coming with us. Just across the yard. We're eating at Mom and Dad's tonight."

Gabe stared at him, uncomprehending.

"Family dinner," Luke explained. "My sister wanted to get together with everybody tonight, and Mom jumped at the opportunity to welcome you home."

THE KITCHEN WAS full of people. And food. And noise.

"Let me get you a beer," Luke said, plunging into the crowd around the refrigerator.

Gabe had really nice memories of the Fletcher family. But there were a lot more of them than he remembered. Plus, he figured their welcome might be different now that he wasn't some eighteen-year-old boot facing deployment but an ex-Marine with six tours and an arrest record under his belt.

But that didn't stop Mrs. Fletcher from grabbing him and hugging him tight. "Gabe!"

He put his arms around her carefully. Her head came to the middle of his chest. The hair he remembered as mostly black was now a vibrant red.

"It's so good to see you," she said, drawing back to arm's length. Her eyes were damp.

Shit, in another minute, she'd have *him* crying. "You, too, Mrs. Fletcher." He glanced at Luke's dad, a retired career Sergeant Major. "Mr. Fletcher."

Tom Fletcher jerked his chin upward and gave him a dead-eyed drill-instructor's stare. Okay. Not so different from his last visit.

Mrs. Fletcher patted his arm. "Call me Tess."

"Yes, ma'am." *No way.*

"Josh, get those dogs away from the dip," she ordered.

The tall teenager chatting with Taylor grabbed one of the two dogs running around underfoot and hauled it toward the back door. Luke's nephew, Josh. The last time Gabe had seen the boy, he'd been around . . . seven? Eight?

"Come on, Shorty," Josh said.

It wasn't clear to Gabe if he was talking to Taylor or the dog. Kate had disappeared across the room, leaving Gabe with Matt and his wife, a young leggy blonde whose name he didn't quite catch.

Everybody was talking at once. Gabe was relieved when Luke came back with the beer.

"What can I get you, Allison?" Luke asked.

"I'll stick with iced tea, thanks," she said. "School day tomorrow."

Gabe could tell she was about ten years younger than her husband. But . . . "You're a student?" he asked.

She smiled. "Even worse. I'm a high school English teacher."

"Meg, what about you?" Luke asked. "Glass of wine?"

His older sister shook her head. "I'll pass, thanks."

Allison's eyes widened. "Oh, my God, that's it. That's the announcement!"

Matt glanced down at his wife. "What announcement?"

"The reason Meg and Sam wanted us all to come to dinner tonight," Kate said from across the room.

Tess turned from the stove, spatula in hand. "Sweetheart, are you—?"

"Pregnant?" Meg finished. She nodded. "Yep."

The tall dude next to her, with wavy dark hair and lots of teeth, took her hand. Gabe recognized him from the day before, when Luke had introduced them outside the bakery. Sam Grady, the contractor. Meg's fiancé.

There were shrieks. And hugs.

Gabe edged out of the way, clutching his beer as every female in the room swooped on the mother-to-be like seagulls on a bag of chips.

"Why didn't you say anything?" Tess demanded.

"We just confirmed with the doctor today," Sam said.

"Kind of early to be telling everybody, then," Luke said.

Meg's face was pink. "Not everybody. Just family."

Not my family, Gabe thought.

He didn't want to intrude on the Fletchers' happy moment.

But he didn't know how the hell to extract himself without making the situation even more awkward.

"Of course you wanted to tell everybody," Allison said.

Tess nodded. "You'll want to move up the wedding date now."

Meg's mouth jarred open. "But everything's planned. We reserved the venue."

"For October," Tess said.

"But I ordered my dress."

"No offense, Aunt Meg," Taylor said. "But I don't think your dress is going to fit in seven months."

"Not that you won't look beautiful, anyway," Allison said. "But—"

Sam put his arm around Meg's shoulders. "We'll work it out. We haven't had time to think ahead that far."

"Seems to me you should have done your thinking before you got pregnant," Tom said.

"Daddy. It's not Sam's fault."

Tom snorted. "He's the father, isn't he?"

Meg rolled her eyes. "Of course he's the father. I just meant . . . Well, I'm not the first member of this family to, um . . ."

"Get knocked up before you got married?" Josh supplied cheerfully.

Matt cuffed his son's head lightly.

"Three for three." Luke grinned and hugged his sister. "And here we all thought you were the smart one."

"I think it's wonderful news," Mrs. Fletcher said firmly.

"I'm old enough to babysit," Taylor said.

"Too bad your ugly face will scare the baby," Josh said.

She grinned and stuck out her tongue.

"I would love to have you babysit," Meg said. She shot her nephew a pointed look. "Both of you."

Gabe took another pull on his beer. He counted at least four separate conversations bouncing back and forth between the Fletchers like beach balls at a rock concert, everybody in everybody's business while the kids bickered amiably in a corner. It was nice, sort of, just a little . . . overwhelming. Somebody had let the dogs back in, and the cream-colored mutt had backed the old shepherd under the table and was trying to coax it to play. Gabe figured the stray locked up in his motel room would have fit right in.

He was less sure if he did.

"Get you a refill?" Sam asked.

"I'm good, thanks," Gabe said. Mr. Fletcher was still watching like he was waiting for Gabe to drop and give him fifty pushups. "Is it always like this?" he asked Sam.

"Pretty much." His gaze met Gabe's with unexpected sympathy. "Of course, it's not every day they find out their only daughter is pregnant."

Gabe raised his bottle in salute. "Congratulations."

"Thanks."

Meg escaped her sisters-in-law to join them, slipping her arm through Sam's. "That's it, we're eloping."

"Seen your name on a lot of signs since I got here," Gabe said to Sam. "Grady Real Estate. That you?"

"My dad. I'm on the construction side."

"What is it you do, Gabe?" Meg asked.

"He's a Marine," Mr. Fletcher said.

Gabe threw him a quick look. *Once a Marine, always a Marine*, was the saying. But he hadn't expected the old man's support. "Discharged," he said. "Three years ago."

"Before the drawdown, Gabe was the combat lifesaver on my squad," Luke said.

"Is that like a corpsman?" Sam asked.

Gabe cleared his throat. "Not exactly. Navy corpsmen are the real medics. I mostly just tied guys up so they didn't bleed out."

He had fastened tourniquets on dozens of shredded limbs during his months in the sandbox.

"Don't let him fool you," Luke said. "In a firefight, the corpsman can't get to everybody. I saw Gabe slice open a buddy's throat once to keep him breathing."

"Gross," said Taylor.

"Cool," Josh said.

"It wasn't a big deal," Gabe said. "There wasn't any other option."

"You saved his life," Luke said.

That's what he did. What they all did. Gabe shrugged.

"I'm going to enlist," Josh said.

Meg frowned. "Not this again."

His stepmother, Allison, looked over from her conversation with Mrs. Fletcher. "After college," she said.

"I'm tired of school," Josh said. "I want to travel."

"Joining the Foreign Legion," Mrs. Fletcher muttered. Or something like that.

"Sorry?" Gabe said.

"Because his heart is broken," Taylor said in a singsong voice. "His girlfriend moved to France."

Color tinged Josh's cheekbones. "That doesn't . . . She doesn't have anything to do with it. I'm almost eighteen. I want to see the world."

"You need an education first," Meg said.

Josh's face turned stubborn. "I can get the training I need in the Marines."

"It's not the training that counts when you get out. It's the certification," Gabe said.

They all looked at him. Shit. Hadn't he learned the hard way to keep his mouth shut?

But he wasn't in jail any longer. He had the freedom now to speak his mind, to offer an opinion.

He cleared his throat. "You can have all the skills and experience you need. Like, to be an EMT. But if it's not documented, if you don't have that piece of paper, you can't get a job."

"The GI Bill will pay your tuition, though, won't it?" Meg asked. "So you could get certified."

"Yeah." He'd thought about enrolling when he got out three years ago. Before he figured out that EMTs didn't make nearly as much money as oil workers.

They were all still staring at him. It should have felt awkward. Intrusive. Hell, it did feel awkward.

But that was just the way the Fletchers were. *Everybody in everybody's business.* Piling on. Weighing in. They were treating him like one of the family, almost.

"What are you doing now, Gabe?" Tess asked.

Their interest made him want to live up to their expectations. To be worthy of the way they saw him.

He looked at Luke's wife, Kate.

And maybe to change the judgment in her eyes.

He held his beer tighter. "Actually, I'm looking for work," he said to Sam. "You got anything?"

Sam raised his eyebrows. "I might. Why don't you stop by the office tomorrow morning and we'll talk."

"I SHOULD SAY goodnight to Taylor," Luke said a few hours later after they had returned to his cottage. "Sure you won't stick around?"

Gabe shook his head. "Got to rest up. I've got a job interview in the morning."

Luke grinned. "Let me know if you need a reference."

He disappeared down the short hallway, the fluffy white cat trotting at his heels like a dog.

Kate stood. She was wearing her lawyer face again, distant and polite. "Thank you for coming," she said to Gabe. "I'll see you out."

He let her escort him as far as the door, out of earshot of the hall, before he turned. "You don't like me much."

Something flickered behind the coolness of her expression. "I don't know you."

"But what you do know you don't like."

"Luke likes you. He's a good man. His family are good people. They've all welcomed you here." Her gaze met his. "Don't disappoint them."

Hell. He should have been offended. Maybe he was. But he liked her directness. He liked her for having Luke's back.

"He means a lot to you," Gabe said.

Her mouth softened. Her eyes never wavered. "Yes."

"Then we have one thing in common," Gabe said. Maybe more than one. *They're* good people, she'd said. As if she didn't quite count herself as one of them. As if she wasn't quite as good. Or as trusting. "He means a lot to me, too."

She exhaled, some of her tension escaping with her breath. "You're not what I was expecting."

"You're not what I expected, either," Gabe admitted frankly.

She smiled, and he saw what must have attracted Luke in the first place. "You don't like lawyers?"

Gabe thought of the ambitious prosecutor who had delayed his trial for eight long months. The defense attorney who had billed him in quarter-hour increments until all his money was gone. "You know the problem with lawyer jokes?" he asked.

She arched her brows. "Lawyers don't think they're funny?"

He nodded. "And no one else thinks they're jokes."

She laughed. *Thank God.*

"Luke said you do a lot of work with abuse victims," Gabe said.

This close to Lejeune, she must see a lot of veterans' families crack under the stress of deployment. Or the painful readjustments when husbands and wives came home.

Not that he had any intention of comparing scars. Whatever Luke might think about Gabe's tendency to shoot off his mouth now and ask questions later, Gabe wasn't handing Kate that particular stick to beat him with. Everybody knew the children of abuse were more likely to grow up to be abusers themselves.

"Yes." She hesitated. "Luke said you were at the bakery the other day."

Gabe nodded, wondering at her apparent change of subject. Where was this going? "We had coffee."

"You went back today."

Jesus, gossip traveled quickly in this town. "That's right." A thought struck him. "Are you a friend of Jane's?"

"I'm her lawyer."

Hell. His stomach muscles tensed.

He cocked a look at her, trying to make light of this new

information. "What, did she need a restraining order against her crazy-ass ex-boyfriend or something?"

Kate met his gaze coolly. "I really couldn't say."

"Her ex-husband," Luke said, returning from putting his daughter to bed. "He gets out of prison next month."

Boom. Jane was married. Had been married, Gabe corrected. To a scumbag con who probably knocked her around.

No wonder she looked at him like she'd seen a ghost.

"Is that a friendly warning?"

"Just a heads-up," Luke said. "In case you were tempted to play hero again."

Luke knew him well. Too well. Gabe had always been a sucker for a woman in distress, even on patrol when the woman in question could be a hostile, when his instinctive impulse to protect was not only foolish but might prove dangerous.

He shook his head. "I've learned my lesson. I need to get my own shit in order. I'm not looking to borrow somebody else's problems."

Especially not a big-eyed blonde in need of rescue.

"Just as well," Luke said. "Jane's been through a lot already. Her daddy is feeling protective."

"And so are her friends," Kate said.

Gabe laughed.

"What's so funny?" Luke asked.

"Nothing," Gabe said. *Not one fucking thing.* "I got a cop on my ass and a lawyer trying to give me advice. I might as well be back in jail."

Seven

"WE PARKED THE construction trailer out back," Sam Grady told Jane two days later. "You won't even know we're here."

Ha. He had to be kidding. Jane drew in her breath, surveying the men assembled on the porch behind Sam.

She was grateful—of course she was—that he had found a crew to start work on her enclosed porch. She knew the older man, Jay Webber, who had a fondness for chocolate doughnuts, and young Tomás Lopez, Marta's son.

But . . .

"Except for the banging," Gabe, the third member of the crew, offered. "You might notice that. And when we start sawing a hole in the wall."

She glared.

He grinned as if he had no idea how much she hated having her space invaded. Or maybe he just enjoyed getting her hot and bothered.

He held her gaze, his smile softening as if inviting her to share some private joke.

He had shaved, she noted inconsequentially, his bad-boy

stubble scraped away to a mere whisper of texture along his jaw. His hair was clean and tied back. With all the angles of his face revealed, he looked harder but somehow younger, too. His mouth was well-cut and firm, his lips faintly chapped. Would they feel rough or smooth? Would his beard be hard or soft? Her fingertips tingled, her skin prickled all over with the urge to find out.

Her flush deepened. She curled her fingers into her palms. *Oh no.*

"No holes," she said.

"Just in the siding," Sam said. Trying, like the prince he was, to make everybody around him comfortable, to make her feel better. "We need to get down to the plywood to attach the frame to the house."

"Where's the door?" Gabe asked, not trying to make her feel better at all. *The jerk.*

"On the outside," Jane said. "So customers can go around from the porch." *Why am I explaining myself to him? It's my shop.*

"Fine for them," Gabe said. "How were you planning to get back and forth from the kitchen?"

"Through the front door." The same way she always had.

"Waste of steps," Gabe said.

Sam's sharp eyes narrowed, as if he could see through walls to the restaurant. "I originally suggested combining the two dining spaces."

Wait a minute. He was supposed to be on her side. "And I told you I can't afford to lose any inside seating."

"If you replaced that big middle window with a sliding door, you wouldn't be giving up much," Gabe said. "One table. Two, tops. Better traffic pattern for you, better view for your customers."

The possibility shimmered before her. She could almost see it, the front of house opening to the enclosed porch, the porch opening to the garden, the sea shining in the distance. *Perfect.*

Her throat constricted. So did her heart.

She had already invested all she could afford in this expansion. Why tempt fate by grasping too hard, by reaching too far, by wanting too much?

"The plan is fine the way it is. I'm not going to spend another week and another two thousand dollars on a door."

"I can get you the door at cost," Sam said. "Add, say, one day to reframe the opening, and then drywall and paint on top of that."

"Thanks, Sam." She smiled at him. "That's very generous. But I can't afford to close the dining room while you knock a hole in the wall. And I can't do food prep with construction dust everywhere."

"Of course," Sam said gracefully. "Your choice."

Gabe cocked his head. "What time do you close?"

Wasn't he listening? Why didn't he simply accept her limitations, the way Sam did?

"We're open seven A.M. until four P.M. Six P.M. in season."

Gabe glanced at Sam. "I could put in some time after hours. Be a late night, but I could get you framed in and buttoned up by the time you open."

Sam raised his brows. "Overtime?"

"No charge for labor."

Jane's breath went. He would do that for her? Why would he do that for her? "I don't take—"

"Charity. Yeah, yeah, you said." His hazel eyes glinted. "So pay me some other way."

Her breathing hitched again as she imagined all the ways he might expect payment. "What did you have in mind?" Damn it, was that her voice, so breathless? So weak?

"Murphy." Warning in Sam's voice.

"Muffins," Gabe said, ignoring him.

Jane blinked. "What?"

He shrugged. "Pay me in muffins. Or chocolate chip cookies. Or dog food. Whatever you want."

She searched his eyes, trying to see behind the slouch and the smirk. She wasn't used to men offering to do nice things for her without expecting something in return. Was he serious?

Something moved in the yard behind him. The black-and-tan dog, scratching vigorously at a camouflage bandanna that someone had tied in place of a collar around its neck.

That *Gabe* had tied, she realized. He was taking care of the dog now. Was it possible this hard, lean former Marine was trying to take care of her, too?

The thought made her warm all over.

And wary. She wasn't a dog. She didn't need anybody taking care of her.

"You can do this in one evening?" she asked him. Buying time.

His lips tightened, almost as if she had offended him. She winced. Maybe she had. And then he grinned. "Unless you want me to stick around longer."

Her cheeks flamed with relief and annoyance. At least, she assumed that sudden heat was annoyance.

"Gabe's uncle was a contractor," Sam intervened. "Gabe apprenticed with him in high school."

So Sam trusted him. Well enough to hire him, at least.

"And you're okay with this?" she asked Sam.

Sam looked amused. "It's his time. It's your bakery."

Jane hesitated. She could see that damn door so clearly in her mind, how many steps it would save, how much better it would be.

"We're pouring the footings today," Sam said. "If you want time to think about it, I can pull the crew, put them on another project tomorrow. Course, I can't promise when they'd be back."

"You get me the door, I can put it in tonight," Gabe said.

Jane's heart beat faster. "Tonight?"

Gabe glanced at her. "So you can stay on schedule. We need the door in place so we can install the ledger board before we start framing."

She had no idea what he was talking about. But Sam was nodding as if it all made sense. She trusted Sam.

She looked at Gabe, all lean, honed strength and attitude, and wished she could trust him, too.

Or maybe she wished she could trust herself.

She realized she was holding her breath and let it out in a rush. "Tonight," she said. "Thank you."

"MAN, YOU GOT balls," Tomás said later that afternoon. "Telling the boss how to do his job."

Balls, but no brains, Gabe thought. First day on a new job, he had planned on keeping his head down, his nose clean, and his mouth shut.

Yeah, because he was so *good* at that, he thought derisively.

Gabe had the initiative and the experience to be a good Marine. What he didn't have was the ability to sit back and take orders from some dickhead officer with more rank than sense throwing his weight around. *The incompetent leading the unwilling to do the unnecessary*, they used to quip in Afghanistan.

Grady, despite his air of privilege, his expensive haircut and pricey watch, wasn't a dick. He didn't seem to give a shit how well Gabe played with others as long as he got the job done.

Gabe was grateful to Grady for giving him a chance. But, shit, no door?

When Gabe used to do remodels with his uncle, Uncle Chuck would go on and on about work flow and efficient use of space. Jane must spend all day on her feet already. What good was her fancy new deck addition if it forced her into taking a thousand unnecessary steps a day?

Gabe hadn't figured on challenging the boss on Day One. But Sam, surprisingly, had agreed.

It felt good that Grady trusted his judgment.

"He seems like an all right guy," Gabe said.

"Sam? He's a prince," Jay Webber said, trundling over with

another wheelbarrow of wet cement. "If you pushed, he probably would have paid you that overtime."

Gabe drove his shovel into the thick cement. He already owed Grady for giving him a job. He didn't want to owe him for helping Jane. He wanted to do this thing for her himself, his gift to her. Every time she looked at her shiny new doors, every time she saved her feet by walking from the counter to the tables instead of dashing around in the rain, he wanted her to think, *Thank you, Gabe*.

God, he was such an asshole.

"I got what I needed," he said.

"Right, right. You got the door." Webber winked. "And a night with Sweet Jane."

Gabe thwacked the back of the shovel down, tamping the wet cement. Better than bouncing it off Webber's head.

Even with a drill, digging holes and mixing cement was hard, dirty, sweaty labor. The sun climbed as they worked, warming the air and threatening to dry out the concrete before they got the posts set properly. Webber and Tomás disappeared for a break around noon, taking the truck, leaving Gabe behind.

"Sure you don't want to come?" Tomás offered before they drove off. *Nice kid.*

"Nope. Thanks." Gabe had plans for lunch. "You could bring me back a burger, though. And another for the dog."

"That's a pit bull, man. You sure one burger will be enough?"

"It'll have to be, until I get to the store to buy kibble."

In the meantime, the mutt was filling up on Jane's cat food.

"Okay."

Gabe handed a twenty to Tomás through the open window.

"I thought Jane was paying you in sandwiches," Webber said from the driver's side.

Gabe shook his head. "I don't expect her to feed me all the time."

Webber grinned. "Maybe she'll pay you back some other way."

Another woman, another time, Gabe would have laughed and agreed. Hell, he'd even teased her about it.

With everybody listening in.

His mistake.

She had to live here, on this island where everybody knew everybody else. She deserved better than to have her name linked with his.

Don't react. Don't overreact. Anything you say will only make the talk worse. He gritted his teeth, locking the words behind them.

But his body language must have done some talking for him, because Webber lifted his hands from the steering wheel, palms out in the age-old gesture of appeasement. "No offense, man. She's a nice girl."

She was nice. And kind and soft and sweet and sexy as hell. According to Kate, she'd already been married to some scumball in prison, yet she'd managed to get out of that relationship and make something of this place. Make something of herself.

He unlocked his jaw. "Too nice for me," he said lightly.

Too good for me.

The truck drove away.

Gabe turned on the outside hose to wash his hands. The dog lapped water from his cupped hands before it lunged, swiping its wet tongue over Gabe's face.

He sputtered, pushing it aside. "Hey."

The dumb mutt barked, like this was some game he'd invented for its amusement. Lunge. Lick. Bark.

"Knock it off."

They wrestled. The hose dropped. The dog danced, splashing water everywhere.

"Stupid bastard," Gabe said, straightening with a final pat. "I suppose you'll want a water bowl and chew toys next."

The dog lolled its tongue, grinning.

Gabe looked at the sky. Time to get to work.

He strode up the bakery steps, doing his best to wipe his

boots, leaving chunks of mud on the front doormat. Shit. Dirt streaked the thighs of his jeans. His shirt was wet, too.

Jane, behind the counter, looked fresh and sweet. He wanted to get his hands on her white apron and mess her up.

She glanced over as the bells above the door jangled. Her eyes skated over his torso before she jerked her gaze back to his face. A blush stormed her cheeks.

Well, well. He fought a grin. Maybe the wet T-shirt wasn't so bad, after all.

"Gabe. What can I do for you?" she asked.

The bakery breathed around them, releasing the warm scent of vanilla, rich chocolate, and pungent coffee. The hunger stirring his gut became a throb. He wanted to take a bite of something. Someone. Jane.

Jerking his head toward the window, he said, "I'm here to look at your space."

"Thank you, but . . . Can't it wait? It's lunchtime."

He looked around. Sure enough, about a third of the pretty painted tables were occupied, mostly by women, most of them staring.

He liked women, but he was clearly outnumbered. He stuck his thumbs in his jeans, stubbornly standing his ground. "That's why I'm here. I want to take some measurements while the guys are at lunch. I won't get in your way."

She frowned. Hell. She was going to throw him out. "What about your lunch?"

Not throwing him out. Nope. Not at all. She was concerned about him.

Or concerned about having to feed him. *Let's not lose our heads here.*

He grinned at her. "Tomás is bringing me something. I'm good."

He was great. He was in. He pulled the tape measure from his pocket, aware of her watching him as he crossed to the far wall, as he stretched to measure the height of the ceiling, as he crouched to run the tape along the floor. He turned, angling his body for her. Possibly he even flexed a little. *Look all you want, cupcake.*

He felt her come up behind him, a subtle rise in temperature, a whiff of cinnamon and sugar floating on the air. He took a deep breath, his muscles swelling for her attention.

"Why are you measuring the whole wall? You said the door wouldn't take up more than two tables."

He exhaled. *That's right, dickhead, she's watching to make sure you don't screw up.* "When it's installed, yeah. But I need to build a frame first to brace the weight of the roof when I take out those windows."

Her brows pleated. "But you'll take it down tonight, won't you? After the door is in?"

She wasn't busy enough that the loss of a few tables would make a damn bit of difference. But . . . Okay. He could see how it might bother her, having some stranger messing up her space, knocking a hole in her wall. He knew how it felt to have everything you'd worked for wrested away. Maybe she needed reassurance. Maybe she wanted to reassert control.

"I can. Or I can leave it up until the inside wall is finished. If I tack up some plastic, it would keep most of the mess out of your shop."

Those big gray eyes regarded him gravely. "That's very thoughtful."

"Hey, I'm a thoughtful guy."

Her gaze stayed steady on his. The corners of her mouth curved in a tiny smile. "You know, I think you might be."

She retreated behind the counter, leaving him stunned and staring after her.

BY THE TIME Webber and Tomás were packing to go, the side yard of Jane's Sweet Tea House resembled the bombed-out rubble of an Iraqi town. Swathes of plastic and rocks covered the ground where the new deck would go. Piles of lumber, dirt, and sand edged the perimeter.

Progress, Gabe thought with satisfaction, stretching his tired muscles.

He wondered if Jane would see it that way.

Webber emerged from the construction trailer. "We're outta here."

Tomás waved, pitching an empty water bottle to the ground with the construction debris before heading to the truck.

Gabe thought of Jane's neat-as-a-pin bakery, the planters bright with flowers on the front porch. Imagined her reaction to trash practically on her doorstep. "Pick it up," he said quietly.

"What?" Tomás asked.

Gabe sighed. The boy wasn't much older than Gabe had been when he reported to Parris Island. He jerked his chin, indicating the discarded plastic bottle.

Tomás grinned and scooped it up, shooting it overhead in the direction of the trash can like a basketball player at the buzzer. It rattled to the ground. Close enough.

"Boss says he'll be by later with the door." Webber winked. "Have fun tonight."

The truck rumbled away, giving a wide berth to some kids walking three abreast along the side of the road. On their way home from school, Gabe guessed. They were messing around the way boys do, with large gestures and piping voices that wouldn't change for at least a few more years.

As Gabe watched, the big boy in the Charlotte Panthers cap said something to the small, skinny one.

The little kid's hands curled into fists. The third boy bumped his arm, nudging between them. Normal kid stuff, Gabe told himself. Nothing to do with him, nothing he had to get involved in.

Panthers Hat said something else, and the smaller boy dropped his book bag on the grass and lunged, knocking his pal in the middle to the ground. The big kid fended him off, laughing.

Gabe laid his two-by-four on the ground. "Hey, guys."

The three boys looked over, startled.

"We got a problem here?" Gabe asked.

The kid on the ground scrambled to his feet.

"This little twerp shoved me," the Panthers fan said.

The little twerp was red-faced and breathing hard, clearly close to tears.

"He hurt you?" Gabe asked.

"Hell, no," the bigger kid said, affronted.

"Then stop whining. And you . . ." Gabe turned to the skinny boy. This wasn't his first fight, Gabe observed. He had a fat lip, still scabbing over, and a bruise on his cheek. "What are you, stupid? This kid's twice your size. He'll kick your ass."

"Yeah, twerp," the big kid said.

Gabe shot him a look.

The kid turned pale. Any second now he'd start bawling for his mother.

Gabe shook his head in self-disgust. *Big tough Marine terrifies nine-year-old boy.* Wouldn't Officer Clark love to hear that one?

This was why he should never get involved.

The bakery door banged open.

Jane stood on the porch. "Aidan! What happened? Are you all right?"

The skinny boy hung his head, his brown fringe of hair falling in his eyes, his shoulders rising around his ears.

Busted. All of them.

"He started it," Panthers Hat muttered.

Yeah, it's the little kid's fault, Gabe wanted to say, but as the only other adult present, he figured that probably wasn't appropriate. "You know these kids?"

"Ryan Nelson, Christopher Poole, and Aidan." Jane met his gaze, her soft chin lifting slightly. "Aidan's my son."

Her son. Hell.

Gabe looked at the skinny kid with the bangs. "Nice to meet you, Aidan."

Aidan scowled.

"Does somebody want to tell me what's going on?" Jane asked.

Aidan cast Gabe a wild look.

Gabe could relate. He remembered—*God*, did he remember—what it was like when the adults around you didn't understand, when you were always getting into fights, when your own mother was disappointed in you.

Aidan held his gaze, his expression caught between furious and pleading.

Yeah, Gabe remembered.

"Oh, you know," Gabe said, although he was pretty sure Jane didn't have a clue. "Just guy stuff."

Eight

JANE LOVED HER customers.

But at the end of the day, she wanted them all to go home.

At the table she reserved for the island's seniors, old Leroy Butler was working his way slowly through a slice of carrot cake and the daily Sudoku. A group of teenagers sprawled around the two four-tops in the corner, pretending to study.

Jane knew they were only here because they didn't have anything better to do. Nowhere else to go.

Like poor Aidan, settled in the corner, smearing cookie crumbs over his spelling homework.

And, yes, okay, there was that pang. She had built this bakery from—well, from scratch, taking on a terrifying amount of debt to start, working all hours while Aidan napped in his crib or played behind a makeshift barrier of flour sacks. No matter how exhausted she was, or how much Aidan's presence sometimes interrupted her work, she took a bone-deep satisfaction in knowing that she could keep her baby with her, she could be the mother her own mother had chosen not to be. Jane's Sweet Tea House was her dream, made in the image of the home she had yearned for as a child, full of warmth and acceptance and the smell of baking cookies.

She wanted desperately to re-create that mother-child bond, to get it right at last, from the other side. But the older Aidan got, the less confident she was. Jane had no model for how to be a mother to a growing boy now that hanging out at the bakery with Mom wasn't cool anymore.

Other children had parents who worked, of course. Christopher's mom was a teacher, his dad, Jimmy, a park ranger. Cynthie Lodge, another single mom on the island, had two kids, held down two jobs, and was going to school for an associate's degree in dental hygiene. So, yes, Wonder Woman. But then, Cynthie could count on her boyfriend's support and her mother's help.

Travis hadn't liked it when Jane started working. *Your job is taking care of me*, he had said, his eyes glittering. *All of a sudden that's not good enough for you?*

At the time, with bills stacking up and the eyes of the town on her, she had really believed she didn't have a choice. They needed the money.

But there was no escaping the fact that Jane's job had contributed to their marital problems.

Maybe her dreams were selfish. Maybe Travis had sensed even then that there was a small part of Jane that wanted to escape what her life had become, that was relieved to slip out of their apartment every day to wash dishes and scrub vegetables in the Brunswick's kitchen. Maybe he realized that her job gave her a measure of freedom, a sense of worth. She knew he resented it when she started to bring home more money than he did.

And maybe Lauren was right, and the nights when Travis drank too much and exploded had nothing to do with Jane, with what she did or didn't do.

Jane topped off Leroy's coffee and straightened, her free hand rubbing the small of her back.

Thank goodness for her dad. Maybe Hank wasn't very good at hugging or talking or doing laundry or braiding hair. But he took Jane in when Travis left them, right after Aidan was born. When she got up at four in the morning to go to the bakery, when she worked late at night, when she drove to the mainland to deliver someone's wedding cake, he never complained about watching his grandson.

Today, though, Hank's shift didn't end until five, and Jane was closing alone.

Or not closing.

Not exactly alone, either.

The bells over the door jangled, and Gabe strode in, bringing the smells of the outside with him.

She shivered in awareness.

He cocked his head, his long hair free around his lean face. "You ready for me?"

Her mouth dried. The rest of her flooded with heat. *So ready. Not ready. What was the question again?*

"I can get started anytime." Gabe smiled. "Sam dropped off your door."

Of course. The door. Her construction project. Jane pulled herself together. "I still have customers."

Gabe spared a glance toward the tables of teens, Leroy with his newspaper, Aidan with his homework. "Looks to me like you're subsidizing study hall."

"I don't mind," she said honestly. "It doesn't cost me anything to have them here. As long as there aren't paying customers waiting for a table."

He stuck his thumbs into his belt loops. "You still have to pay rent."

He'd surprised her. Again. Most people assumed that buying a cookie or a cup of coffee entitled them to sit in the shop all day.

"There's not much for teenagers to do on the island in the off-season. No malls. No multiplexes."

"They've got a whole beach right on their doorstep."

"It's still too cold to swim without a wetsuit. At least here they're warm and with their friends. Hey, Leroy." She turned to smile at the older man. "Can I box up that leftover cake for you?"

Leroy Butler shook his head. "Didn't leave anything but crumbs today."

"Then how about a cookie to take home? On me."

"That would be real nice. Thanks." Leroy glanced at Gabe. "Everything all right?"

The old sweetheart. He was looking out for her. She patted his arm. "Everything's fine. Gabe here is doing a little work for me." She handed Leroy the bag. "I'll see you tomorrow, okay?"

"So do you babysit the whole island?" Gabe asked when Leroy had left. "Or just everybody who comes in?"

"Leroy lost his wife right before Thanksgiving," Jane explained. "Emphysema. He needs a cookie every now and then."

Gabe shook his head, smiling. "You're something, you know that?"

That's what Travis used to say. *Jesus, Janey, you are really something.* But the words sounded different coming from Gabe.

His gaze warmed. "There it is," he murmured.

"What?" She swiped self-consciously at her face. Flour? Chocolate?

"Your smile."

"Oh." She pressed her fingers to her hot cheeks.

"When you smile . . ." The look in his eyes warmed her all the way through. "You've got a great smile."

"My dad says I have my mother's smile," Jane said before she stopped to think.

"Your mom must be a real pretty woman, then."

Oh. She just *melted* at the compliment, her insides as gooey as chocolate. Which was exactly the kind of reaction that would get her into trouble. "I wouldn't know. I haven't seen her in years."

"How old were you when she . . . ?"

"Left us? Eight." Six months older than Aidan.

"That's rough."

"It's fine." She was fine. She was over it. She wasn't that confused child anymore, so hungry for attention, so desperate to be needed, that she would jump into another reckless relationship with another unsuitable guy.

"Still . . . Eight years old." Gabe glanced at Aidan, bent over his spelling words in the corner. "That's pretty young to be on your own."

"I wasn't on my own. Dad used to make me go to our neighbors' house after school. I had to beg him to let me stay home alone."

She had been so scared, she remembered. So determined to prove to her father that she could be trusted, that she wouldn't let him down.

That she wasn't like her mother.

"We had rules," she said, counting them off on her fingers. "No friends over, ever. No going out, no answering the door. Homework first, only one hour of television, and call him in an emergency."

His mouth twitched. "Sounds boring."

"I wasn't bored. Lonely sometimes." *Shoot.* She hadn't meant to say that.

"So you taught yourself to bake."

She blinked, surprised by his perception. "Yes. Well, not all at once. At first, I just wanted to make dinner."

But her efforts had seemed to make her father happy. She, Jane Clark, could make people happy with her food. It was a revelation. After that, she never wanted to do anything else.

"Ever burn the house down?"

She shook her head. "I was always careful." Which made her sound totally dull and meek and unexciting. Not that she was looking for excitement, she told herself. Oh, no.

"What about you?" she asked.

"I can heat soup from a can," Gabe offered.

"That sounds very . . ." Words failed her.

"Healthy?"

"Efficient," she said.

He grinned. "That's nothing. You should see me order pizza."

An answering smile tugged her lips, and just like that, his green-and-gold eyes went dark as molasses. *When you smile . . .*

Oh, God.

She tugged the end of her braid, as if she could yank some sense into her head. "Actually, I wasn't asking about your cooking skills."

He looked interested. Like, *interested* interested. "Yeah?"

"Yeah. I mean, no. I mean . . ." Her tongue tangled. What was she asking? What was she thinking? It wasn't like they were friends. He was here to work on her enclosure, not swap stories of their childhoods.

"Go ahead. Ask." His eyes met hers. *Definite interest.* "I'll tell you anything you want to know."

She gazed at him helplessly, her heart thudding with possibilities.

Why are you helping me?

Did you really kill a man in a bar fight?

Do you want to have sex?

No, no, no. She cleared her throat. "Tell me about you."

"I grew up in Brightmoor. That's Detroit," he added in response to her obviously blank look. "Shitty neighborhood. Not much home life generally. Lucky for me, my uncle took me in."

She tried to recall what Sam had said. "Is he the one who taught you to be a carpenter?" she guessed, ridiculously pleased when he nodded.

Gabe nodded. "Uncle Chuck. My mom's brother. He took me around in his truck with him, kept me off the streets and out of trouble. Mostly." His grin flashed, making nerves all over her body tingle. "I would have landed in jail a lot sooner if it weren't for Uncle Chuck. He was a great guy."

Ignore the tingling. Remember the jail part. Don't be stupid. "Was?" she repeated.

"He died of this massive stroke. When I was seventeen." Gabe's voice scraped as if he hadn't used it in a while. As if he were sharing things with her that he didn't usually say.

As if maybe her telling her story had made it possible for him to tell his, the way friends do.

Jane caught herself. This was wishful thinking, the kind of stupid fantasizing that got her into trouble. Seeing things in people that weren't really there. Making up a relationship in her head based on yearning and attraction instead of reality.

"We were on a job together, fixing some rotten windows," Gabe said. "Uncle Chuck didn't feel so good, so I went up on the ladder." There was still that trace of . . . something in his voice, deep and intimate. "He made this sound . . ." Gabe broke off, and Jane's heart broke a little, too. "Nothing they could do, the doctors said."

"I am so sorry."

Gabe shrugged, so much like Aidan when he was pretending not to care that she wanted to put her arms around him and give him a big hug. Rub his back. Kiss the top of his head, his cheek, his . . .

Except he wasn't Aidan, and she was an idiot. "You must miss him very much," she said softly.

"Miss him. Missed having a job."

"So instead of being a contractor, you decided to join the Marines."

His face closed. "Something like that. Yeah."

"How did your parents feel about that? Your mother?"

He gave her a funny look. Jane flushed. Because, yes, dumb question. What mother alive wanted her son to get shot at?

"She was fine with it." He looked at the big wall clock hanging above the wedding cake display. "Aren't you supposed to kick everybody out now?"

Subject closed, his tone said. End of discussion.

Okay.

She should have been relieved. She had Aidan and her

bakery. She had freedom and security. She wasn't jeopardizing those for a man again.

Gabe Murphy was a threat to her in ways that had nothing to do with his broad shoulders and big hands, his muscled arms and history of violence. He made her feel things. Want things. That liquid tug of sympathy, those flashes of understanding, were more seductive to her than sex.

Not that she would turn down sex, if he offered.

That is, she would, of course she would, but . . .

Crap. Heat swept her face.

Gabe stood watching her with that unreadable expression, a glint in his eyes that hadn't been there a moment ago.

She couldn't begin to guess what he was thinking.

Just as well, Jane acknowledged. Because her own thoughts scared her enough.

GABE PRIED THE big double window from its frame. Son of a bitch must weigh three hundred pounds. Getting it out was a two-man job. But there was just him. Unless he counted Jane, inside doing some kind of prep work in the kitchen. And her son, taking half-assed shots at a rusty basketball rim attached to a pole by the carport. Outside its shadow, the dog dozed in the late afternoon sun.

So, just him.

The dribble, dribble, *thunk* of the ball alternated with the solid *thwack* of Gabe's mallet. He pounded again at the jamb—the dog raised its head from its paws at the noise, ears on alert—and tugged again at the bottom. Wood creaked. Cracked. His arms took the weight as the window broke loose, his legs bracing as he lowered it to the ground.

The kid missed a shot and went running after the ball. Gabe half hauled, half slid the heavy window to the side, ready for the Dumpster. The light glared off the glass, pink and gold. He looked at the sky. Six o'clock. Gabe's stomach, spoiled by two whole days of regular meals, growled.

He wondered if Jane had plans for dinner.

Not that he had plans to ask her out. He'd never in his life had to buy a woman dinner in exchange for sex. And while he'd never hooked up with anybody's mother before, he had this idea that you didn't take a kid along on a date to a restaurant. At least not a first date. He'd have to ask Luke how he had managed with a kid.

Not that it mattered to Gabe. He had no business getting involved with a woman like Jane.

The problem was she stirred him, rousing old hungers to life. She was so soft, all of her round and pink and touchable, that she woke all his crazy caveman protective instincts. The last time he'd acted on those instincts, he'd spent nine months in jail.

Which was another reason to stay away from her. She had an ex-husband with a restraining order who was getting out of prison in a month. A kid to raise. A business to run.

And a badge-wearing, gun-toting daddy who wanted to run Gabe out of town.

He had come here to find his feet, to make a fresh start. To figure out what he was going to do with the rest of his life.

You could get certified, Meg Fletcher had said.

He shook the thought away. The GI Bill covered tuition—he was fuzzy on the details—but he needed a real job to pay the bills. Anyway, chasing a piece of paper to prove he knew what he already knew, starting at the bottom with a bunch of fresh-faced premeds who had probably never dealt with anything more life-threatening than a hangnail . . . Not for him.

He had enough baggage of his own without taking on Jane's.

But there was that moment, God, that moment, when she looked at him with those soft gray eyes, when all his muscles clenched and every cell in his body whispered, *Yess*. That look that said she was interested in him, like he was worthy of her interest. *Tell me about you.*

He whacked the guide board into place. He needed to get laid.

Because what were the odds, really, that a woman like her would give a guy like him the time of day?

From what he'd seen of her today—with the teenagers, with the old guy who'd lost his wife—bakers must operate like bartenders, making them all feel better, making them all feel special. Treating them all with that same warm, focused attention, feeding them all out of her bounty and the goodness of her heart. Maybe she was simply being nice to him. Or worse, felt sorry for him.

He set the depth of the circular saw and ran it up along the board, buzzing through the cedar shake siding.

No wonder that his sex-starved brain, his eager dick, mistook her sympathy for something else. He'd probably imagined that moment of electric awareness.

But he hadn't imagined that blush.

Gabe released the trigger, stopping the saw. So . . . Yeah. There was that.

He moved the ladder to work on the other side. From the corner of his eye he could see the kid, Aidan, creeping closer.

The pull of power tools on the American male, Gabe thought.

When he was that age, he used to sit on an upturned bucket, watching Uncle Chuck at work. Even then, his uncle found him things to do, little shit that would make him feel useful.

At least let me take him for the day, Uncle Chuck would say to Mom, lowering his voice to avoid waking Pop, sleeping it off in the next room. *He'll be safe with me.*

And Mom, moving stiffly, a bruise on her arm like the shadow of a hand, would wince and agree.

You must miss him very much.

His throat burned. Ah, Christ. He couldn't afford this kind of distraction. Not unless he wanted to lose a finger. He blinked and went back down the ladder.

The kid stood watching from a few yards away, eyes gleaming beneath that straight fringe of hair.

"Circular saw." Gabe held it up for inspection before

swapping it for the next tool. "Reciprocating saw." Like he was doing freaking show-and-tell at the kid's school. "You don't touch either one. Got it?"

The kid nodded, solemn as an owl.

Gabe cleared his throat. "Good."

He went back up the ladder. Sawdust flew beneath his blade. The vibration shook his hands. The noise filled his ears and rattled his brain.

When he had finished the cut near the header board, he climbed down the ladder and grabbed the crowbar, prying away the cedar shakes to expose the sheathing beneath. He picked one up, winged it away. Both the dog and the boy turned their heads to watch its flight. Pry, tug, toss. It was dirty, tedious work, but the stack of shingles grew slowly, along with his sense of accomplishment.

"You missed the pile," Aidan said.

Gabe pushed up his safety goggles. "You think you can do better?"

"Can't do worse."

Gabe bit back a grin. "How old are you?"

The boy's chin stuck out. "Seven and a half."

Anybody who still counted their age in months was too young to work with splintering wood and rusty nails. But it wasn't Gabe's job to explain that to the kid. "How about you work on your jump shot instead?"

"The hoop's too high."

Gabe eyed the hoop, which listed slightly below regulation height. In Helmand Province, he and his buddies had spent some downtime shooting a soccer ball at a tire mounted on the combat outpost wall. Of course, they were all over four feet tall.

"You're not shooting from the pocket," Gabe said.

Aidan looked blank.

"Get your elbow under the ball. Up and down," Gabe instructed, demonstrating in the air. "Yeah, like that. Now raise your arm. See? Straight line from your eye to the ball to the basket."

Aidan glanced at him uncertainly.

Gabe bit back a grin. "Don't look at me. Look at the target. Good. Bend your knees. Now shoot."

The ball arced short of the rim.

"Not bad." Gabe corralled the ball before it could roll into the pile of shingles and bounced it back to the kid.

"I missed."

"So you need a little practice."

Movement at the back door. Even before Afghanistan, before jail, Gabe had always had excellent peripheral vision. His body tensed and then relaxed. *Jane.*

The mutt, recognizing the source of its food, lunged joyfully to greet her.

Jane stiffened instinctively, thrusting out her hand to deflect its nose from her crotch. The dog cringed, head shy.

"Easy," Gabe called.

Jane shot him a dry look. "Are you talking to me? Or the dog?"

He grinned. "Both."

She took a deep breath—*Hello, breasts*—and reached out gingerly. The mutt ducked its head before submitting to her touch.

Gabe watched her fingers stroke the dark fur, an unfamiliar yearning tightening his chest. "Lucky bas—" He remembered the kid in time and shut up.

"Is that your dog's name?" Aidan asked. "Lucky?"

"Uh." Gabe cleared his throat. "Yeah." Why not? He had to call it something.

Jane sidled around the dog, her gaze slipping past Gabe to the edge of the construction. "Is everything all right out here?"

Her view was blocked—mostly—by the corner of her building. But all she had to do to see the full extent of the destruction was step into the bakery's dining room. Gabe had done his best to protect the space with tarps and plastic curtains, but demo was always messy.

"It's all good," he promised. Which wasn't much reassurance, but it was all he could give her. For now.

She regarded him with those wide, considering eyes, still absently petting the mutt panting at her side. *Stroke, stroke.* Every muscle in Gabe's body sat at attention and begged. "Aidan's not getting in your way, is he?"

What? Gabe shook his head, trying to dislodge the image of those fingers on his skin. "Nope."

"Mr. Murphy's teaching me how to make a jump shot," Aidan said.

Jane tilted her head. "More guy stuff?"

She didn't *sound* annoyed, Gabe thought hopefully. "You never played basketball when you were a kid?"

Color tinged her face. "Do I look like a basketball player to you?"

"Well . . ." Given permission to roam, his gaze dipped down to her amazing breasts, her round, full hips. He'd pick her to play on his team any day. He grinned. "You're a little short."

"Mom, watch!"

Aidan threw the ball, which rattled off the rim.

Gabe snagged the rebound. "Almost there, sport. Try again." He watched the kid fumble. "Like this." He got behind Aidan, adjusting his stance, positioning his arm. "Ball in the pocket. Eyes on the basket. This hand—your free hand— you're not throwing with this hand, okay? It's just there to guide the ball. Right. Now bend your knees. And . . . shoot."

Aidan launched the ball.

This time Gabe followed it to the basket and tipped it in. "Good job."

The kid beamed, cracking his split lip. "Go, team!"

"Yeah." Jesus, he had a smile like his mother's. "Nice assist." Gabe bounced the ball back to him. "Do it again."

"Show me." Jane's voice was quiet and firm.

Gabe's head snapped around. "What?"

"Would you show me, too, please?" Her cheeks were pink, but she didn't back down.

He liked that about her. Liked damn near everything about her, in fact. Which was why this was such a bad idea.

"Why?"

She raised her shoulders in a small, frustrated shrug, which did nice things to her chest. "Because I need to do things myself. I can play with him. I can help him. I'm his mother."

Aidan's mother. Hank Clark's daughter. It would be really, really stupid of Gabe to get involved.

But the kid's daddy was in prison. It couldn't be easy for her, trying to be both mother and father to the boy.

"Sure. Fine." He took a deep breath, inhaling vanilla and . . . and something. He could do this. It wasn't like teaching her to shoot pool, bending her over a table . . .

Or baseball, getting up close behind her, teaching her to choke up on a bat . . .

His mind blanked.

Fuck. He was just getting his life back under control. He was not losing it over soft, appealing Jane Clark.

The fact that he wanted to bone her into next week didn't mean he couldn't teach her how to shoot a damn ball.

Even if she did smell good enough to eat.

"So, you want to shoot the ball into the basket," he said.

The corner of her mouth indented in one of those tiny, controlled smiles. "Yes, I figured that's why it's called basketball."

She was killing him. "Right. Okay. Stand with your feet about shoulder-width apart. Line your fingertips up with the long seam of the ball. Don't grip so hard." Did that sound dirty to her? Because, with her sweetness filling his head, with all that softness close enough to touch, it sounded dirty to him. "You want a little air here. Like this." He demonstrated. "Balance the ball on one hand."

"Your hands are bigger than mine," she complained goodnaturedly, but she followed his instructions, stretching her small fingers to span the ball.

Gabe frowned, laying one finger on a small discolored circle near the crease of her thumb. "What's this?"

She glanced down, distracted. "Oh. A burn."

"And this?" A series of thin silver scars at the base of her little finger.

"It's nothing. Just a cut."

More than one. A slippery knot tied itself in his gut. He'd figured her hands would be like the rest of her. Smooth. Unblemished. Or like her pastries, pretty and perfect. But this close he could see they were covered in nicks and burns, calluses and scars.

"How did you cut yourself?" he asked, dreading her reply. Already knowing her answer.

Inside, he felt like he was freaking five years old again, trying to make sense of the noises in the night, the bruises on his mother's throat, her arm. *"You hurt yourself, Mommy?"*

"It's nothing, honey. Hush. Mommy bumped into a door."

Or, *"I tripped on the stairs. It was an accident."*

Never, *Daddy backhanded Mommy onto the floor*, or shoved her hard against the cabinets or knocked her down and made her bleed.

"I don't remember," Jane said. "It must have been an accident."

The knot tightened.

See, this was the reason he couldn't let himself care. The real reason he wouldn't get involved with any woman soft enough, vulnerable enough, weak enough to live with an abuser. To lie about it, to make excuses for him.

He'd tried to protect his mother, and she'd thrown him out of the house. He'd tried to defend Dani Nilsen and spent nine months in jail. He couldn't do this anymore. He'd already proved he wasn't anybody's knight in shining armor.

At his continued silence, Jane glanced at him sideways. "I guess that sounds a little strange."

Not strange at all. Familiar. The knot moved into his throat, threatening to strangle him.

"It's just . . . I'm a baker," she continued. "I'm surrounded all day by knives and stoves and mixer blades and pots of boiling caramel. I'm so used to burns and cuts I don't even notice them anymore."

"A baker," he repeated stupidly.

She flushed a little. "My job's not all fondant and royal icing, you know."

He hadn't known. He hadn't thought.

He looked at her small hand again, seeing it differently. Seeing her differently, her injuries transformed from the secret symptoms of abuse to signs of strength, souvenirs of a mission, like a Marine's battle scars.

He had the stupidest impulse to bend his head and kiss each mark, the callus where her knife must rest, the purple burn inside her wrist.

He swallowed, forcing a grin. "So, you can handle yourself in the kitchen. Let's see what you can do on the court, cupcake."

Nine

GABE WATCHED JANE chase after the ball. Which she did a lot, since neither she nor the kid could shoot worth a damn. The ball clanged against the rim and ricocheted off the gravel.

Do I look like a basketball player to you? she had asked, an unexpected edge to her tone, that flash of humor in her eyes. A cupcake with attitude. He liked that.

Watching her was definitely entertaining, like enjoying the cheerleaders instead of the game. When she jumped, when she ran, everything under her apron bounced and bobbed.

She was a good sport, though, flushed and smiling, brimming with energy even at the end of whatever kind of day she'd had. As if spending time with her son, playing two-on-one basketball on a rusting hoop against the handyman, was her idea of a good time. She touched Aidan sometimes in passing, ruffling his hair, bumping his shoulder, adjusting his grip the way Gabe had shown her, and Gabe's whole body clenched in longing.

His throat tightened. He couldn't remember the last time

somebody had touched him that way, with casual affection. Tess Fletcher, maybe. His uncle.

Lucky barked and danced around them, making little openmouthed runs at the ball. As if anything the humans were chasing must be edible, and the dog wanted in on the action.

Aidan laughed, high-pitched, gleeful.

Gabe widened his stance, his elbows on his knees, pretending to guard the basket while he made himself short enough for them to shoot over. "Come on, show me what you've got."

Jane's gaze met his, her face shining with joy and exercise and laughter, and he went temporarily blind, as if he'd stared too long at a pink, gold, round sun.

She said something—his ears registered sound—but he couldn't hear actual words. So, temporarily blind *and* deaf.

Which meant he was basically fucked in an ambush situation. He almost didn't care. He couldn't look away.

"You got a license for that dog?" Hank Clark said behind him.

Gabe's muscles bunched, his body registering the threat before his mind caught up. He straightened slowly. Turned.

Clark stood at the edge of the gravel, arms crossed, face like a minefield, rutted and dangerous.

Yep. Fucked.

Aidan stumbled over the ball. He picked it up, looking silently from his grandfather to Gabe, alert in the way that children learned to be alert to the tension in the air. The dog's ears were forward, its eyes wide.

Hell.

Gabe had always had problems kowtowing to authority. Nine months ago—hell, three days ago—he would have told the old man to take his license and shove it. But things were different now. New job. Clean slate. Gabe was different. People trusted him now—Luke, Sam, Jane. He couldn't let them down. He would not let himself down.

There was no honor and no satisfaction in taking down

a country cop thirty years his senior. Especially not in front of the cop's daughter and grandson.

He took a deep breath and shifted into parade rest, eyeballs front, hands out of trouble at the small of his back. "No, sir."

"It's Lucky, Grandpa," Aidan said.

Hank spared his grandson a brief glance. "Lucky, huh? We'll see." He fixed his glare on Gabe. "Mutt got a name tag? Rabies tag? Collar?"

"No, sir." Some of the best DIs and worst officers in the world had busted Gabe's balls. He had learned long ago that there was no point in making explanations or excuses. The suspicious father in front of him wouldn't accept them in any case. *Just answer the questions. Keep it simple, stupid.*

The mutt's ears shifted back and forth. Its tail tucked close to its body. Gabe knew how it felt.

"What is that, a pit bull?" Hank asked.

Jane and the kid both looked at Gabe.

"He was a stray," Gabe said. "Until two days ago."

"Figures," Hank growled. "No telling what sort of diseases it's picked up running around. Or you, either."

Gabe gritted his teeth, forcing himself not to respond.

Jane squeezed her son's shoulder. "Aidan, run in and get your backpack. Dad, I don't think this is an appropriate discussion to have right now."

Gabe and Hank both looked at her, taken aback by her intervention. Aidan set down the ball and ran into the house. The screen door banged behind him.

Lucky flinched at the noise and slunk closer to Gabe, body lowered, hackles raised.

Hank recovered first. "It looks vicious. Somebody has to protect my grandson."

"Dad, they were fine. They were playing," Jane said.

She was *defending* him. She was standing up for *him* against her father. Okay, for his dog, but still, it gave Gabe hope.

"You want the boy to get rabies?" Hank demanded.

"Of course not. And he won't." But there was a little pleat between her brows. Her finger crept up to twine in her braid.

Gabe unclenched his jaw enough to speak. "I'll take care of it."

There must be a vet on the island. Luke would know. All Gabe had to do was pay for the shots. And a collar. And a license.

Shit. This was why he should keep his mouth shut, why he shouldn't get involved. He was supposed to be getting his life back on track, not throwing his time and money away on a dog.

"There's an animal hospital in Beaufort. You could make it in an hour. If you had a car," Hank added with a gleam. "You should go there."

Permanently, his tone implied.

The old bastard. "You got a problem with my dog being here, *sir*"—Gabe packed the word with all the aggression he couldn't express—"I'll deal with it. You got a problem with me, you can take it up with my boss."

Hank snorted. "I don't need to talk to Sam."

Gabe held his gaze. "I meant your daughter. I'm doing this for her."

"Gabe is installing the door as a favor," Jane said. Taking his part again. He didn't need her protection, but it felt nice, all the same. "On his own time. For free."

"If you believe that, you're stupider than I thought," Hank said.

Jane's cheeks flushed ugly red, like he'd slapped her.

Lucky growled, very softly, responding to Hank's tone of voice. Or maybe to Gabe's sudden stillness.

He dropped his hand, gripping the bandanna around the dog's neck. He didn't have a hope of holding the dog back if it decided to give him the slip. One twist, and Lucky could be free. Serve the son of a bitch right if the dog bit him in the ass.

Except then Lucky would be locked up for sure.

And Jane wouldn't thank him if his dog attacked her

father, no matter how offensive the old man was. Especially when he was only trying—damn it—to protect his daughter and grandson.

So for Jane's sake, for the dog's sake, Gabe held on.

"Did Grady even do a background check before he hired this guy?" Hank demanded. "Because he didn't come to us."

"Grady doesn't need police permission to put me on his payroll," Gabe said.

"Which is why we got a problem in this country," Hank said. "Bunch of transients and criminals taking jobs from ordinary folks."

"Dad," Jane protested.

Gabe shot her a look. She hadn't objected when Clark insulted her. But she was quick enough to speak up when he attacked someone else.

Hank shifted his weight, not quite meeting her eyes. "What? I'm just saying you don't know anything about this guy."

Aidan came out of the bakery, his backpack slung over one thin shoulder.

"Get in the car. We're going out for pizza," Hank said. He looked at Jane. "You, too."

Jane crossed her arms over her apron, a feminine echo of her father's pose. "I'm not leaving Gabe here alone."

Hank gave a short nod. "You want him supervised, fine. You take Aidan on home. I'll stick around, keep an eye on things."

Gabe ground his teeth together. He hadn't signed on to spend his evening with the chain gang boss. But what could he say? The guy was Jane's father. Objecting would only prove that the son of a bitch was right, that Gabe was using the job as an excuse to be around her, as an opportunity to score.

Jane hugged her arms tighter. For comfort? Or strength? "My bakery, my responsibility." Her voice was quiet but firm. "I appreciate you taking Aidan, Dad, but I'm staying."

Her starch surprised Gabe. Maybe it surprised Hank, too, because after a few more grumbles, he got into the squad car.

"Thanks, Dad."

"Don't be too late," he said gruffly.

She touched her fingers to the car door, a kiss of flesh to metal. "I'll call you."

She hugged Aidan good-bye. He squirmed and climbed into the back like a little model prisoner. Looking out the window at Gabe, the boy raised his hand, fingers curled in a tiny wave on the other side of the glass.

Something in Gabe's chest expanded, his lungs, his heart, pushing against his ribs. He winked.

The boy smiled.

And Hank drove them away.

"Well." Jane wiped her hands on her apron. "That was . . ."

Awkward, Gabe thought.

At least the dog hadn't bitten anybody.

"He doesn't mean to be . . . That is, he's concerned," Jane said. "He's just not very good at expressing himself."

Gabe raised an eyebrow. "I'd say his concerns came through loud and clear."

She bit her lip. "I know he can be a little overprotective. After my mom left, it was just him and me. And then him and me and Aidan. It's hard for him to respect my personal boundaries."

"Personal boundaries," Gabe repeated.

"That's what Lauren says. Lauren Patterson. She's a counselor at the school?"

Her voice rose a little, like she was asking a question. Like he made her nervous or something. Like he could turn vicious, like his dog.

Gabe winced a little. "I get it. No worries. I can respect the hell out of your personal boundaries."

She searched his face, those big gray eyes wide and doubtful. "If you don't want to install the door now . . ."

"Not right now."

Her expression fell. "That's okay. I understand."

Gabe frowned. From her reaction, you would have thought he was leaving her in the lurch, with a hole in her wall and the door leaning against the side of the building.

"I need to frame the new opening first," he explained. "Might take another hour. Maybe two."

She blinked. "You're not mad?"

"Why would I be mad?"

"Because my father insulted you."

A smile tugged his mouth. "I've been cussed out by the meanest drill instructors on the planet. You want to insult me, you're going to have to try a lot harder."

Her face, her whole body, relaxed. Cautiously, she smiled back.

"I don't blame your dad for busting my chops," Gabe continued. "Doesn't matter how old you get, he still sees you as his baby girl. Me? I'm a drifter with a rap sheet."

"But you were found not guilty. I heard . . ." She closed her lips tight.

He ought to be grateful the gossips had acquitted him. But no amount of talk changed the facts.

"A guy is dead. That's still on me."

She met his gaze straight on. "Did you mean to kill him?"

He didn't expect her to understand. "I'm a Marine. I'm trained to win. You go into a fight, you make sure when the other guy goes down, he doesn't get up to fight again."

"Why were you fighting?"

Gabe massaged the back of his neck with one hand. He should be used to repeating the story by now. To the cops, to the lawyer, to the judge. But he didn't want to talk about that night. He didn't like to remember. He sure as hell didn't want to go into all the gory details with a woman he was trying to . . .

Well. With a woman he liked.

On the other hand, Jane wasn't looking to convict him, wasn't asking just to feed the local gossip machine. He was hanging around her place. Her son. He owed her some kind of explanation.

"I came out of the bar," he said. That night, he'd stayed until closing time, reluctant to return to the quarters he shared with five other guys, the trailer that always smelled of old socks, French fries, mold, and sweat. "And I heard her. Dani."

He'd thought at first she was doing it with her boyfriend in the alley. There was precious little privacy in a fracking town. No lover's lane, no empty motel rooms. He'd seen her with the guy a couple of weeks before. But . . .

"There were four of them." Holding her down, egging one another on. "The first guy I pulled off hit the wall head-first. When the other three ran off, he was still lying there."

"It was an accident," Jane said.

Gabe frowned. "Not an accident. I told you, I'm trained—"

"To protect people," she said. "You didn't want him dead."

He looked down at his big, callused hands, still grimy from tearing out the window. "No," he admitted.

After he'd checked on Dani, after he'd stripped off his jacket to wrap her in, he'd actually tried to revive the son of a bitch until the sheriff arrived.

"I screwed up," he said.

"You made a mistake. Everybody makes mistakes. You shouldn't be judged your entire life because of one error in judgment."

He stared at her. She was serious. She actually believed him. Believed in him.

Her earnest expression faltered. "Unless that's what you think. Unless you believe that everybody gets what they deserve. You know, a woman works in a bar, wears the wrong clothes, marries the wrong guy, she should accept the consequences."

"Hell, no," he growled. "Dani wasn't asking to be raped. It was four on one."

"I wasn't talking about Dani," Jane said.

Understanding burst in his brain, her words smacking him upside the head like a two-by-four. *Everybody gets what they deserve. A woman marries the wrong guy, she should accept the consequences.*

She had a restraining order against her ex. He knew what that meant. He *knew*, and the knowledge made him sick, in his heart and in his gut.

He wanted to tear apart the man who had hurt her, to strike out at anybody who thought they had a right to judge her.

Slowly, he uncurled his fists. He couldn't fix this problem by beating on it. "There are mistakes, and then there's just bad luck. The guy you married . . . Did you love him?"

"I was nineteen," Jane said. "But yes, I did. Which makes me an idiot."

"Nope, it makes you nineteen." The age of wishful thinking, of believing you were invulnerable. The age of most of the recruits who came to Parris Island hoping to belong to the brotherhood or save the world from terrorism or escape shit at home. "It means you went into it for the right reasons. He turns out to be a shit, that's on him. You've got nothing to be ashamed of. You did what you did out of love."

"So did you."

He shook his head. "It wasn't like that. I didn't love Dani. I barely knew her."

"That makes what you did even more special. You chose to put yourself at risk, to lay down your life, for a stranger."

She made it sound almost religious. Which was a laugh. If there was a God, He hadn't paid much attention to the child Gabe. Now that he was an adult, Gabe figured he was returning the favor.

"I just reacted," he said. "It's my training."

Jane's eyes shone. "It's you. You're a good man. You did the right thing for the right reasons when you had nothing to gain."

Ah, Jesus. He stared at her, shaken. In all his life, no woman had ever looked at him that way, like he was . . . *a good man.* No woman had ever said that to him before.

He swallowed the lump in his throat. "Nothing to gain and nothing to show for it."

"That woman you saved, Dani . . . She wouldn't agree with you. I'm sure she appreciates what you did."

He looked down at his hands again. "She wouldn't testify," he said, real low.

"What?" Jane asked, like she hadn't heard him correctly.

He cleared his throat. "She wouldn't testify against them. That's why the DA was able to get so many continuances."

"Was she from around there?"

"Dani? Yeah."

"Maybe she felt trapped," Jane suggested. "She could have been afraid. She has to stay in that community. She has to live with whatever decisions she made. That doesn't mean she wanted what happened to her or that she isn't grateful to you for stopping it." Jane reached out and took his hand, wrapping her small, scarred, capable fingers around his big, rough ones.

"You saved her," she said with a little squeeze. "And one day, she may look back on that, and it will give her the courage to save herself."

She might as well have squeezed his heart. Except that his heart was swelling too large for his body, pressing against his ribcage. He couldn't breathe, all of the room in his chest taken up by his rapidly expanding heart.

It slayed him that after all Jane had been through she was still so stubbornly hopeful, so determined to see the best in everybody. Including him. It made him want to be that guy that she imagined, to live in her world. "Not every woman's as brave as you are."

"I'm not brave."

"You saved yourself. You changed your life." The way Dani wouldn't. The way his mother hadn't. He admired her so much. "You left your ex."

Her eyes flickered. "No, I didn't."

He didn't want to hear it. "You got a divorce. You got a restraining order."

"Only after Travis left us."

His too-big heart was pounding in his chest, flooding his

brain with blood, making it hard to think. He struggled to understand. She didn't leave him?

Her chin raised. "Go ahead. Ask the question."

"What question?"

"The one everybody asks. Why did I stay?"

"I know why you stayed."

"Because I was afraid," Jane said. "Afraid of what he would do, afraid of what people would say, afraid of being abandoned. Trapped, like Dani." She smiled sadly. "So, you see, I'm not really brave at all."

His chest was tight. *Maybe she felt trapped*, Jane had said about Dani, but she could have been talking about Gabe's mother. She could have been talking about *herself*.

He cleared his throat. "Because you thought you could make things better. Because you thought that was on you, to fix things. To fix him. You made the choices you felt you had to make back then."

"It didn't feel like a choice," she whispered.

"You can't judge yourself by what happened when you got knocked down," he said. "What matters is what you do when you get back up again. You're amazing."

She looked at him with those wide gray eyes, a funny little smile curving her lips. He wanted to kiss her so much. "Do you ever listen to yourself?" she asked.

"What?" he demanded defensively.

"You can't define yourself by who you were when you were down. What matters is what you make of yourself when you get back up again."

He frowned, confused. "That's what I just said."

She folded her arms. "You should have a little faith in yourself. Luke believes in you. Sam trusts you."

"Yeah? What about you?" He met her eyes, challenge in his own. "Do you trust me, Jane?"

JANE'S GAZE LOCKED with his. Her heart swelled like a soap bubble in her chest, fragile and shiny.

Gabe stood in the slanting sunlight like a wall, casting a long shadow. His broad shoulders braced against an invisible burden, his work-hardened hands were loose and open at his sides. She was snared by the contrasts of him, the long hair the color of burnt caramel, the dark beard already shadowing his jaw, his easy smile and intense eyes.

Her type, she'd thought, before she knew any better.

But he was stronger than Travis. Tougher. Rougher, too.

Life had beaten him up and knocked him down, but it had not broken him. She admired the way he played the hand he'd been dealt. No complaints. No excuses. He was patient with Aidan. He was kind to his dog. He hadn't provoked a fight with her father or walked away.

It was just too bad that being around him made her quiver like a bowl of pastry cream.

She wanted to trust him. But living with Travis had slowly eroded her faith in her own judgment.

Could she risk her hard-won independence on another mistake?

"Everybody deserves a second chance," she said, struggling to breathe. "Even . . ."

"Somebody like me?" he finished dryly.

Her heart thudded. "I was going to say someone like me."

The air thickened like honey. The sun had sunk to the level of the trees. A faint breeze came off the sea. A nervous chill chased up her arms. She shivered, wondering what he'd do if she burrowed against him to borrow his heat.

"Careful." His voice deepened. "I'm the guy your dad warned you about, remember?"

Jane licked her lips. Even knowing it would be a mistake, she wanted to surrender to the attraction pulsing between them. To give in. To let go. To believe. "You don't scare me."

"Yeah?" He moved closer, and the air around her warmed by at least ten degrees. Didn't stop the goose bumps, though. "Maybe I should," he murmured.

He lowered his head without touching her, giving her enough time and space to stop him.

If she wanted to.

If she didn't stop him . . . Nerves jumped in her stomach. Well, she would deserve everything she got.

He was so close, his breath brushing her lips. Heat radiated from his body. He smelled delicious, like salt and sun and testosterone. She wanted to lick him, the crease of his neck, the hard curve of his shoulder. All over. His mouth hovered over hers, tempting her to take a bite. If she raised on her toes . . . If she leaned in, just a little . . .

She didn't move, her heart pounding in longing and panic. She'd told the truth. She wasn't afraid of him, exactly. But she was terrified of making another mistake.

He cupped the back of her head, his fingers sinking into the hair beneath her braid, his calluses delicately abrading her scalp. She jerked once and was still, absorbing his touch.

He brushed his lips against the corner of her mouth, over her hot cheek to the vulnerable hollow below her ear. She closed her eyes, embarrassed by the frantic beat of her pulse. He nuzzled her earlobe. Took it and bit, very gently. Her mouth opened on a short, shocked gasp of excitement.

He kissed her, his mouth taking hers, nudging for entrance, sliding inside, tasting her with slow, devastating restraint. She was softening in ways she barely remembered, clenching in places she'd almost forgotten.

He teased her to play, a nibble of her lips, a flicker of his tongue, a promise of pressure, a hint of heat.

He was so hot.

He made her hot, too. She was burning up inside, all her air gone, her fear evaporating in flames. She kissed him back, running her hands up his arms—his biceps flexed under her palms—to cling to his shoulders. He felt so good, solid and warm. She sagged, giddy with lust and lack of oxygen, weak with relief. After everything, she could still want this. Want him. Still respond like a normal woman with a normal woman's desire.

How long since she'd been kissed like this? Wanted like

this? He caught at her lips, stroking her open, licking into her mouth, until she was melting in his arms, her thoughts dissolving, her knees wobbly. She pressed closer, flattening her breasts against his chest, trying to get close, closer, feeding on the taste of him, dark and addictive as coffee.

His hands slid under the hem of her T-shirt, rough against the bare skin of her back. She was exquisitely aware of his fingers, stroking up her spine, of his body, muscled and solid against her smaller, softer one. She wrapped her arms around him as if she were drowning, rolling her hips against the thick ridge of his erection, rocking them both.

He made a deep sound low in his throat and gripped her waist.

Yes. The word washed through her brain, surged through her body. She was floating in warmth, carried away on a tide of sensation. *Do it.*

A small, cognizant part of her, standing above the flood, recognized she did not want the choice. If he swept her off her feet, then whatever happened—the responsibility, the blame, the possibility of mistake—wasn't hers alone.

His fingers pressed tight, warm, electric. He pulled her against his hard, aroused body, the friction shocking all her secreted nerve endings to life. She felt the charge deep inside before he eased her hips away, breaking their connection.

She stared up at him, bereft of contact. Of comfort.

Gabe's face was taut, his breath escaping in short, rough pants.

"Why don't I scare you?" he said. "You scare the hell out of me."

JANE STARED UP at Gabe, her pupils dark and dazed, so far gone he couldn't be sure his words had penetrated.

He could have her now. The realization seized him, shook him like a dog with a bone. They didn't need a bed. Hell, they wouldn't even have to get undressed.

Jane's mouth curved in a small, provocative smile. "You say that like it's a bad thing."

She was teasing him. He fought the urge to grin at her like a fool. But he liked that so much, that she would tease him after he'd just kissed her brains out. He liked the sly humor that lurked beneath her calm surface, the quiet strength under her pinup girl looks. He liked everything about her.

God, he was so fucked. Not fucked, he amended quickly. Not going to be fucked.

"I think it's kind of flattering," she added. Her smile faded a little in the face of his continued, stupefied silence. "Not that I want to scare you."

Right.

"I have to get back to work," he said.

Her mouth, full and bruised-looking from his kisses, jarred open. He almost closed his eyes so he wouldn't have to see what he was giving up. "Why?"

His blood pounded, hard and primitive. *Because if I don't I'm going to take you inside and bend you over a table. Take you up against the wall.*

He tried to force some circulation back to his brain. "Because that's why I'm here. I need to bang"—*Not* bang, *don't say* bang—"this out."

She tilted her head, regarding him with grave, gray, considering eyes. "I see."

He was afraid she did. He started to sweat, running scared.

"Do I get any say in this decision?" she asked.

"There's no decision. We're not doing this."

His words stung color to her face. Her soft chin firmed. "I'm not offering to marry you and have your babies. It was only a kiss."

It was more than a kiss and they both knew it.

"It was a mistake," Gabe said.

Her flush deepened. But, being Jane, she continued on bravely. "If I did something wrong . . ."

"What? No. It was fine." *Fine?* God, he was such an ass-hole. She deserved so much better. How about *fantastic?* *Amazing.* The thought of her, hot and round, soft and sweet, in his arms, almost destroyed him. "You were great."

She looked confused. He couldn't blame her. He was confused himself.

"Not a mistake that way," he explained. "I liked kissing you. I like you."

"Then . . ."

His jaw set. There was no help for it. He was going to have to tell her the truth.

"I can't do this," he said tightly. "I can't do this with you. I'm one paycheck away from being homeless."

"I'm not interested in your paycheck." She sounded . . . hurt? Insulted?

He was getting this all wrong. He was trying not to hurt her, damn it. "It's not just the paycheck. I come from noth-ing. I'm fresh out of jail. You deserve better. More."

"You sound like my father."

Gabe winced. He supposed he deserved that. But he was doing the right thing—trying to do the right thing—for both their sakes. Any relationship with Jane would involve her kid. Her skinny, scrappy, appealing kid who was currently not Gabe's problem.

And then there was Jane's father, who could make him-self Gabe's problem at any moment.

Getting involved would only set up both of them—Gabe for failure and Jane for disappointment.

"Your dad has a point," he said. *Damn it.* "The thing is, I can't be with you, with anybody, right now. I've got a lot of shit to deal with. Probably more than I can handle. You have enough going on without taking on my problems."

Her chin went up. "Fine."

"Good." They understood each other. Gabe tried to feel glad about that instead of tense and miserable. Suppose he hadn't stopped. Suppose he'd hoisted her in his arms, her legs wrapped tight around his waist, and carried her into the kitchen? Laid her down on a counter, peeled her jeans from her sweet . . .

"Perfect," she said and went inside and slammed the door.

Ten

A WEEK LATER, the sounds of construction penetrated the bakery walls, rattling the windows like gunfire. *Pop pop. Bang bang. Rizzzzz.*

Jane set her teeth and concentrated on tying string around a bakery box.

The place wasn't exactly jumping. But business was picking up. More vacationers taking advantage of off-season rates, more property owners coming to see how their rental houses had fared over the winter. Her regulars dropped in, buying doughnuts after church and special-order cakes to celebrate this birthday or that anniversary.

But this Sunday morning, they did not linger as they usually did over lattes on the front porch or brunch in the dining room. Nobody wanted to dawdle in a construction zone. Even the seniors had abandoned their usual table.

At least she had fewer tables to bus. A good thing, since she was working alone.

The whine of the saw cut through her concentration. Not alone.

Gabe and the crew had shown up around ten, after most of the early-morning joggers and beach walkers had come and gone. Sleeping off Saturday night, Jane thought, and wondered how Gabe had spent his off-hours. Not that it was any of her business what he did or who he did it with.

He didn't want to get involved with her, fine. She could still feed him. Nobody ever turned down her food.

Every day this week when the crew showed up, she'd had breakfast waiting. Egg sandwiches with thick Canadian bacon and tangy hollandaise. Glazed sticky buns the size of lunch plates, oozing butter and cinnamon. Ham and cheese brioche, flaky and melting. Jay and Tomás had fallen on the food with thanks and gratifying hungry sounds. And Gabe had given her a long, measuring look, as if he suspected her of wanting to poison his coffee.

Heat surged to her face. Not that she ever would.

The tic behind her eyeballs pulsed in counterpoint to the nail guns outside. She had been up since four this morning. Normally she enjoyed the quiet, productive hours as the sky shimmered from gray into gold. But this morning she felt beaten, exhausted. For the past eight nights, she'd tossed and turned, her mind replaying that ~~knee-weakening heart-shattering~~ stupid kiss.

How could Gabe kiss her like that and then stop?

Okay, she understood why he had kissed her. He was a guy. She was blond and had boobs. Sometimes that was enough.

But she couldn't get past the way she had responded, arousal blooming inside her like proofed yeast, soft and hungry.

Or why he had left her shaking with desire and frustration.

"Extra-large decaf soy, no-foam, sugar-free vanilla latte," ordered Suzy Warner.

Awful drink. Everything about it artificial. But there was no arguing with an acquired taste, Jane had learned. People wanted what they wanted.

And didn't want what they didn't. Her mind skittered to Gabe. Her jaw clenched.

The pop of a nail gun filtered through the newly installed patio door. *Don't look.*

"Make that to go," Suzy said. "Extra hot."

Jane kept her smile in place. "Of course. Emmalee?"

Emmalee Swanson, Suzy's walking companion, jerked her attention from the double glass doors, where Gabe and Tomás were outside propping up a ladder. "Oh, a Glorious Morning Muffin, please. And a large coffee."

Jane pulled a cup from the stack and reached for the bottle of syrup. "Coming right up."

Suzy took off her sunglasses to inspect the dining room. "What a mess. Bless your heart. I'm surprised you're even open."

Jane tamped the shot with a little more pressure than was strictly necessary. "Actually, the crew's been very considerate."

Before Gabe left on Friday night, he'd cleared away the chunks of old drywall, tearing down the temporary frame he'd built to support the weight of the roof. But the raw wood stood out like a wound in the smooth-skinned walls, the wiring exposed like bare nerves.

"How long are they going to take?"

"End of the week," Jane said, steaming the soy milk. "You'll have to come back and see our new patio space."

"It's a wonderful view," Emmalee said. "Is that Marta Lopez's boy outside? My, he's grown up fine. Who's that with him?"

Jane resisted the urge to look. "Gabe Murphy."

Suzy's eyes swiveled like a ghost crab's, dark and beady. "The convict?"

Her voice was loud enough to attract attention. Lauren Patterson, behind her in line, raised her head from her phone.

"He's a friend of Luke Fletcher's," Jane said. "They served in the Marines together."

"I heard he killed a man out West someplace."

Jane snapped the lid on Suzy's latte. "He was acquitted."

"Well, you know what they say. No smoke without a fire. I wouldn't have him around my place. I'd be afraid I'd be murdered in my bed."

"I'd like him to come around my bed," Emmalee said. "Look at those arms."

That long, lean body, those rippling arms, those hard, competent hands.

Bang bang. Jane flinched. *Pop pop pop.* Like nails on a chalkboard, but much, much louder.

"Let me give you a hand," Lauren said, sliding behind the counter with a loaded dishpan. "Hi, Emmalee. Suzy. How was your walk?"

Jane took advantage of the interruption to serve the next customer. By the time she'd bagged their order—one cheese Danish, one chocolate chunk scone, and half a dozen cupcakes—Lauren had loaded the tray of dirty dishes into the dishwasher and was checking the levels in the milk pitchers.

Lauren had worked part-time at the bakery last summer, when she was supposed to be writing a follow-up book to her first bestseller about her experience as a hostage in a bank robbery. According to Marta Lopez at the police station, Lauren was actually sort of famous. She didn't need to work for tips and wages.

"You don't have to do that," Jane protested.

"I enjoy it. And you've got your hands full." Lauren shook the thermos of half-and-half before unscrewing the top. "I didn't think the season started until Memorial Day."

That's right, Jane realized. This was Lauren's first spring on the island. "Things start to pick up around Easter. I've already hired more help."

"Thalia?"

Thalia Hamilton, Josh Fletcher's girlfriend, had worked for Jane last year.

Jane swept crumbs from the counter, running an eye over

the tables. "I e-mailed her. She's not sure yet if she's staying in France this summer. So I hired another girl for the front of house, and someone to help me in the kitchen. He's a dishwasher at the Brunswick now, but he wants to train as a pastry chef. I'm really flattered he's leaving the restaurant to work here."

"Of course he wants to work with you." Lauren refilled the sugar dispenser. "You're the best. Don't you make all the desserts for the Brunswick?"

Jane flushed, pleased and surprised. She was competent. In her whole life, nobody had ever called her the best at anything. "Except for the gelato. And the crème brûlée." She watched as Lauren grabbed a rag and the bottle of sanitizer from under the counter. "Here, I can do that. You go home to Jack."

"Jack's directing traffic out of the Methodist church parking lot."

"In that case . . ." Jane wiped her hands on her apron. "Do you have a minute to stick around? I did want to talk with you. If you have time."

"Absolutely."

The bakery bells rang as more customers straggled in, a father with three little kids, a young couple stuck together at the hip.

As Jane filled the father's order, the boy behind him in line hooked one arm around his girlfriend's neck, pulling her closer. She leaned into his side, tucking her fingers into his back jeans pocket. Something about the way they touched each other, so casual, so confident, so *young*, made Jane's throat ache.

She swallowed and looked away, focusing on the father's order. "Sorry, we're all out of bear claws. How about an apple fritter instead?"

Pay me in muffins, Gabe had said. *Or chocolate chip cookies. Or dog food. Whatever you want.*

What she wanted apparently wasn't on the table.

She bagged the apple fritter along with the last two

cinnamon buns and a chocolate chunk scone and handed them across the counter. "Have a nice day. What can I get you?" she asked the young couple.

"What do you want, babe?" the boy asked.

She snuggled closer under his arm, pressing her breasts to his side. "Whatever you want, babe."

Jane gritted her teeth. It wasn't Gabe's fault he'd stirred her up and then refused to do anything about it.

Okay, yes, it was.

But he was right about one thing. She wasn't some teenaged girl hanging on to her boyfriend. She was a grown woman. She had enough going on in her life without getting her panties in a twist over Gabe Murphy.

She rang up the couple and then counted her remaining pastries. Two apple turnovers, three berry muffins, four scones.

"Are you all right?" Lauren asked.

It was almost time to flip the OPEN sign to CLOSED. Should she risk running out? Or bake another half dozen Danish and risk throwing some away?

"What?"

"You seem distracted," Lauren said.

"I'm fine." She could always give the leftovers to Lauren. Or to the crew outside. *Eat* that, *Gabe Murphy*.

Which sounded vaguely dirty. Sexual. She flushed.

"You need to take something home with you," she said to Lauren. "What about the lemon ricotta tarts? Jack likes those."

"Sweetie, I would never say no to your tarts. But you don't have to pay me in pastry." Lauren smiled. "Contrary to what you may have been taught, help doesn't always come with strings attached."

Jane opened her mouth to explain. Shut it again. She wasn't paying Lauren back, exactly. Feeding people made her feel good. Made her feel valued on a deep, human, fundamental level. Everybody needed to eat. Why shouldn't she be the one who got to feed them?

The bell over the bakery door jangled, and Gabe walked in, bringing the scent of the outdoors into her warm, fragrant bakery: sea air and sweat, freshly cut wood and machine grease. Man in tool belt. Ridiculously hot. Whatever he'd been up to last night had not involved shaving, because the sexy pirate stubble was back, tempting her to test it with her thumb. Her breath came faster. Beneath her apron, between her breasts, a sheen of perspiration formed.

He nodded to Lauren. To Jane. "Heard you're closed tomorrow."

The simmering inside her bubbled over into speech. "It's Monday. We're closed every Monday. It's usually a slow day anyway, and I need the time to catch up on paperwork. Plus, you know, it's nice to have one day off a week."

Lauren glanced at her, clearly wondering what provoked her babbling. *Why are you talking? Shut up, shut up.*

Gabe sent her another long, level look. "Forecast is for rain. Sam's pulling the crew to install cabinets on some upfit in town."

Ashley Ingram's coffeehouse. Jane clamped a lid on her boiling emotions, fighting to match his cool delivery. "All right. I appreciate you letting me know."

"I told him I'm taking a personal day. Got some business in the morning. But I can be here in the afternoon to do your drywall."

Oh. Her knees just melted. "I . . . Thank you. That's really nice of you."

He gave her a long look. "Just finishing what I started."

Her heart quivered.

"Really?" she asked sweetly. "Because I thought that wasn't happening."

His eyes shuttered. He turned without another word and walked away.

"Wow," Lauren said as the door closed behind him. "What's up with you? That was almost snarky."

Jane opened the cash drawer, hoping Lauren wouldn't

notice her hot face. "Nothing's up. Why would you think anything was up?"

"You said you wanted to talk."

"About *Aidan*," Jane said. "I was wondering . . . That is, I hoped . . . Did you have a chance to talk with his teacher yet?"

"Caught her in the break room on Friday. I should have told you first thing. The good news is, he's doing well in class. Sylvie says he's paying attention and following directions."

"I check his homework. His grades are good."

"His grades are great. Socially, he's on the quiet side, but he has a couple of friends he usually plays with at recess."

Jane nodded. "Chris Poole and Hannah Lodge. But what about the fighting?"

"Sylvie hasn't seen anything that concerns her. Some roughhousing on the playground, but that's not unusual."

"Bullying?"

"Not that she's observed." Lauren hesitated. "Of course, teasing is common at this age. Sometimes it's a way for children to cement their own social status. Boys especially are very conscious of their rank within the group. So they look for weaknesses, things that may set another child apart."

Jane's stomach pitched. "Like not having a father."

Lauren's eyes were warm and sympathetic. "Or having a father in prison."

"I read that book you gave me. We talked about it. But Travis left us right after Aidan was born. It's not like his dad was part of his life before."

"I know it doesn't seem logical. Or fair. But kids don't always react logically. Have you seen any change in Aidan's behavior at home? Acting out, difficulty sleeping, or issues with eating? New fears? Bed-wetting?"

"Nothing like that."

"Well, that's good," Lauren said, her tone encouraging. "Kids are pretty resilient. It might do him some good to talk with someone, though."

Which was the nicest possible way to say, *Your kid needs a shrink.*

"Would you talk with him?"

"If that's what you want."

"Will the other kids tease him? If you pull him out of class?"

Lauren patted her arm. "I'll find a way."

"Thanks." Jane rubbed at a nonexistent spot on the counter. "My dad thinks I'm making a mountain out of a molehill."

"Is that what you think?"

"I think Aidan keeps things bottled up inside. I think he needs to find a way to talk about what happened last summer."

"When Travis tried to kidnap him."

Jane winced. "Yes." It wasn't only Aidan who bottled things up inside.

"Maybe you need to talk about it, too," Lauren said gently.

"I'm fine," Jane said. Times like this, she missed Mom more than ever. She hadn't had a mother's care, a mother's love, a mother's guidance for such a long time. How could she know if she was doing the right thing for Aidan? "I just wish I knew how to help him."

"You care. That's the important part. Just listen. It would help if you could model good communication at home," Lauren said. "Set an example. Talk about your feelings."

Jane thought of her dad in his recliner watching ESPN. "I'll try."

"Aidan needs to know he can come to you to talk about anything. Even if it's scary or hard to say."

"Okay."

"Good communication doesn't just happen. It takes timing and practice. Sometimes you have to start by sharing the small stuff and work your way up."

"Small stuff." Jane nodded. "You bet."

"Want to give it a try?"

"Now?"

"No time like the present." Lauren leaned against the back of the counter, helping herself to a cookie sample. "Why don't you tell me about you and Gabe?"

Jane smiled. "Nice try."

"Come on, this is practice," Lauren reminded her.

Jane felt her color rise. She glanced around the nearly empty bakery. "There's nothing to tell."

"You've been seeing a lot of each other lately."

"I see all the crew."

"Jack says you and Gabe were alone together last Friday night."

Which meant Dad had been complaining to the chief of police. Jane winced. "He was just being nice. He installed that patio door."

"Was that all he did? Because when he came in a minute ago, you could cut the tension with a knife."

Dear Lauren. Jane was willing to share her failings as a parent. Anything to help Aidan. But her crappy love life? Not so much.

On the other hand, Lauren had every reason to be suspicious, every right to be concerned about the consequences of Jane's poor choices, man-wise. When Travis came around the bakery last summer, demanding money and threatening to take Aidan away, Lauren had been hurt trying to stop him. Jane *owed* Lauren.

She owed Gabe, too. Whatever he'd done—or not done— he didn't deserve Lauren's suspicions.

"It's nothing." Jane lowered her voice. "He just . . . He kissed me, okay?"

A pause, while she pretended to count the twenties in the cash register. Her heart measured the time in beats. *Thud. Thud. Thud.*

"Did you want him to kiss you?" Lauren asked at last.

Her blood got hot even thinking about it. "I don't know. Maybe." No, that wasn't fair to Gabe, either. "Yes."

Lauren made an interested hum. "And . . . ?"

"And nothing." Jane slapped the cash drawer shut. *Ping.* "It was a mistake."

"Why do you say that?" Lauren asked gently.

Because that's what he called it. The memory stung heat to Jane's face. "Because I'm no good at it. I don't have any experience. I send out the wrong signals or something."

Lauren's dark eyes were concerned. "Jane . . . did he pressure you? Because you need to feel comfortable setting boundaries with a new partner. It's important for you to feel satisfied and safe."

Jane wiped her hands on her apron. "Are you talking about sex?"

Lauren smiled. Shrugged. "Occupational hazard. I'm a therapist. We're always talking about sex."

"Because I'm fine with sex," Jane said. At least, she thought she would be, if she ever got the chance. "He didn't push. It was the opposite of pushing. He kissed me"—the memory of his mouth, warm and sure and urgent, surged through her like a wave—"and then, for a week, nothing."

"Ah."

Jane flushed. "What does that mean?"

Lauren took another cookie. "That maybe you're ready for more than kisses?"

"I don't know what I'm ready for," Jane muttered. And now she would never find out. Darn it.

"Mm. I call bullshit."

"Excuse me?"

"When Gabe stopped, how did that make you feel?"

This was so humiliating. "I don't know. I don't go around analyzing my feelings. I just want to hit him with a sauté pan."

"You're angry."

"Oh, no," Jane said automatically. She didn't get angry. She was too afraid of driving people away.

Anger was unproductive and volatile. Dangerous. Expressing anger only made other people mad at you. Made Dad withdraw deeper into himself and his recliner, made Travis explode. It was better, safer, not to feel at all.

"You sound angry," Lauren observed.

"Well, I'm not," Jane snapped. "I'm . . ." *Hurt. Disappointed. Frustrated.* "Furious," she blurted out.

Oopsy. Maybe she was a little mad after all.

She stared at Lauren, waiting for the sky to fall. Outside, the nail gun rattled against the sheathing of the house.

"Well, that sounds honest. And perfectly healthy to me," Lauren said.

Jane blinked. "It does?"

"Absolutely. You're both single, healthy adults, with adult needs. You have every right to be up-front with him and expect him to be up-front with you."

"He was up-front," Jane said. "He told me he wasn't interested in a relationship."

"After he kissed you."

Jane nodded. She understood the brain chemistry of pleasure and reward, how to tempt a sweet tooth with sugar or tease an appetite with salt. But Gabe's kiss was like chocolate, smooth, rich, dark, delicious. The cravings it provoked were almost unhealthy.

"So you're not the only one sending mixed signals," Lauren observed.

"He . . . I . . ." She swallowed. "He kissed me like . . ." Her hands, her capable, scarred hands, fluttered in the air, helpless to describe his kiss. "He's a really good kisser," she said lamely. "I thought, if he wants me . . . Well, why not? Let him do it. And instead . . ." She drew a sharp breath. "He backs off and tells me I have too much going on in my life already. Like I'm too stupid to decide for myself what I want."

Lauren raised an eyebrow. "'Let *him* do it'?"

"It. You know." Jane flapped her hands again. "Let him sweep me off my feet."

"Mm. Are you angry because you wanted him to take

control so that you wouldn't have the responsibility of making the decision?" Lauren asked. "Or are you angry because he did take responsibility and you didn't get what you want?"

Yes. Darn it. "Both," she admitted.

"You do understand that those are incompatible positions?"

Jane looked at her hands. Oh, look, another burn. She rubbed at it absently. "I guess."

"So, what are you going to do about it?"

"About what?"

"About your feelings."

"I reckoned I'd do what I usually do," Jane said, deadpan. "Ignore them until they go away."

Lauren laughed. "Or you could ask yourself, what do I want? What's the behavior that will get me what I want?"

"You sound like a therapist."

"I am that." Lauren held her gaze. "I'm also your friend."

A rush of affection tightened Jane's throat. "I know. And I'm grateful."

"Hey, I get something out of this relationship, too."

"Yeah. Cookies."

"Your friendship." Lauren grinned. "Not that the cookies aren't a nice bonus. But you're an amazing friend. And one of the kindest people I know."

"Stop. I'm not so amazing."

"I know it's hard to feel amazing. Especially when someone who should have loved you unconditionally, all the time, makes you feel unlovable."

Jane had read the books. She knew that one of the effects of living with abuse was lowered self-esteem. She swallowed the tightness in her throat. "I'm better off without him."

"Without Travis? Absolutely. I was talking about your mom."

Jane stared at her in shock.

"You know, my dad died when I was a teen," Lauren said quietly. "After that, I was so afraid that somebody else would leave me that I put up with a lot of shit. From guys, especially. It took a lot of work—and Jack—to teach me that I deserved more."

"I'm sorry about your dad," Jane said.

"Thanks. But my point is, you don't have to settle. Gabe Murphy could be a really nice guy. But maybe he's not the right guy for you right now."

Jane's chest hollowed. As if she'd lost her breath or something equally precious. Vital. Which was stupid. How could she lose something she'd never had?

Only a kiss.

Only a moment when she'd felt charged, shiny, electric from the inside out. She'd felt *hot*.

Jane bit her lip. "You're probably right."

Of course she was right. Lauren was her friend. She only wanted Jane to be happy.

Sex would make you happy, whispered the devil inside her.

Jane hushed it. Making a play for Gabe now, especially when he'd told her he wasn't interested in a relationship, would be every bit of the mistake he'd called it. She felt sad—*You're angry*, the devil said—about that, but she couldn't ignore the reality of her life.

She was Hank's daughter. Aidan's mom. She couldn't go throwing herself at a man just because he had muscled arms and a glint in his eyes, because he was a good kisser and kind to dogs, because he made her feel reckless and rebellious and alive again.

She boxed the lemon ricotta tarts for Lauren to take with her. Slowed work to look out the window.

Gabe was braced on the ladder outside, his long body extended, saying something that made Tomás grin.

Jane's pulse kicked up.

What do you want? Lauren had asked.

She wanted to be a good mother, Jane reckoned.

She wanted to be a good baker, for her bread to feed her

neighbors, for her cookies to comfort them, for her cakes to be a part of every island celebration.

She wanted . . .

Gabe reached overhead, his T-shirt pulling loose from his jeans, revealing the hard, furred ridges of his abdomen.

Her mouth went dry. Oh, she wanted.

Eleven

THE RAIN FELL, flattening the grass and flooding the ruts in the parking lot, turning the blues to gray and the grays to black.

The gloomy weather suited Hank's mood.

"You won't make the rain go away by glaring at it," Marta said.

He turned from the window to scowl at her. With her bright lips and nails and honey-toned skin, she looked like a tropical sunset, warm and vivid. Her blouse was pink. Her bold gold earrings glinted against the reddish tint in her dark hair.

Something stirred inside him. Annoyance, maybe, or relief at having a target for his frustration.

"Shouldn't you be typing something? Or filing?"

She raised her elegant brows. "It's Monday. Nothing happens on a Monday."

"Where's Jack?"

"At the high school, showing his drunk-driving-accident slides to all the seniors before prom. And before you ask, Luke ran over to the mainland with his friend Gabe. Something about an animal license," she added with a pointed look.

Hank grunted. At least the son of a bitch wasn't at Jane's.

Jane was a good girl. Never a moment's trouble until she took up with that no-account ex, Tillett. She'd proved herself to be a fine mother, a hard worker. But there was something in her—a bit of her own mother, maybe—that made Hank uneasy. A restlessness, a recklessness, that made her a target for the wrong kind of man. Assholes like Travis Tillett. Troublemakers like Gabe Murphy. She deserved better. More.

But had she listened to him? No.

Maybe she would have listened to her mom.

He prowled to his desk and back again. Shoved his hands in his pockets. It chafed a man when he couldn't do better by his daughter.

"If you can't sit down, go home," Marta said.

"I'm on call."

"So, if something happens, I will call you. You don't have to stay here."

His jaw set mulishly. "Maybe I like being here."

"I can tell. If you like it so much, why didn't you take the chief's job when the town council offered it to you?"

He used to be surprised by her knowledge of the island and everybody on it. Not anymore. Made her a damn fine dispatcher, to tell the truth.

"I'm too old," he said. *Too tired.*

"What are you, sixty-four? Sixty-five?"

"Fifty-nine," he snapped, and then realized he'd been had when her eyes laughed at him.

"Not so old, then. You could live another forty years."

Coming home every night to the same damn recliner, the same damn sportscasts with the announcers getting younger every year. Or fighting off age with hair dye and capped teeth. "I'd rather be dead."

"Be careful what you wish for. My husband died when he was only forty-one."

That shocked him into contrition. "I'm sorry." He really was. "I didn't know."

"You never asked."

"I always figured . . ." He saw boggy ground ahead and stopped.

She swiveled in her chair, crossing her legs. Nice legs. "That my husband left me?"

He scowled. His wife had left him. Though a man would have to be useless or stupid or both to leave a woman like Marta. "It happens."

Her face softened. "Yes, it does."

Hank didn't want her pity. "I guess I figured you must have kicked his sorry ass out."

She smiled, but sadly. "No."

"How old were your boys?" She had four sons. He knew that much.

"Alex and Mateo were in high school. Tomás and Miguel were little boys—eight and two."

He didn't know the older ones. But he'd seen the younger two around. "Good boys. You've done a good job with them."

She shrugged round shoulders. Maybe she didn't want pity, either. "We got by. They are good sons. Hard workers, like their father. The older two got scholarships to college. My point is, you are hardly too old to start something new. I was fifty-two when I accepted this job."

Because she wanted a challenge, Hank remembered Jack saying. Before that, she'd worked at Grady Real Estate. Started as a cleaning woman, ended up as office manager. She'd been Jack's first hire as chief of police.

"See, that's why Rossi should be Chief," Hank said. "I wouldn't have hired you."

Her eyebrows raised. "Because I am a woman? Or because I am Mexican American?"

Heat crawled in Hank's face. He guessed he deserved that. "Because I'm an old dog. Too set in my ways. I would have gone on the way things were before, using the county dispatcher. Jack was the one who went to the town council and got the funding for the job. I couldn't have done that."

"You don't give yourself enough credit. People listen to you."

"My daughter doesn't," he was surprised to hear himself say.

Outside the windows, the rain continued to fall, wrapping them in a gray curtain of sound.

"You are worried about her."

He opened his mouth to deny it. Nodded instead.

"Tomás says they are working at the new coffee shop today. Is Jane concerned it will take away from her business?"

It was so far from what Hank had been thinking that he goggled. "What are you talking about?"

"Ashley Ingram's place. Down on the harbor. It could be competition for Jane."

He rejected the idea instantly. "Jane doesn't have anything to worry about. She's a great little baker."

"She is. But I assumed that was why she was expanding her dining space."

Hank frowned. "She didn't say anything to me about that."

"Do you two talk at all?"

"We don't need to talk," Hank said defensively. "Jane knows if she needs anything, she can come to me. The problem is, she's too damn proud. Stubborn."

"Your daughter, proud and stubborn?" Marta widened her eyes. "Imagine."

A grin tugged at his mouth. He turned it hastily into a scowl. "Like this drywall thing today," he said. He didn't know shit about installing drywall, but he could've done something. "I offered to go over there to help, but she told me no. She'd rather have that Murphy fellow hanging around."

"Maybe because he knows what he is doing," Marta said.

"He better not be doing it with my daughter."

"Isn't that up to her to decide? She is an adult woman, yes?"

Hank couldn't argue about that. Didn't like to think about it. So he grumbled, "She wants him to work around her place, I can't stop her. But she's not coming home for dinner."

"Poor Hank." There was a gleam in Marta's eyes he wasn't entirely sure he liked. "You will have to feed yourself tonight."

"I can feed myself. I feed me and the boy all the time." Best not to mention that on the nights Jane wasn't home in time to start dinner, she'd usually prepared something ready for him to heat in the oven.

"Do you mind watching your grandson?"

"No, Aidan's a good boy. Good company." At least one good thing had come out of his daughter's lousy marriage. "Besides, I'm not watching him tonight. He's going over to a friend's house."

Those big, dark eyes regarded him thoughtfully. "You are lonely."

Hell, yeah. "No."

"It's all right. I get lonely, too." She smiled. "Mostly for the company of someone my own age."

His heart thundered. "You get that here," he pointed out. "Company, I mean. People coming in and . . . People." *Me.*

"Maybe you should come over tonight," she said. "Since you don't have anything better to do."

"To your house," he said, just to be sure. His blood rushed in his head. She was widowed. She was lonely. He liked her, despite the sparks that flew between them in the office. Or maybe because of them. He wondered if she brought all that attitude to bed.

"For dinner." Another curve of those bright lips, warm and amused. "And for the companionship."

"DON'T LOOK AT ME like that," Gabe said.

Lucky sighed and dropped his head on his paws. The mutt had spent the morning being poked, prodded, and vaccinated like a Marine facing deployment, enduring the vet visit with abused dignity. The treats and attention afterward had helped. So had the ride home in Luke's truck. But as soon as the dog grasped that Gabe was abandoning him alone in the motel room, the sulks started.

"Sorry, pal. You'll just be in the way."

Usually Gabe took Lucky with him to the job site, but he was working inside today. Not that Jane would throw the beast out into the rain, but Gabe wasn't taking advantage of her soft heart. In any way.

Lucky's gaze, dark and mournful, tracked Gabe to the door.

"I'm leaving you for your own good."

The dog turned its head away.

Fine. Try to do the right thing and everybody hates you.

He locked the door behind him.

"Any mail for me today?" he asked at the front desk.

Bob didn't look up from his magazine. "Nope."

Not today, not yesterday. Not ever. Gabe didn't know why he bothered. His mom never replied to his postcards. Never made that call, the one that said *I'm sorry* or *I forgive you* or *I'm leaving that bastard* or *Come home.*

He went out into the rain. Luke's truck was still parked in front of the building.

Gabe stopped. "Hey."

"Thought I'd give you a lift to work."

They'd marched through worse than rain. But Gabe didn't see any point in getting soaked and tromping muddy work boots all over Jane's clean floors.

"Thanks." He got in.

Luke slid him a look. "You're spending a lot of time at the bakery these days."

"I'm finishing up a job."

"Heard the rest of the crew moved on. Taking your own sweet time because you like the scenery?"

Gabe's jaw tightened.

Another quick, assessing glance. "Whatever you're up to, you've got Hank's shorts in a bunch."

"Nothing happened," Gabe said. One kiss. One kiss that rocked his world and lit up his system like tracer fire in the desert sky at night. "And you can tell Daddy nothing's going to happen."

"She turned you down," Luke said, his voice almost sympathetic.

"No."

It would be easier if she had.

Gabe had lost his head over a woman twice before. Rushed into a situation thinking he could make a difference, believing he could save them.

It hadn't gone well for him. Either time.

Kissing Jane had been a bonehead move. A mistake.

Though she hadn't felt like a mistake in his arms, he remembered reluctantly. She felt soft and firm, smooth and silky. He touched her and he instantly went hard. Hell, he didn't even have to touch her. All he had to do was catch her scent, sweet and hot as something from the oven, and he wanted to lick her, suck her, eat her up. The generous way she kissed him back, that little noise she made—*so help me, God*—tore at his control.

He almost hadn't stopped, and that scared him. His response to her was too intense. Too much. She was too much for him.

Being around her this past week made him feel like a kid at the grocery store, peering in the bakery case, leaving dirty handprints smudged on the glass. Or like a horny adolescent staring out the detention room window at the pretty cheerleader, who had smiled at him the day before, flirting with the quarterback at the edge of the practice field.

He was sick of looking and not buying, tired of needing and not having.

Luke's fingers drummed the steering wheel. "Let your Sergeant break this down for you. You're attracted. She's attracted. Her father hates your guts. So you've got a choice to make, Marine: Do you try to satisfy Jane? Or do you satisfy Hank? Because you can't make both of them happy."

"No choice," Gabe said. "They're both ticked at me now."

"You still have to pick your battles," Luke said. "I can already tell you you're not going to win any ground with Hank. So I wouldn't waste my ammunition there."

"I'm not taking a shot at Jane, either."

"I won't argue with that, but . . . why not?"

"I got my first paycheck Friday. Put down a week's deposit at the motel."

Luke frowned. "Yeah, so?"

He didn't get it, Gabe realized. Their shared service made them brothers. But even the bonds of blood and battle couldn't change their lives before the Corps.

He didn't expect Luke—with his solid family and their century-old inn and his reputation as Hometown Hero—to understand. But he tried to explain anyway. "If you don't count jail, that motel room is the closest I've had to a fixed address in years. I'm trying to turn my life around here. This thing with Jane . . . I'm not looking for that kind of complication. I'm not ready."

"You mean, you don't want it bad enough."

Gabe flushed. He wanted Jane. Imagined having her in just about every way a man could have a woman.

But she wasn't a fucking hill to be taken. He respected her, the way she raised her son, ran her business, fed strays and the elderly. She had made something of herself, something solid and fine and permanent.

"I need more to offer her than a motel room." More than good intentions and great sex.

"Is she asking for more?"

No. And maybe that stung, a little. "She deserves more."

Luke grunted. In agreement? "Two years ago, I would have told you there was no way I was ready for a daughter. When I got home, I'd never had a relationship with a woman that outlasted a deployment. I sure as hell didn't have a clue how to be a daddy. But good things come on their own schedule, not some timetable you set up in your head. I had to accept that." His grin flashed. "And then I had to talk

Kate into accepting me. It took time to earn her trust. Taylor's, too."

Easy for Luke to say. *No clue?* His mother was strong, his father was decent, and his family was frickin' perfect. He'd grown up with their example.

Gabe looked down at his father's big hands at the ends of his thick, scarred wrists and slowly uncurled his fists.

He'd grown up with an example, too. Luke had no idea what Gabe carried inside him. What he was capable of.

"Jane's got no reason to trust me. Hell, I don't trust myself."

"You always did step on your own dick," Luke said with rough affection. "You want to walk away, that's your business. Just make sure you understand what you're walking away from. And where you're going."

Gabe nodded without speaking.

He was done with running away. He had a chance to build something here if for once in his life he was careful and smart, if he considered the consequences before jumping into action.

But when he was with Jane, when he kissed her, he lost his head. He just . . . *wanted.* She looked up at him with those big gray eyes and that full, sensitive mouth, and he forgot everything else he was supposed to be doing and thought about doing her instead. Spread out on a counter. Up against the wall.

That kind of desire was dangerous. Like waving a red flag in front of a bull. He couldn't afford that loss of control.

The best thing he could do for both of them was to keep his distance.

THE SOUNDS OF Gabe working pierced Jane's kitchen, the whine of the saw and the whir of a drill gradually replaced by the rasp of a compound knife.

By seven o'clock, she was a mass of nerves, anticipation swarming over her skin like mosquitoes on a hot summer night, making her jump. Itch.

She opened the bottle of wine to breathe. It was a good

Italian red, with nice undernotes of smoke and spicy rosemary to cut through the richness of the meat, but what if Gabe didn't like wine? Most of the men she knew were beer drinkers. Travis used to drink a six-pack every night. More on the weekends.

She set the bottle on the stainless steel counter with a little clink. She was *not* thinking about her ex-husband tonight.

If Gabe wanted beer, she could offer him a beer. She wanted wine. In fact, she could use a glass right now. Or two. Because if she drank enough, she could probably find the courage to go through with what she was planning. Alcohol lowered inhibitions, didn't it? *I was drunk*, she could tell herself in the morning. *I didn't know what I was doing.*

Except she did. After days (years?) of denying her feelings, she knew exactly what she wanted. And she'd made a plan to get it, too.

She eyed the wine again. Nope. If she started drinking now, she'd burn the steaks. Then they'd never get to dessert, and all her hopes and efforts would be wasted.

The oven timer buzzed. She pulled out the Gruyère potato casserole and reset the temperature to three hundred fifty degrees. The steaks, stuffed with oysters, were ready for the pan. She'd reduced the amount of garlic in the compound butter and replaced the sautéed tatsoi greens she'd originally planned to serve with crisp haricots verts. A manly, meat-and-potatoes meal with enough fancy touches that she'd put something of herself in every bite.

Nothing subtle about this menu.

Or about her intentions, either.

She sucked in her breath, picked up the tray loaded with plates and flatware, and pushed through the swinging door.

Gabe was cleaning his tools, scraping the wide blade of the drywall knife against the rim of the bucket. His hair was tied back in a stubby ponytail. A few shaggy strands escaped, softening his strong profile against the stark white of the newly plastered wall.

Perfect timing. She exhaled, trying to ignore the jumping

of her stomach. "It looks good." Her voice sounded almost normal. "Are you all finished?"

"For tonight. It needs another coat." He straightened (*So tall.* Her heart gave a little bump.) and wiped his hands on his thighs, leaving white streaks against the denim.

Outside, the rain ran down the double glass doors in streaks and spatters of light, casting a sparkling veil of privacy against the dusk.

Jane swallowed. In her fantasies, she said something witty and sophisticated now, something that would make her plotting unnecessary.

But faced with the solid reality of Gabe standing, waiting, watching her with dark, hooded eyes, she was struck dumb, dry-mouthed with nerves and desire. She gripped her tray tighter.

"Something smells good," he said.

His voice released her from her unwelcome paralysis.

"Dinner." The single word made her feel better. She might not remember her lines, but she could cook.

He looked down at the two place settings on her tray and then back at her face, his expression almost grim. *Not* the reaction she was going for.

She set down the tray and planted her hands on her hips. "You won't let me pay you any other way. So you'll eat my food and like it."

His face relaxed, a smile starting deep in his eyes. "Yes, ma'am. Can I clean up first?"

Relief weakened her knees. "Is fifteen minutes enough?"

He nodded.

She beamed back at him and then whisked herself back into the kitchen before she could lose her confidence. Before he could change his mind.

What do you want? Lauren's words replayed in Jane's head as the steaks sizzled in the hot iron skillet. *What's the behavior that will get you what you want?*

Of course, Lauren probably hadn't been talking about seduction. Because that's what this meal was—an invitation to indulgence, a campaign against the senses. Jane might not be successful like Meg or smart like Lauren or confidently sexy like Cynthie.

But in her kitchen, she had power.

She slid the steaks into the oven to finish while she tossed the green beans in lemon butter. Grabbing the wine and two glasses, she returned to the dining room.

Gabe was standing by the table. He had washed his hands and arms and probably his face as well. Water slicked his shaggy hair, deepening its caramel color. His lashes were dark and spiky against his lean face as he studied the fat white pillar candle between the two place settings.

At her entrance, he looked up, his eyes intent. The wariness was back. "Worried the power will go out?"

Her cheeks heated. She stuck out her chin. "I like to be prepared."

His gaze went to the wine in her hand. "So I see." Was there a trace of amusement in his voice? "You want me to pour that?"

"Unless you want a beer."

"No, this is fine. Good." Their fingers brushed as he took the bottle. Her heart did a little jig in her chest. "You shouldn't have gone to this much trouble."

"I wanted to."

Another long, assessing look while the rain drummed on the tin roof and her blood pounded in her ears. Okay, so he wasn't falling on her like Lucky on a bone. But he hadn't run away yet, either.

She held his gaze, everything zinging and tingling and trembling inside her. She could do this. She wanted to do this. She just needed to feed him first.

"Don't go anywhere," she said, and escaped back into the kitchen to check on the steaks.

The steaks were perfect, charred outside, pink inside, the melting compound butter mingling with the briny flavor of the oysters. The potatoes were creamy and fragrant, the edges crispy and golden.

Gabe ate a third of his steak and dug a sizable dent in the potatoes before coming up for air. "You cook like this every night?"

She gulped her wine. "Pretty much," she lied.

"So what made you decide to be a baker?"

"I love baking."

"Yeah, but this . . . this is amazing. You said you learned to cook because you wanted to make dinner. You could be a chef someplace."

He actually listened when she talked. He remembered what she told him. A warm, golden glow settled inside her. Or maybe that was the wine.

She took another sip. "I don't have the temperament to be a line cook."

"What do you mean?"

"I worked for a little while at the Brunswick. Dinner shift in a restaurant kitchen . . . It's chaos. Everybody's yelling, rushing, trying to do three or five things at once. Cooks love that. They like working like crazy until midnight or two in the morning and then partying until four and then crashing and sleeping late and going into work to do it all again. They love the heat. The sweat."

"The adrenaline rush."

She blinked at him, surprised by his understanding. "Yes."

"You get that on a mission," he said. "It's hard to come down from."

"Do you miss it? Being a Marine."

"I miss being part of something bigger than me." His eyes were dark. "Having what I do matter. When I got out, I should have—" He broke off. "Water under the bridge."

She reached across the table to touch his arm. "What you're doing now, building things, that's important, too."

He shifted in his chair, uncomfortable or impatient with the turn of the conversation.

She tried again. "This addition is important to me."

He raised his gaze from her hand on his arm to meet her

eyes. "Happy to help out. But let's not kid ourselves, cupcake. Construction isn't exactly life-or-death stuff."

"Providing shelter? That's satisfying a basic human need."

His lips curved. "Like feeding people."

She flushed and pulled her hand back, grabbing her wineglass. "I make cupcakes."

"You make people happy," he corrected softly. "I've been watching you boxing up birthday cakes, giving cookies to the kids, slipping extras to those old geezers in the corner."

"A lot of the island seniors live on fixed incomes," she explained.

"Whatever. You get off on helping people."

"You make me sound unselfish. I'm not. I opened the bakery for me. Because it suits me."

He watched her with flattering intensity. "Because of your son."

"Because of Aidan and because . . ." She took a breath, her chest expanding, opening under his regard. His attention coaxed things from her, words, thoughts, feelings. "I like the quiet. In the morning, when I'm the only one here, and everything is under my control . . . I love that. I like knowing exactly what has to be done for things to turn out just right. I like the weighing and the measuring, the predictability of it all." She broke off to take another sip of wine. "Well, you know."

"Not really."

She leaned across the table, resting her weight on her elbows. "But you need the same precision, don't you? In building and in baking. 'Measure twice, cut once,' isn't that what you say?"

"My Uncle Chuck said it all the time." Gabe's smile took a wry twist. "Especially when I screwed up."

She grinned back at him, pleased to have found a point of common ground. "When you screw up on the line, you can usually adjust. Cooks can always tweak a recipe. It's harder to recover from a mistake in baking. Well, unless you cover everything in fondant," she added. "But the good thing about baking is you can always start again. There's no rush the way there is in a restaurant kitchen."

"Isn't that the problem? No rush," he explained in response to her questioning look. "No risk. No fun."

His gaze caught hers, snaring her like a fly in honey. For a moment, she couldn't breathe.

"I have fun," she protested. "Cooks dismiss bakers because we're not 'spontaneous.'" Her fingers made air quotes around the word. "But there's an art to baking. You can take the same basic recipes, the same few ingredients—flour, sugar, butter, eggs—and transform them. It's like magic."

He leaned back and picked up his fork, releasing her. "If you say so."

"I can do more than just say so." She moistened her lips, dry-mouthed with longing, trembling with daring and indignation. *No risk? No fun?* She'd show him. She pushed back her chair. "I'll prove it to you. Wait here."

Twelve

JANE STUDIED HER naked body in the door of the big walk-in refrigerator, her reflection distorted by the stainless steel. Probably a good thing. Otherwise she might chicken out. Her breasts, freed from support, looked awfully large, the nipples pink and prominent.

Like a cow, Travis had told her once, back when she was nursing Aidan.

She shivered despite the heat of the kitchen and the residual glow of the wine. Well, that's what happened when you took off all your clothes. There was probably a draft somewhere. After a moment's thought, she undid her braid, combing her hair forward with her fingers to fall over her shoulders. That was better, but she was still all bare below, her pale, soft tummy and the springy patch of hair between her thighs. She squeezed her legs together, as if that would make them look thinner or stop her knees from shaking. She hadn't had sex in years. What if she was no good at it?

Her pretty dessert sat plated and ready on the counter,

its three-layered glossy perfection mocking her silly hopes and fears.

Jane took a deep breath. *Just do it. Before the chocolate shavings wilt, before you lose your nerve, before Gabe gets tired of waiting and goes home.*

She picked up the plate. And then put it down at the last minute to tug on her white chef's apron, pulling her hair free of the bib, wrapping the ties around her waist. That was better. There was still a considerable draft around her backside, but at least her front was covered.

Positioning the plate at chest level, she turned to face the door. It was highly unlikely that any islanders were standing outside in the dark and the rain, peering through the bakery windows. But she was taking a big enough gamble here without risking flashing her neighbors.

"Gabe?" His name squeaked out like air escaping a balloon. She cleared her throat. "Could you give me a hand in here?"

His chair scraped back. She caught a blur of movement through the portal before the door swung open.

"Sure. What do you—"

He stopped dead on the threshold, his eyes widening to take her in, traveling from her face to the dessert in her hands to her bare feet and back again, slowly. "What's this?"

She blushed all over. Wasn't it obvious?

"Chocolate mousse cake," she said, her cheeks burning. "With chocolate ganache, raspberry sauce, and whipped cream."

His lids lowered as he regarded the plate. All the necessary components were there: the main, the sauces, the fresh berry garnish. And one more.

Gabe plucked the wrapped condom from the chocolate icing with two fingers and held it up. "Never saw this in a dessert before."

This was torture. She wanted to hit him with the cake. Or run and hide in the walk-in until her full-body flush faded. In, say, a week or so.

She stood her ground. "I told you, I like to be prepared."

A muscle ticked in his jaw. "Jane . . ."

He was going to say no. "Don't say no."

"Looking at you right now, like this, 'no' is not the word that springs to mind. Are you sure you know what you're doing?"

Jane exhaled. "Well, I thought I was seducing you. But if you have to ask, I'm obviously not doing a very good job."

He took a step toward her. "The apron's a nice touch," he said, an undernote of laughter in his voice.

She closed her eyes in humiliation. "I wasn't going to wear it. Or anything. Bring food and show up naked, that was the plan. It wasn't supposed to be this hard."

"Oh, it's hard," Gabe said wryly, so close she jumped.

She opened her eyes.

He was standing right in front of her. She could reach out and touch him, except she was still clutching the stupid plate, holding out the slice of cake she'd labored over like a piece of her heart.

He was smiling a little, but his eyes were dark and serious. "This is a really bad idea. I don't want to hurt you."

Tenderness welled inside her.

"It's okay," she reassured him. "It's only . . ."

Sex.

But the lie stuck in her throat.

"It is what it is," she said. "This is what I want. I don't need anything else."

Liar, whispered a small voice in her head. She used to dream of so much more, simple, girlish dreams of a man to love her and share his life with her and build the family she longed for together.

But in this moment, shivering with heat and anticipation, Gabe almost in her grasp, this would do. This was enough. She would make it be enough.

His smile deepened at the corners. "Then I better make it good. Your cake"—he grasped the plate—"looks great."

"Thank you," she said breathlessly.

"But right now . . ." He took the dessert, setting it on the counter beside her. "It's in the way."

Her heart moved into her throat. She swallowed. "Okay."

He braced his hands on either side of her hips, trapping her against the counter, within the circle of his arms. Attraction prickled along her skin, rained down inside her like a shower of sparks. Without the plate to anchor them, her hands wavered and then fell. He captured them, pressing them to his chest. His shirt was still damp. She flexed her fingers against resilient muscle. His heart thumped under her palm, hard and strong.

"So, this plan of yours . . ." He stroked her hair away from her face and over her shoulders, dropping soft, tantalizing kisses on her cheekbone, her cheek, the corner of her mouth. "How does it go?"

She parted her lips, seeking the pressure of his. "What?"

His breath of amusement against her skin raised tiny goose bumps up and down her arms. "Never mind. We'll figure it out."

His mouth caught at her upper lip, stroked at the bottom one, easing her open, sinking inside. She absorbed the warm, delicious friction of his tongue, the taste of him rich and heady as wine. His clothed body brushed hers, all that heat and weight and hardness leashed. Contained. Pleasure sank into her, rich and dark. Under the stiff fabric of her apron, her nipples puckered.

"So pretty," he whispered against her mouth. He circled the point of one breast delicately through her apron before he lifted his hand away. "In your plan, did I do this?"

Something cool dabbed the side of her breast. Jolted, she looked down. Whipped cream. He spread a dollop through the open side of her apron before tugging the bib down and away, bending his head, licking her clean with one warm, lazy stroke of his tongue. *Oh, my.*

With his eyes on hers, he reached for the plate. He fed her cake with his bare hands, trading bites for kisses.

"Wait." She grabbed his thick wrist. "I can't eat all your cake."

His slow smile weakened her knees. "You went to all this trouble. You deserve to enjoy it."

She trembled. She didn't cook for herself. She fed other people.

The idea that she should please herself, that she could indulge herself, that she deserved to enjoy herself, felt wrong. Wicked. Seductive.

Shifting her hold, she caught Gabe's hand in both of hers and sucked his thumb into her mouth, salt and chocolate, rough and smooth, creamy and hard melting together.

He choked out a curse, moving his hand to cradle her breast, teasing the tip with his wet thumb until it puckered for him, tight and rosy, and then he plumped up her breast and sucked it into his mouth.

Her body clenched, arching to give him better access as he worked her with soft pulls. Need spiraled deep in her belly. He suckled one breast and then the other, alternating smears of cool, smooth cream with the warm, greedy pressure of his mouth. She grabbed at his hair, like damp silk between her fingers. Clutched at his T-shirt, dragging it up to run her hands over the hot, smooth skin of his back. He lifted her up, her bare bottom on the stainless steel worktable.

She yelped.

He stilled. "Too much?"

She smiled in apology. "Too cold."

He laughed. "Right." Stepping back, he stripped his T-shirt over his head.

She swallowed. His body was lean and hard all over, his chest lightly dusted with dark hair.

He caught her staring and grinned.

Heat scalded her.

"You are so sweet," he murmured. "I want to taste all of you. All over."

She jerked in shock and arousal. "Um . . ."

His eyes were bright and devilish. "Not in the plan?"

"Well . . ."

His warm hands engulfed her knees. He pushed them apart, making a place for himself between her legs.

She tried to press them together as he reached behind and over her, spreading his T-shirt over the work surface. His care in protecting her back from the cold metal warmed her as nothing else could have done. But . . .

"You don't need to do anything for me," she said. "I'm a vanilla kind of girl."

He stuck his finger in the dessert. "This is chocolate."

She snorted before she could stop herself. "Well, yes. But I made it for you."

The glint was back. He dropped to his knees. Kissed the inside of her thigh. "I can share."

She sucked in her breath, squirming in embarrassment, trying to get away, hitching to get closer. "Okay, that's nice, but—"

"You ate my cake," he said.

Lowering his head, he breathed her in. Inside, she was melting, burning, her mind and bones dissolving. Spreading her wide, he kissed her in earnest. She moaned. It was good, he was so good, so shameless and delicious, that she lay back, covering her eyes with her arm, sinking into the darkness, letting him do whatever he wanted. What she wanted. His mouth was so hot and skilled, his fingers inside her, twisting, thrusting, making her crazy, making her come. Her dangling toes curled, her muscles clenched. She reached for him, aching and unfilled.

"Please." Her body strained. She fumbled, unable to get a grip on his broad shoulders, on his smooth skin. "I want . . ." *You. Please.*

He surged upward, moving over her, taking her mouth again, sharing the taste with her, chocolate and sex. She shivered, hungry and shaking. His zipper rasped, his buckle clanked as it hit the floor.

"I'm here. I've got you, baby."

The condom package ripped, and he was there, where she was wet and swollen for him.

Her stomach tensed in a moment of purely feminine doubt as he took himself in hand, as she felt him nudge for entrance. But he eased inside her slowly, in short, shallow thrusts, giving her body time to stretch and adjust to his, kissing her temple, her eyes, her mouth, whispering how good this felt, how hot she was, how sweet, until something inside her softened and surrendered, yielding to his possession.

He sank deep. The slow, thick slide shuddered through them both. She gripped his back, her hips lifting to him, wanting his weight. Craving more.

His breath hissed. His eyes blazed. "Jane. Baby. It's been a while. I can't . . ."

Her fever climbed. The rasp of his beard, the scent of his skin, the cold, hard metal and hot, wet friction all blended and flowed together like flavors in her head. She was brimming with sensation. She tightened her legs around him, twisting under him, struggling to take more. Gabe groaned and shoved deeper, harder, faster, and her climax boiled over, flooding her, spilling to the tips of her fingers, the ends of her toes.

He held still and hard inside her, riding it out, wringing the last, luxurious spasm from her flesh, before he thrust again and again and took his own release.

GABE LAY STUNNED, mind blown, heart pounding, absorbing the shock.

Like the moment after a bomb went off, when you waited for your senses to function and your breath to return so you could see how the world had realigned around you and check for body parts.

Except his world felt oddly right.

And his body parts hadn't been this happy in a long time.

He raised himself to look at Jane, soft and round and mostly naked under him, apron dragged down around her breasts and up around her thighs, all of her smeared in chocolate. Beautiful. Edible. His. His body stirred, wanting her all over again.

He had to get out. Before the condom leaked.

He'd had no intention when he came over here today of fucking her. *Not fucking*, he thought, trying to find a word that wasn't bland or insulting. Screwing? Making love. Anyway, he had no intention of doing it. Doing her. But when he walked into the kitchen and saw her standing there, blushing and brave with her carefully prepared cake and silly apron, her strong bare shoulders, her cute naked feet . . . Hell, he was only human. And male. There was no way he could resist her.

Not that he'd tried very hard.

No going back now. So he would improvise. Adapt.

She hitched one shoulder, wriggling against the table, her neck at an awkward angle. That couldn't be comfortable, he thought, trying to feel guilty and feeling grateful instead.

He caught a strand of her hair between his fingers, pulling it away from her lips. "You okay?" His voice was husky.

Her cheeks were pink, all of her pink and sticky and delicious. "Fine. You?"

"I'm good." *Great. Never better.*

"Your, um . . ." She tried to sit up. Winced. "Your elbow's on my hair."

"Sorry." He moved his arm, helped her sit up and slide off the table.

She wobbled and he had to catch her, which was nice, her body pressed against his.

He ought to say something. Something smooth and sincere that would convince her that sex with him wasn't a terrible mistake. Something besides *Thank you, God*, or *How soon can we do this again?*

But looking at Jane drove all the words from Gabe's head. She was so . . . pretty.

She tugged at her apron, not quite meeting his eyes.

"Thanks for dessert," he said abruptly.

Her blush flared. "You're welcome."

God, he was such an asshole.

He had to do better. She deserved more. Some praise or reassurance, maybe.

"Your cake was really pretty." He fastened his pants and took her hand, her small, warm, capable hand, in his. "Sorry I messed it up."

"That's okay." Her head was still bent, watching his thumb stroke over her knuckles. "I liked it."

With his free hand, he picked chocolate icing from her hair. "I kind of messed you up, too."

Her mouth curved in that small, secret Jane-smile before she met his eyes. "I liked it," she repeated.

His chest expanded. He grinned at her like a fool, holding her hand. "Guess you want to go clean up." *Or we could do it again*, he almost said.

He didn't want to let go of her hand. He didn't want to let go of her, period. Not now, not ev—

Ah, hell. He was doing it again. Over-committing. Jumping in too fast, too deep. All he had to offer—all she said she wanted from him—was sex. What was he hoping? That she'd be so impressed by his technique that she'd keep him around long enough to act out all his fantasies? The one with her bending over the counter, for example. Or straddling him in the chair. Or . . . He shook his head, disgusted with the direction of his thoughts.

But maybe she'd consider coming back with him to his motel room.

"I . . . Yes, I should," she said.

His heart stopped. Had she read his mind?

She reached for her neatly folded jeans on the counter, and he shook his head to clear it. *Dickhead.* She was replying to his comment about washing up.

"Right," he said. "You do that. I'll wait."

And maybe that was the right thing to say after all, because she smiled at him as she gathered up her clothes and disappeared in the direction of the women's restroom.

Nice ass.

Not that he was going to see it again tonight.

His T-shirt was hopeless. He balled it up and put it with his jacket in the other room. The candle still glowed on the table, its light flickering over the remains of dinner.

He had never in his life had a meal like that before. Steak and potatoes, sure, but not a five-star gourmet restaurant meal with candlelight. And cake.

He blew out the candle. The smoke curled up in the quiet room.

She'd done this, all of it, for him.

His throat tightened, a funny pressure in his chest. This went way beyond a sandwich and a cookie in a brown paper bag.

It is what it is. I don't need anything else.

Then why go to this much trouble? Not out of charity or just to say thank you. Not only for sex. Hell, if she wanted him for sex, all she had to do was ask.

Which meant . . . Damned if he knew what it meant. But he was smiling as he stacked the plates and carried them into the kitchen.

OH. DEAR.

The mirror in the women's room provided a clearer reflection than the door of the walk-in. Jane winced. Much clearer.

Puffy lips, raccoon eyes, beard burn on her throat, chocolate icing in her hair . . . and in other places that were much harder to wash in the tiny room's only sink. She looked like she'd been to a rave at Willy Wonka's.

She retrieved her panties from the pile of folded clothes. Still clean. She spared a guilty thought for Gabe's T-shirt.

Seriously? demanded her inner Sunday school teacher. *You had sexy times with a near stranger on the kitchen prep table and you feel guilty about some chocolate smears on his shirt?*

She hushed the voice. She was a capable, fully grown woman. She'd even bought condoms. Yes, okay, she'd gone shopping at the Piggly Wiggly on the mainland where no one would see her and talk, but she took responsibility for her actions. She could have sex with a man she wanted.

Fabulous sex, her seldom-used girl parts reminded her. Her reflection blushed and smiled in agreement.

Jane gave herself a mental shake. The point was, she was almost thirty years old. She'd read those books Lauren loaned her. She knew about the rush of chemicals released in the brain during sex. She was old enough not to mistake sex for love. Smart enough not to look for something that wasn't there. She could handle a no-strings hookup with Gabe Murphy.

He'd warned her. *I don't want to hurt you.*

It is what it is. Thrilling. Tender. Fabulous.

She tugged her shirt on over her head, sneaking another glance in the mirror. Her eyes were soft and dreamy. A sappy, satisfied smile curved her lips.

But she was realistic. She was not going to romanticize a onetime kitchen encounter intended to relieve her sexual drought. She yanked her hair into a ponytail, fastening it with the band around her wrist. Chemistry be damned. Everything would be fine as long as she didn't lose her head.

Or her heart.

She returned to the kitchen. And gaped.

Holy chore-gasm.

There he was, standing shirtless at the wash sink, scrubbing baked-on crust from a casserole dish. No doubt about it, he looked . . . Well, he looked amazing, okay? Male perfection, all bare muscled back and chiseled arms and testosterone. And a tattoo on his left shoulder blade—helmet, rifle, and boots. The battlefield cross.

Her heart contracted painfully, like it was trying to squeeze its way out between her ribs. All the lies she'd been telling herself about being practical and sensible went flying out the window.

Here was a man caring enough to protect her back with his shirt and wash her dishes. To take care of a stray dog. To take time with her son. To carry his losses with him, inked into his skin.

He wasn't a stupid chemistry experiment or a handy way to reawaken her sleeping inner slut.

He was himself. Gabe. And beneath his tough-guy façade, he was vulnerable, too.

He glanced over his shoulder and caught her staring, and, oh, the look in those eyes . . .

A quirk tugged at the corner of his mouth, making her insides quiver. "What's the matter? Never seen a guy doing dishes before?"

She stuck out her chin. "I worked in a restaurant kitchen. I've seen lots of guys wash dishes."

His smile deepened. "Should I be jealous?"

Up close and personal, he looked even more like a seductive fantasy brought to life, from the bad-boy stubble and the glint in his eye to the happy trail that ran down his ridged stomach and under the waistband of his jeans. Unbuttoned, she noticed. Well, she couldn't help looking, could she? Bubbles slid down his corded forearms into the water.

She rolled her eyes. "Like you have anything to worry about. You must know you're perfect."

He met her gaze, his expression unreadable. "No. Don't make me into something I'm not."

"I won't. I can't. I did that with my ex," she explained. She had believed she loved Travis. She'd really thought he loved her. She had wanted so desperately to make them a family that she'd lied to her father. Worse, she'd fooled herself. "I meant, perfect physically."

"Right." A flicker of something in his eyes, gone before she had a chance to identify it. "And you're beautiful."

A puff of disbelief escaped her. "You don't have to say that."

"It's true."

Pleasure warmed her from the inside out. A blush washed up her face. Unable to hold his gaze, she ducked her head and grabbed a dish towel. "Here, let me dry."

They stood side by side in front of the triple sink, close enough that she could smell his skin overlaid by the clean scent of soap. He smelled delicious. Jane could feel her resolve and her dignity dissolving. She wanted to bury her face in his neck and just inhale him.

And those muscles . . . The lovely way they slid under his skin as he reached for a pot . . .

She cleared her throat. "I guess you had to stay in good shape in the Marines."

Gabe slanted a look at her, a wry twist to his mouth. "I got out of the Corps almost three years ago. I used to work out in my cell. There's not much else to do in jail except read. Or watch TV in the common room, but that gets old fast."

"I like to read," she offered. "Not that I have much time for it."

"What do you read?"

"Whatever Lauren gives me. Self-help books, mostly. Cookbooks." Her blush deepened. "Romance novels."

But Gabe, to her surprise, nodded. "They had those in the jail library." A pause. "Some of them were pretty good."

She goggled. "You read romance?"

He shrugged. "I told you, not a lot to do. There was this series about Navy SEALS, Troubleshooters or something, that I liked a lot."

She nodded eagerly. "Suzanne Brockmann. I like those, too."

Because whatever struggles the characters endured, whatever mistakes they made, the heroines were strong women who fought back, who found their happy ending.

It almost gave Jane hope.

Huh. Maybe that's why Lauren gave them to her.

Standing beside Gabe with the sound of the rain on the roof was almost unbearably domestic. The brush of his wet arm against hers made her knees wobble.

She held her breath, afraid to say anything and spoil the moment.

Gabe voiced what she was thinking. "This is nice."

She turned to him, driven by desperation, the words rising from deep inside, spilling out. "Gabe . . . why are you still here? What do you want?"

He met her gaze, his eyes dark and steady. His body tightened. Her heart pounded to the rhythm of the rain. So serious, that look. What was he thinking?

He exhaled, the tension leaving him suddenly, or maybe it was still there, transformed. His mouth gentled, smiled. "Got any more cake?"

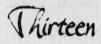

Thirteen

THE RAIN DRUMMED on the porch roof of Marta Lopez's little bungalow, almost drowning out the noise from the television inside.

Marta's gaze lifted from the cellophane-wrapped bouquet in Hank's hands to his face. "Very nice." Her lips curved in a warm smile. "Maybe there is hope for you after all."

Hank cleared his throat, pleased with his forethought in stopping by the grocery store. His ex-wife used to complain he wasn't the flower-buying kind. But when a woman invited you over for dinner and—what had Marta called it?—adult companionship . . . well, he figured he shouldn't show up empty-handed, that was all.

Should he kiss her?

But she stepped back out of the doorway, and the moment—if it was a moment—was gone.

"Come in." She took the flowers. "You know my sons."

Hank stopped in the act of wiping his feet. *Her sons?*

"Tomás, Miguel, say hello to Officer Clark."

Well, hell.

Two young men sprawled in front of the television in the living room. The one on the couch got reluctantly to his feet and kicked the sole of the younger one's shoe until he got up, too. From their expressions, they were about as glad to see Hank as he was to see them.

He nodded. "Boys."

"Hi, Officer Clark," said the shorter one. Miguel, still in high school.

The older one, Tomás, jerked his chin in greeting.

"I'll put these in water," Marta said, disappearing through a big archway. He could see a table, already set for dinner, on the other side.

The boys shifted uncomfortably.

Hank glanced at the TV. The anchors on *SportsCenter* were bantering about Louisville's chances in the Sweet Sixteen this weekend. So the evening wasn't a total loss.

He dropped into a chair.

"They don't know shit," Tomás said, settling back on the couch.

Hank slid him a look. "Brackets busted already, huh?"

He grinned sheepishly. "Yeah. But I'm doing better than Miguel."

"Hey, all my Elite Eight are still in the tournament," Miguel said.

"Who's your Final Four?" Hank asked, and they talked about Duke and whether Michigan State had a shot this year until Marta came back with the flowers.

There was already a vase on the table, but she replaced those flowers with the bouquet Hank had brought. He was relieved to see his was bigger.

Marta looked from Hank to the television, a smile twitching her lips. "Do you want to help me in the kitchen or watch ESPN?"

"Is this a test?" Hank asked warily.

Her smile broadened. "I prefer to think of it as an opportunity."

Miguel rolled his eyes. Tomás said something in Spanish, and Marta laughed and answered in the same language.

Damn it. Hank didn't understand what they were saying. Didn't know what he was doing here. He hauled himself to his feet.

"You always have a chaperone?" he asked after he had followed Marta into the kitchen.

"On a first date?" Marta widened her eyes at him. "Of course. Mami would insist."

So this was a date. Some of the tension left his shoulders. "Bet the boys couldn't keep their hands off you when you were young."

Marta raised her brows. "As opposed to now, when I am so old?"

Hell. "I didn't mean . . ."

Her smile reached right inside him and twisted him up. "Hank, relax. I am teasing you." She turned to adjust the heat on the stove. "The truth is, I do not entertain very much. It is always the boys' friends who come over. I am a single parent. You know how that is."

Hank nodded. After Denise left him, he didn't have the time to chase after another woman. Or the heart.

"Jane didn't have many friends over. Couldn't," he said. "I was working most of the time."

Even when he wasn't, she had always been a quiet kid. Solitary, like him. He remembered with a queer tug of his heart the way she used to sit for hours at the edge of his vision while he watched TV. He'd never known how to talk to her. And she never said much. Never asked for much of anything, except when she was little and begged him to let her stay home alone.

You can trust me, Daddy, she'd said.

And he had. Until Tillett.

"I was lucky," Marta was saying, stirring a pot. "Alex and Mateo were in high school—old enough to watch the younger boys. They were company for one another. But they had their own activities. Football—soccer—cross-country, after-school jobs . . . It seemed like all I did was drive them places. At that age, everything is work and your children."

And sometimes work was an escape from your only child, from the reminder of how badly you'd screwed up your life at home.

"I should have done more with Jane," Hank said. "Been around more. I wish . . ." He shut up. It was all water under the bridge anyway.

Marta's eyes were shrewd and kind. "You are doing more now, yes? With your grandson."

"I guess." Hank stopped himself, barely, from shuffling his feet. "What are you making?" he asked, changing the subject.

"Green mole chicken."

Green chicken? "Smells good," he said.

Marta smiled. "It tastes even better." She lifted a lid, releasing a cloud of steam and unfamiliar aromas, and dipped in a spoon. She stood close, almost between Hank's feet, and lifted the spoon to his mouth. "Taste."

He accepted the spoon cautiously between his lips.

"Well?" she demanded. She was usually so bossy, he forgot what a little thing she was, short and curvy. She smelled spicy and unfamiliar, like her chicken.

He swallowed. "Not bad."

Her eyes sparked. Her lips parted. "'Not *bad*'? Not—"

He put his hands on her waist and kissed her, which shut her up. Her mouth was soft and warm as she kissed him back, her body round and firm. He tightened his hold on her waist.

She made a little noise in her throat and stepped back. He released her instantly. They stared at each other. His heart pounded. Seemed her breathing was faster, too.

She licked her lips. "Needs salt."

He bit down on a grin. "Seemed pretty perfect to me."

Her smile was something to see.

She turned away and grabbed a napkin-covered basket off the counter. "Here." She thrust it at him. "Take this to the table. It's time for dinner."

There was one of those Catholic crosses hanging on the wall of the dining nook. Hank didn't see how staring at Jesus crucified was supposed to aid a man's appetite, but he bowed his head as Marta and the boys said some kind of grace and crossed themselves.

Marta banned cell phones and television at the dinner table, but there wasn't a lot of yapping. Her sons shoveled in their food with the healthy appetite of young males, leaving Hank free to do the same. The rice was red, the chicken was green, and there were oranges and olives in the salad. Garlic in everything. But it all tasted fine. Good. He said so. Marta thanked him.

Miguel finished eating first, carrying his empty plate into the kitchen and wandering back toward the television.

"All done with your homework?" Marta asked.

"Yep."

"What about your chemistry test on Friday?"

"I'll study tomorrow."

"You are working tomorrow night. You'll study now."

"Ma . . ."

Marta arched an eyebrow. Hank knew that look from the station. The most whiny-ass, entitled tourist in the world had been known to fold when faced with the power of Marta's raised eyebrow.

With a heavy sigh, Miguel fetched his backpack from under the end table by the front door. "What about dessert?"

"Ice cream," Marta said. "I'll call you."

"Next time, you should bring dessert," Miguel said to Hank. "You know, instead of flowers?"

Hank met Marta's eyes, heat creeping under his collar. Was there going to be a next time?

She shrugged, a smile playing around her mouth.

"I'll think about it," he said gruffly.

"Jane, she makes great desserts. She did this Key lime pie for the restaurant last week? It was really good."

Hank felt a glow of pride at this praise of his daughter. "You work at the Brunswick," he said.

"Yeah. Twelve hours a week."

"As long as you keep up your grades," Marta said. "Go study."

"My grades are good enough," Miguel said, letting his book bag slide, trying to put off the inevitable. Like a prisoner squaring off with a guard to delay the long walk to the electric chair. "We can't all be lawyers like Alex."

"She's not saying be a lawyer, stupid," his older brother said. "But maybe you want to go to college."

"Papi didn't go to college. You didn't go to college."

"Because I got a good job now. But Gabe says you got to plan for the future. To think beyond the next paycheck."

"Your friend Gabe is very wise," Marta said. She narrowed her eyes at Hank. "Did you just growl?"

"No," he growl— That is, he grumbled. Maybe his voice was pitched a little lower than usual. So sue him. "You talking about Gabe Murphy?"

"Yeah. We work together," Tomás said. "More than a week now. Sam hired—"

"I know who he is."

"He's a good guy."

"He's trouble. I don't trust him."

Marta's brows rose. "And yet he's working at your daughter's bakery."

He wouldn't be if Hank had any say. But he'd lost that argument. His jaw set. "Jane's her own woman. She makes her own decisions."

"You don't believe that," Marta said.

Hell, no.

"I don't want to talk about it," Hank said.

Marta's eyes were deep and soft. "I understand. It's hard when your children grow up."

She turned the conversation to other things while Tomás

cleared the table and Miguel went upstairs to do his despised chemistry homework. Later, there was ice cream.

But some of the shine had been rubbed off the evening, and Hank knew why.

It was that Gabe Murphy's fault.

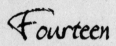

Fourteen

IN THE KITCHEN, Jane heard the door bells chime and then . . . nothing.

"Lindsey?" she called.

"I'm on break," the teenager yelled.

Jane sighed and wiped her floury hands on her apron. She turned back to the baker's bench, where Rudy Jackson, her other new hire, was learning how to prep for the following day. "After you get the cinnamon rolls formed, you need to cut them. An inch thick. And then you place them, twelve rolls to a half sheet, about this far apart," she said, demonstrating with her thumb and forefinger. "Okay?"

Rudy scratched his bandanna, eyeing the long rectangle of dough slathered with butter and layered with brown sugar and cinnamon. "Sure. No problem."

His standard response. He was either incredibly quick on the uptake—*Please, let him be quick*—or overwhelmed.

Jane was feeling fairly overwhelmed herself. Hiring staff was supposed to make her life easier. But at least in the beginning, it made everything more complicated.

Like sex.

She pushed the thought away.

"You have any questions, you come get me," she told Rudy.

"No problem."

With a last anxious glance at the dough, Jane headed for the front, where Lindsey Gordon sat at a table, texting.

Over by the display cakes, Meg Fletcher waited, looking sharp and put together and vibrating with nervous energy. Despite moving back to Dare Island almost a year and a half ago, she still acted like she lived in New York City. She had conducted her initial wedding cake consultation the same way Jane imagined she operated her public relations company—with fierce decisiveness and attention to detail.

"Hi. We need to talk about my cake order," she said as soon as Jane appeared.

Even for Meg, this was abrupt. Bride nerves, Jane thought, and smiled reassuringly. "Let me get your folder. But I think you're all set. October, right?"

Meg looked tense. "There's been a change of plans."

"Oh." *Uh-oh.* "Well, if you want to change your order, we still have plenty of time."

"No." Meg's blue eyes welled with sudden tears. "We don't."

Jane's stomach sank. She genuinely liked Meg. And Sam. They seemed like the perfect couple—smart, determined, devoted. If the wedding was off . . . If Meg had changed her mind . . . Or Sam had . . .

They had everything going for them. If they couldn't make a relationship work, what chance did ordinary mortals have?

She glanced around the nearly empty bakery. "Lindsey, we're pretty quiet. Why don't you go home for the day?"

"Do I still get paid for my last fifteen minutes?"

"No. But you can make up the time tomorrow."

"Great."

While Lindsey clocked out, Jane arranged two lemon-iced sugar cookies on a plate and brought them to Meg. "Sit down. I'll get you some coffee, and we'll talk."

Meg sniffed mightily. "No coffee."

"Okay." Jane pressed a napkin into her hand and led her to a nearby table. "Tea? Chocolate? Let me get you something."

"I'm fine." Meg sat, dabbing at her face. "I just . . . My stomach's upset."

"I'm sorry."

"It's not your fault. It's hormones."

Jane blinked. "Hormones."

Meg stuck out her chin. "I'm pregnant."

"Wow. That's awesome! Congratulations."

"Thanks. Twelve weeks." Meg took a deep breath. "We're moving up the wedding to May."

"I'm so happy for you. What wonderful news."

Meg dried her eyes. "It really is. I'm happy, too. I'm thirty-seven years old. The doctor said I might have trouble getting pregnant. Which is why I went off my birth control pills," she added wryly.

"So this isn't really unexpected," Jane said.

"It kind of is. We were using condoms." Meg blew her nose. "Mostly. And then last week we had our first ultrasound, and it's twins."

Jane gaped. "Twins!"

Meg laughed. "I know, right? You look the way I felt. Those two little heartbeats. And Sam . . ." Meg's face, her whole body, softened as she spoke her fiancé's name. "He was holding my hand. He actually had tears in his eyes. It was pretty freaking amazing."

Aw, that was just so sweet. Jane felt a definite twinge of . . . not envy. Wistfulness, maybe. Not because of the babies, although she had always dreamed of more children, brothers or sisters for Aidan. But it would be so nice to have a Sam in her life, holding her hand.

Okay, not Sam.

Because despite Sam's truck, his building business, and carefully cultivated good ol' boy charm, Jane couldn't imagine a life with him. The things she would be expected to wear and say and do as the wife of Sam Grady, things that came so naturally to Meg, would fit Jane like a bad pair of jeans—chafing in all the wrong places.

Sam would always be thoughtful. Polite.

He wouldn't tickle her sense of humor with inappropriate remarks or irritate her to the point of snapping back. He didn't make her want to brain him with a frying pan one moment and jump his bones the next. He'd never stood at her wash sink, elbows deep in suds, the top button of his jeans unfastened and a drop of water sliding down his . . .

Her breath shuddered out.

Focus, Jane.

"Do you think four tiers is too many?" Meg asked. "We're not expecting everyone to be able to make the wedding. Not on such short notice."

"We can change the size of the tiers and keep the same design," Jane said. "You can give me a final headcount about a week before the wedding."

"That would be great."

"Let me get your order, and we can go over it together."

In the kitchen, Rudy was still filling pans with tomorrow's cinnamon rolls.

"Those look great," Jane said. "When you finish each tray, get it in the proofing cabinet with the Danish so they can slow rise overnight in the refrigerator."

"No problem."

Her cake orders were organized by date in a thick binder over the pastry table. Tucking the book under one arm, she filled a mug and carried both to Meg.

"Lemon ginger tea," she said, setting the mug on the table. "No caffeine, and it'll help settle your stomach."

Meg peered into the cup. "Seriously?"

Jane shrugged. Smiled. "Well, I can vouch for the no-caffeine part, at least." She flipped open the binder. "So what date are we looking at for the wedding?"

"We were thinking the weekend between Mother's Day and Memorial Day. Sunday. Say, three o'clock?"

"Perfect. I close at one. I can deliver and set up in plenty of time." Jane clipped the binder and moved the page with cake order and design sketch near the front.

"You're sure changing the date won't be a problem?"

"Not at all." Not much. "Not this early in the season."

"Thank goodness. I was afraid you'd be overbooked and I'd have to serve a tower of Twinkies."

Jane laughed. "Like a croque-en-bouche. It's a French wedding cake," she explained when Meg looked blank. "Choux pastry balls piled into a cone and held together with threads of caramel."

"Yum." She took a cautious bite of cookie. "These are delicious. Do you ever think of expanding?"

Jane glanced through the sliding doors at the rain beating down on the frame of her new patio enclosure. "I am. But things are kind of at a halt right now."

In more ways than one.

"It's the rain," Meg said.

It wasn't only the rain.

She hadn't seen the crew in four days. Or Gabe.

Oh, he'd dropped by. Stopped in for coffee, for lunch. But always when there were other people around, customers or her new staff. They hadn't managed to have a single conversation, let alone sex.

Well, what did you expect?

Nothing, she admitted. She'd been so focused on doing the deed that she hadn't thought beyond dinner and seduction.

She certainly didn't expect everything to change just because they'd had sex. But she wasn't prepared for things to go on exactly as before, either.

"Not expanding the building," Meg was saying. "Growing your business. More wedding cakes. Specialty cakes."

Jane pulled her mind back to the job. "I already do most of the weddings here on the island. If I did more events on the mainland, I'd need a new refrigerator van. And a driver to handle setup."

"You should think about it," Meg said. "It would be good business for you in the off-season."

The bells over the door rattled and chimed.

Gabe filled the doorway, the jacket over his broad shoulders dark with rain.

Lucky tried to follow him inside, only to be brought up short by the leash wrapped around the porch railing.

"Sit," Gabe ordered.

The dog grinned, tongue lolling, tail wagging.

"I mean it." Gabe cocked a finger at the dog and then pointed outside. "Go. Sit."

Lucky heaved a sigh and retreated to the porch, where he collapsed on his haunches.

Gabe glanced over, smiling, at Jane. "Hey."

Instant brain melt.

"Hi." She swallowed, hoping she wasn't drooling as visibly as the dog.

"Gabe! How are you?" Meg asked cheerfully.

He nodded, his gaze still on Jane. "Meg."

Heat rolled through Jane. *Shoot.*

"I wasn't expecting to see you today," she said.

He looked at her, his beautiful hazel eyes unreadable.

"Because, you know, you're . . ." She flapped her hand. "Busy."

His gaze dropped to the open binder on the table. "Looks like you're busy, too."

"We're going over my cake order," Meg said.

He angled his head to see the page. "This it?"

"Yes," Jane said. The cake was one of her most sophisticated designs, a welcome change from the gum-paste shells and starfish that most beach brides requested—four off-set square layers with different textures of silver and white fondant and edible pearls.

"Pretty," he said.

So pretty, he had whispered against her mouth.

A warm glow suffused her chest, pride and embarrassment mingled. "Thank you."

A corner of his mouth quirked up. "Almost as pretty as dessert Monday night."

Hot color scalded Jane's face.

"What dessert?" Meg asked.

"Just something I was trying out," Jane said.

"Really." Meg widened her eyes. "How was it?"

"Good. I'll let you get back to work," Gabe said, looking at Jane. "I just came to tell you I'll be by later to put the last layer of mud on the drywall."

She was pretty sure that wasn't a euphemism.

Her stupid heart beat faster anyway. "I'm training Rudy this afternoon." Meaning, *We won't be alone.*

Another long, unreadable look. "I'll stay out of your way."

"Mom's hoping to see you for Sunday dinner," Meg said.

"You tell her I appreciate that very much," Gabe said.

"Unless you have other plans," she added brightly.

"Don't worry, I'll let you know. You just take care of yourself." That smile tugged at Gabe's mouth again. "All of yourselves."

"Wait," Jane said. "You knew she was pregnant?"

As if she needed another reminder of how quickly gossip traveled on the island.

Gabe winked at Meg. "Second hottest mother on the island. I'll see you," he said to Jane and walked out.

"Whew." Meg mimed fanning herself with one perfectly manicured hand. "If I wasn't hot before, I certainly am now."

Jane was ready to burst into flames herself. Her cheeks, her face, her whole body burned. Thank goodness she'd already sent Lindsey home.

"So." Meg eyed her speculatively. "You and Gabe."

Jane busied herself with the binder. Meg was one of the smartest people Jane knew. She could probably share all kinds of good, hard, practical advice about love.

If Jane wanted to hear it.

Which she kind of . . . didn't.

Monday night had been special. A moment out of time, a secret, selfish indulgence. Sex and chocolate. Fantasy stuff, like one of her romance novels—a harmless escape from her careful, safe, predictable existence. As long as she hugged the memories to herself, she could almost pretend she had made the whole thing up.

But if she talked to Meg, if she dragged her hopes and desires into the light of day, she would be acknowledging they were . . . real.

And then where would she be?

"Come on," Meg coaxed. "You know all my secrets now. Nobody's judging you."

"Maybe not in New York City," Jane said. "Probably nobody cares how you behave in New York. But this is Dare Island."

"Where everybody loves you."

Jane blinked. She'd never really thought of it that way before. She'd always been so concerned with what the neighbors thought. The idea that they weren't judging her, that they were taking a concerned interest—like, say, a mother would, if her mother had stuck around—well, it was nice. "I wouldn't know where to start."

"Start with Monday night."

"Well." She drew a breath. "I made dinner. Here at the bakery."

"Dinner is good," Meg said. "Now get to the dessert."

"Chocolate mousse cake. With whipped cream and ganache."

"You dirty girl," Meg said admiringly. "And then?"

"Then . . . we did it," Jane said.

"In the bakery."

Jane nodded, unable to suppress a small surge of pride. "In the kitchen. On the prep table. And the counter." A quiet little tingle at the memory. "And, um, on a chair."

"I may faint."

"And then . . ." Jane paused, building to her climax. "He *washed the dishes*."

"That's it. I'd like a chocolate mousse cake, please. To go."

Jane grinned, foolishly pleased.

"So, was this a onetime trip to Horny Town or are you two, like, together now?" Meg asked.

"I don't know," Jane confessed. "It's one thing to buy condoms, you know? To tell yourself you're allowed this one night of no-strings adventure. No labels. No commitments."

"No regrets," Meg said.

Jane nodded again. "But the truth is, I never had casual sex before."

"You're twenty-nine years old."

"I got married at nineteen. Travis was my first real boyfriend," Jane said. The only man she'd ever slept with. When everyone else her age was experimenting with sex, hanging out and hooking up, Jane had been coming home exhausted after the dinner shift only to wake up with her husband's weight pinning her to the mattress. Or startling out of sleep to tend to Aidan before his crying woke his father.

"But you've been divorced for years," Meg said.

"And raising a baby alone and living with my father," Jane reminded her. "I don't know how to take the next step. I don't even know what the next step's supposed to be."

"Sweetie, you're not baking a cake," Meg said. "There's no recipe to follow here."

"It's just that everything's so complicated right now with Aidan. And my dad. I'm not looking for anything else at this point in my life."

"Surprise," Meg said. "I wasn't looking for twins, and yet here we are."

"You'll be a great mom," Jane said.

"Thanks. That means a lot, coming from you. But what I'm saying is, good things come along in their own time. Sometimes you just have to accept and enjoy."

"Sometimes things aren't that simple," Jane said.

"No reason to make them complicated. He's coming by later, isn't he?"

"To plaster the drywall."

"There you go, then," Meg said with satisfaction. "When

a man shows up with power tools and paint it's a sign that he's marking his territory. Like pissing on trees."

"But he hasn't said anything."

Meg sipped her tea, regarding Jane over the rim of her cup. "I didn't really know Gabe from before. But he hasn't had the easiest time of it since he got out. From what Mom says, he didn't have the best home life, either. Don't take this the wrong way, okay? But you have this sort of . . . air, you know? Very princess-in-a-tower. Kind of calm. Guarded."

"You mean cold," Jane said, stricken.

"No, no, you're very caring. I was going to say, self-sufficient. Maybe Gabe doesn't think he has anything to offer you. Have you considered that maybe he could use a little encouragement?"

"I showed up naked and carrying a cake," Jane said. "How much more encouragement does he need?"

Meg laughed. "That, I can't tell you. But I do know you'll figure it out."

GABE FEATHERED THE compound away from the joint with broad horizontal strokes, blending the plaster into the wall on either side. This was the third and final application. Slow going, but if he did it right, he wouldn't need to sand the wall and get plaster dust all over Jane's tidy dining room.

He needed to get this right.

And in the meantime, she could just get used to him hanging around.

He knocked the excess mud into the tub and reloaded the trowel. *Ninety percent of life is showing up*, Uncle Chuck used to say.

Right now Gabe didn't have much to offer Jane. But he could do showing up.

Fifteen minutes later, she came out of the kitchen carrying something on a plate. The smell conjured memories of Monday night, sending a jolt straight to his groin. *Chocolate*.

He wanted to strip her naked and search out the scent on her skin.

Yeah, with her assistant working on the other side of the door. Big idea, dickhead.

"Smells good," he said. "Is that for me?"

She nodded. "It's my Death by Chocolate Brownie."

"Thanks. Great name." She was killing him. "Put it on the table, would you? I want to finish this seam."

She set down the plate, but she didn't go away. It was damn distracting.

She folded her small, scarred hands neatly over her apron. "Gabe, what are you doing here?"

It was the second time today she'd said something like that. Like she really didn't know. Or was too polite, maybe, to tell him to move along. He tried not to find that discouraging.

He aimed a smile her way. "If you have to ask, I'm not doing a very good job."

Her eyes widened as she recognized her words from Monday night.

"It's an awful lot of work. When you offered to put in the doors, I didn't realize you'd get stuck replacing the whole wall."

He loaded the trowel again. "Construction's like that sometimes. One thing leads to another. You don't know what you're getting into until you start."

She smiled. "'If you give a mouse a cookie . . .'" He must have looked blank, because she explained. "It's from a children's book. About a boy who feeds a mouse and then the mouse keeps wanting more, and the boy can't get rid of him."

He wanted to smile. Or snarl. He'd never had a woman brush him off with a line from a kids' story before. "You looking to get rid of me, cupcake?"

"No, I just . . . I wondered how long you're going to be here, that's all."

Was she still talking about the drywall?

"As long as it takes," he said. "I want to finish what I started." *What we started.*

He spread compound over the joint as she stood quietly, watching. The memory of her touch ghosted over his skin. His muscles bunched and stretched, angling for her attention. He smoothed the ten-inch trowel knife over the seam, careful not to press too hard. *Easy, easy.*

"Is this a booty call?" she blurted.

He jerked, dragging the trowel through the wet mud, scoring a deep dent. Damn it. He was being so disciplined, so deliberate, so restrained. He was sort of insulted that she hadn't noticed.

He looked over. She was so damn cute, her blond hair slipping its braid, her brow pleated, her fingers twisted together.

He grinned. "I'd have to be getting sex for that."

She flushed a little, but her gaze remained steady on his. "You'd also have to call."

Man, she didn't miss a beat. "I don't have a phone," he explained.

Her flush deepened. "Oh."

"I'll get one."

"You don't need to do that."

"I need one for work anyway." He was saving up for a car, but he could afford one of those prepaid deals. "Something to add to the list."

She smiled ruefully. "I know all about lists."

"Mine's pretty basic. Food, transportation, shelter."

"I thought you had a room at the Fishermen's Motel."

"For now." His first permanent address since getting out of jail. He thought of the postcard that had arrived this morning with RETURN TO SENDER written in an unfamiliar hand. *That* never happened before. An uneasy feeling stirred his gut. He swallowed it down, applying compound with long downstrokes of the putty knife.

"Be nice to find a place with a little more privacy," he said. "Maybe a yard for the dog."

Chances were good she wasn't inviting him home. He sure as hell didn't see himself hanging out watching TV on the couch with her daddy. But maybe she'd come visit him if she didn't have to worry about sneaking past Blabby Bobby at the front desk.

For the first time, Gabe understood why other men got tattooed with the names of their girlfriends, why a guy would drop three months' salary on some flashy ring. Hell, if he had his way, Jane would wear a sign. *Taken. Off-limits.*

But he didn't have the right to make that claim. She might feel differently about having her name linked with his.

"So you're . . . staying," she said. Not quite a question.

He slanted a look at her. "Is that a problem?"

"I'm sorry," she said, though he couldn't figure out what she had to apologize for. "I've never done this before. It's really none of my business."

Flustered, he thought. Was that a good sign or a bad sign?

"'This,'" he repeated without inflection.

"You know. Whatever this"—she waggled her hand in the air between them—"is. This thing we're doing. I don't have any expectations. We both have full, busy lives without adding a lot of complications. I don't want you to think that I'm needy. Or naggy. Or oversensitive. Or insecure."

Gabe knocked the excess mud from the trowel into the tub. "That's a lot of *don't*s," he observed. "What do you want, then?"

"Oh, no." She shook her head. "You first."

A smile tugged his mouth. He figured if he told her half the things he wanted she'd run like hell.

On the other hand, he didn't have a lot to offer her right now. She deserved his honesty, at least. So he gave it to her. "I want to be with you. Everything in my life is temporary right now. But I want to be with you."

She looked in his eyes, her cheeks pretty pink. "You mean have sex again."

"Yeah. Sure. Sex would be good." He laughed, disgusted with himself. "Who am I kidding? Sex would be great. But I was thinking . . . hoping . . . Look, plaster needs a day to dry, especially in this rain. I'll be back on Monday to paint. I thought maybe we could go out after, get something to eat."

He wiped his hands on a rag, his heart banging against his ribs.

"I'd have to get a sitter for Aidan."

Holy shit. She was going to say yes? "He could come with us," Gabe said, before she had second thoughts. "Like, for pizza or something."

She hesitated.

Ouch. Even though her reaction was pretty much what he was expecting, it still stung. But she was a good mom. Protective. It figured she didn't want him spending too much time with the kid.

"Or we could go next Saturday," Gabe said. After he got paid again. "After you have a chance to line something up."

"I'd like that," she said softly.

He grinned, fast and sharp. So she was willing to be seen with him. Spend time with him. *Score.*

"It's a date," he said. Quickly, before she could change her mind. "What time?"

"I, um . . . Seven thirty?"

"I'll pick you up," he said.

Pick her up? Shit, what was he thinking? He didn't have wheels yet.

She smiled and nodded, and he knew. *Jane.* He was thinking about Jane, with her soft gray eyes and slow, secret smiles, her warm generosity and no-quit attitude.

For the first time in a long time, he was thinking about a future.

He really needed to buy that car.

Fifteen

LUKE FLETCHER SAT on the back steps of the Pirates' Rest, shucking corn into a plastic bag between his knees. "Nice truck," he said as Gabe came up the walk for Sunday dinner.

"Thanks," Gabe said.

The sea breeze caught the bag, making it swell and rattle against the ground. Lucky barked. On the porch, the Fletchers' big black shepherd lifted its head, ears swiveling upright.

"Easy," Gabe said, keeping a light hold on the leash. "Is your dog going to eat my dog?"

"Nope. Fezzik's got manners. And we locked the puppy inside until they have a chance to get used to each other."

Fezzik padded over to investigate, tail stirring politely.

Gabe gave Lucky a reassuring pat. "Good dog."

"That's Willy Holling's old pickup," Luke observed as the two dogs sniffed each other.

"His wife wanted it out of the front yard," Gabe said.

"So it's yours now."

"Paid for," Gabe said. "Still have to transfer the title."

"Make sure you do," Luke advised. "Before Hank pulls you over and asks to see your registration."

"I need to get my North Carolina driver's license first. Figured I'd go this week."

Luke looked up from stripping corn. "Sounds like you're staying."

The prodigal son, Gabe thought again. Would his brother welcome him home for good? "Thinking about it."

Luke rose from the steps, wiping his hands on the thighs of his jeans. "Your thinking have anything to do with Jane Clark?"

"It might," Gabe acknowledged cautiously.

"Good luck, then. I got to say, your taste in women has improved."

"Thanks," he said.

"You've got yourself a package deal there. You prepared for that?"

"I can handle her father."

"I'm talking about her son."

Gabe's throat dried. "I don't know, do I? I don't know a damn thing about being . . ." *A father*. Even the word made his insides jump. "Except what not to do."

"That's a start."

"It's not enough."

"At least you get that. Just be sure this is what you want. Because until you know where things are going, you might want to slow down some. For the kid's sake. No point in him getting attached."

Gabe set his jaw, clamping down on an unaccustomed feeling of annoyance. He couldn't be pissed at Luke. His old buddy had done the single-dad thing. He knew what he was talking about. Plus, he and Jane were about the same age. They must have grown up together. Gabe was the newcomer, the outsider, here.

But he couldn't help thinking that Jane didn't need another man running interference in her life. Underneath the soft and the sweet, she was strong and determined. Brave enough to go after what she wanted. Tough enough to call Gabe on his shit. He figured she was capable of making her own decisions, of protecting her own son.

Or maybe he just wanted to believe that.

"I don't know where this is headed," Gabe said. "But I'm not going back."

Luke sighed. "You always did charge into things."

The screen door opened and Kate came out. "While you, of course, are the most patient, the most reasonable, the most easygoing of men," Luke's wife said dryly. "Hi, Gabe."

"Kate."

Luke's daughter slipped out behind her. She smiled at Gabe. "Hey, Mr. Murphy. Daddy, Grandma's ready for the corn."

"Here you go." Luke handed her the bag. "I'm patient," he said to his wife.

She rolled her eyes. "You're relentless until you get what you want. There's a difference."

Luke caught her hand and kissed it. "Got me you, didn't it?"

And Kate, the hardheaded, cool-eyed lawyer, blushed and stood on tiptoe to kiss him.

Taylor made gagging noises.

This, Gabe thought. He rubbed the heel of his hand over his breastbone to relieve the funny pressure on his heart.

Be sure, Luke had said.

This was what he wanted. This laughter, this warmth, this love, this family. He wanted them all with Jane.

Now all he had to do was convince her that he could be what she wanted, too.

AIDAN SAT WITH his after-school snack of milk and cookies, surrounded by stacked tables and chairs covered in drop cloths.

"Like a fort," Jane said, smiling, as she ruffled her fingers through her son's straight brown hair. The gesture made Gabe shiver all over with longing, like a dog.

"I need to get these cakes in the oven so they're ready to

decorate tomorrow. You copy your spelling words and don't bother Mr. Murphy. You can play with your Legos."

The boy pulled his head between his shoulders like a turtle withdrawing into its shell.

"He's no bother," Gabe said.

"Are you sure?"

"Yeah. I could use a hand on those shelves. After he finishes his homework."

That earned him a glance, bright and wary, from the boy, and another smile from Jane. "Well, now that you've talked me into painting the entire dining room, I think we both should give you a hand," she said. "Aidan?"

The boy jerked his shoulder in what might have been a gesture of assent.

"We'll be fine," Gabe said. "Go bake."

He angled his brush along the trim, laying down an even line of paint against the bright white primer.

When he was a kid working with his uncle Chuck, he used to hate painting. He wanted to rip things up and nail things down, to get his hands on power tools. But he wasn't an impatient sixteen-year-old any longer. There was a different satisfaction, he was discovering, in seeing a project through from start to finish, in being able to step back and think, *I made this. It's good. It's done.*

Especially since he was doing it for Jane. He liked the new color she had chosen, a soft taupe that wasn't blue or brown or gray but a combination of all three, like the Sound on a cloudy day. The neutral tone pulled the shades of the outdoors inside, providing a clean backdrop for her pretty cakes and bright pastries.

He finished the door and started cutting in around a window.

"Grandpa told me not to talk to you," Aidan announced. "Because you were in jail."

Gabe's paintbrush bobbled. Well, shit.

He reached for a rag to wipe the smear of paint from the trim. Now what?

He'd never been any damn good at keeping his mouth shut. But even he knew that *Your grandpa can go to hell* was not an appropriate response to a seven-and-a-half-year-old.

"You don't need to talk to pick up a paintbrush," he said evenly.

Aidan drank his milk, sneakers swinging back and forth, back and forth. He wasn't even tall enough for his feet to touch the ground.

"My dad's in jail," Aidan said.

"I heard." Gabe dipped his brush. "That sucks."

Could he say "sucks"?

"Yeah," Aidan said gleefully. "It *really* sucks."

Okay, probably he should watch the language.

"Mom says you go to jail when you break the rules," Aidan said after another pause. "Did you break the rules?"

Gabe's back stiffened, but he kept his tone easy, his grip on the paintbrush light. "Yeah, I did."

Aidan wiped at his milk mustache. The bruise on his cheek had faded to a yellow smudge. His lip was all healed. "What did you do?"

I killed a man. "Got in a fight."

Aidan nodded wisely. "Sometimes you have to stand up for yourself. That's what Grandpa says."

"Sometimes it's smarter to walk away," Gabe said. "You ready to get started on those shelves?"

Aidan jumped up, his sneakers hitting the floor with a smack. "Okay."

Gabe set him up on a corner of the drop cloth with a brush, a small roller, and the already-primed shelves. "Edges first," he instructed. "You want to catch the drips with the brush, like this, see? Then we'll go over it with the roller, get a nice smooth finish."

Gabe pulled over the ladder to cut in around the big picture window, stopping his own work occasionally to praise, to adjust, to demonstrate. "Good job," he said, shifting a finished shelf out of the way, and Aidan beamed.

The kid looked just like his mother when he smiled.

Gabe cleared his throat. "Watch those drips."

They worked together for a while in silence.

"Can you write letters in jail?" Aidan asked. The boy's head was bent, his straight hair flopping into his eyes.

"If you have somebody to write to," Gabe said.

"I wrote to my dad once," Aidan said.

Ah, crap.

Gabe glanced toward the kitchen door, hoping for rescue. Where was Jane? She would know what to say. According to Luke, she had raised her son on her own. Aidan's dad wasn't even in the picture.

But maybe that was the point. Gabe knew from bitter experience that it didn't matter how much of a shit your father was, there was a part of you that still wanted his love. That craved his approval.

"What did your mom think about that?"

"She didn't want me to at first. But he's still, like, my dad, right? He came to get me. Last summer. He wanted to meet me, he said. But he never wrote back."

Gabe lowered his brush, thinking of all the postcards he'd mailed over the past ten years that went unanswered, all the things he'd said and left unsaid, never finding the right combination of words that would turn his mom into a mother like other mothers, a mother who cared. Like Tess.

Like Jane.

But he could remember (couldn't he?) good times, too. His mom bringing him ginger ale in bed once when he was sick. Uncle Chuck taking him to see the Pistons edge out the Bulls.

Aidan wouldn't have those kind of memories with his dad.

"You writing to your dad like that . . . You gave it your best shot," Gabe said. "You stepped up. That was a brave thing, that was a good thing, for you to do. You're a good kid."

"Then why didn't he answer?"

Because he's an asshole, Gabe wanted to say, but that wouldn't help. Probably nothing he could say would help.

He wiped his hands on a rag, choosing his words with care.

"Sometimes dads don't know how to be dads. Your dad, he didn't step up. That's on him. That's not on you."

Aidan dropped his head, his bangs shielding his eyes.

"Hey." Gabe squatted down on his heels, waiting until the kid looked up. "The thing is, the thing you should know is, you've got people who are here for you. Your mom. Your grandfather."

Me, he thought.

But it was too early to say that. Too early even to think it. Too late to take the thought back.

"It's not the same," Aidan said.

"I know."

"You don't understand."

"Yeah, I do. Which is why you can talk to me. And how I know that you will get through this. I'm not saying it will be easy. But you got people who love you who will help. Even one person who's there for you can make all the difference."

Those big brown eyes searched Gabe's face. "Who do you have?"

He was some kid. Gabe rubbed his jaw to hide his smile. "Well, when I was your age, I had my uncle Chuck."

"Where does he live?"

He's dead. "He's in heaven, I guess."

Aidan's brow puckered. "But who do you have now? You need somebody now."

Gabe opened his mouth to reply when something—an indrawn breath, a sudden stillness, a scent like vanilla in the air—dragged at his attention. He lifted his head.

Jane, standing at the entrance to the kitchen.

Their eyes met and held. Held, while the moment flowed and thickened between them. *You need somebody now.*

"I'm working on it," Gabe said.

GABE ROSE FROM his crouch with a long-limbed, easy strength that made Jane's knees wobble. His eyes were dark as molasses, with just that hint of gold and green drizzled around the edges like honey. Sweet. Dazzling.

"How long have you been standing there?" he asked.

Jane swallowed. "Long enough."

Long enough to hear his patience and honesty with Aidan, to lose her breath and a piece of her heart. An almost maternal tenderness moved through her, heavy and fierce.

She wanted him. And he needed her, or he thought he did.

All she had to do was go back to being the old Jane, the one who trusted her happiness and her son to somebody else.

She cleared her throat. Smiled. "How's the painting coming?"

"Good," Gabe said. "Kid's doing a good job on those shelves."

"No drips," Aidan piped.

She laid her hand on his shoulder, bird bones and slight muscle. "I can see that. Nice job. I'd say this calls for pizza."

"Pizza! Yay!"

Gabe smiled slightly. "I can have the walls done by the time you two get back."

He had offered to take them out for pizza before, and she had hesitated. She couldn't decide now if her caution was foolish or selfish—or very, very smart.

She was falling for him. But she had to be realistic. She had a kid to worry about. There was a risk that Aidan might fall for him, too.

At her continued silence, Gabe raised an eyebrow. "Unless you don't trust me with your shop."

"It's not that," Jane said.

She didn't have only her own feelings to consider now, or Aidan's. Now there was Gabe, who deserved better than to be used and dismissed.

Surely she could give him what he wanted and hold back enough to protect herself and her son.

"I reckon you earned pizza, too," she said. "I can handle

a roller. Why don't we finish painting together and eat after?"

Gabe nodded slowly. "I'd like that. If that's what you want."

In the end, she and Aidan were so covered in paint that they decided to have the pizza delivered—mushroom for Jane, pepperoni for the boys. Gabe insisted on paying.

Jane folded her arms. "That's not right. Not after all this work you've done."

"You worked, too."

"It's my place."

"I painted the shelves," Aidan said.

Jane shared a quick smile with Gabe.

"You sure did," Gabe said. "Looks nice, too."

The new color made the bakery look bigger. Brighter. Jane spun slowly in the center of the room, surveying the freshly painted walls with satisfaction.

Satisfaction and gratitude. It had taken her days to paint the place herself when she opened six years ago. She was proud of all she had accomplished on her own. But she couldn't deny the work had gone quicker with Gabe's help.

"It all looks nice," she said.

"Beautiful," Gabe said.

But he wasn't looking at the room.

She blushed to the roots of her hair, warm all over. "Thank you. Well, I . . . I should get Aidan home. It's a school night."

"Sure," Gabe said. "See you, sport."

"You could come, too," Aidan said.

A faint smile touched Gabe's lips. Her gaze snagged on his mouth. He was so handsome when he smiled. "I don't think so. I've got to walk my dog."

"Aidan goes to bed at nine," Jane said. "You could drop by after."

Gabe's dark gaze turned razor sharp. "You want me to come to your house," he repeated.

She nodded, her blood rushing. "Maybe . . . for coffee?"

Not a booty call. They needed to talk, away from Aidan and interruptions.

"You can read me a story," Aidan said.

Her jab of surprise was followed by a tiny prick of envy. Lately, Aidan had grown impatient with cuddling. But often, at the end of the day, he reverted to her little boy again. Even though he was old enough to read to himself, he liked for her to read to him at bedtime. Usually she could squeeze in a hug, too.

Gabe stuck his thumbs in his belt loops, a smile tugging the corner of his mouth. "You got the mouse and the cookie book?"

"Yeah!" Aidan's face changed. Became doubtful. "It's kind of for little kids though."

"I've never read it," Gabe said.

Aidan brightened. "I could, like, maybe read it to you."

"I'd like that." Gabe looked at Jane. "But it's up to your mom."

"Well, I . . ."

"Please?" Aidan said.

She could not resist both of them. Not when her own heart was on their side. She shrugged helplessly. "I guess we'll see you later, then."

"Twenty minutes?"

"Make it half an hour. Aidan has to shower."

Gabe rubbed the back of his neck. "Wouldn't mind a chance to clean up myself."

He patted Aidan's shoulder. Stepped in close—he was so tall—and kissed Jane on the cheek, a brush of stubble and smooth lips, a whiff of paint and warm male. Her insides gave a sudden throb. Her lips parted.

"Thirty minutes," he said and was gone.

Aidan's eyes had widened at the kiss, but he didn't say anything as Jane locked up or in the car or later when they got home.

Was that a good sign or a bad sign?

Jane spooned grounds into the coffeepot, one ear cocked for the shower running upstairs. She had never brought a man around her son before. Maybe if she had, she'd know what to say to him now.

And maybe Aidan wouldn't have been so quick to jump in the car when his father tried to take him last summer.

The doorbell rang.

Her hand jerked, scattering coffee grounds over the counter.

"Sorry," she said breathlessly when she yanked open the front door a few minutes later. "I spilled the . . ."

Tulips.

Her thoughts dissolved. She melted all over, her knees and her spine.

Gabe Murphy stood on her doorstep in an olive-green T-shirt that brought out the color of his eyes, holding a bouquet of yellow tulips. "Spilled the . . . ?" he prompted.

"What? Oh, the coffee." She stared at the cheerful blooms, trying to remember the last time a man had brought her flowers.

Gabe looked at her oddly. "You okay? Not burnt or anything."

"Hm? Oh. No." You didn't bring flowers to a booty call.

"These are for you." He thrust the tulips at her. "Watch the stems. Tess said they'd drip."

She accepted the bouquet, wrapped in a damp paper towel fastened with a rubber band. "Tess Fletcher?"

"They're from her garden."

And you definitely didn't bring flowers from your best friend's mother's garden. Jane raised the tulips to her face, melting a little more, breathing in the fresh green scent with its faint undernote of musk.

"Where's Hank?" Gabe asked.

She blinked. "He's out tonight. Home at eleven, he said."

"Late shift."

"I don't think so." She lowered the flowers. "Honestly, I don't know. Usually, the officers are just on call after nine o'clock. But he's been acting weird lately."

"Weird, how?"

"Well, he's always spent a lot of time at the station, but he's gone even more now. And when he's home, he's kind of distracted." She frowned. "Also, he's been shaving a lot. And whistling."

Gabe's mouth quirked. "Maybe he has a girlfriend."

"Oh, no," she said automatically. "Dad doesn't date."

Any more than she did. *Huh.*

"Twenty years is a long time to go without sex," Gabe observed.

"Yes." She bit her lip. Even eight years was too long. Eight days. "But we're talking about my *dad.*"

"I'm no authority, but it seems to me having a kid doesn't eliminate your sex drive."

Their eyes met. Her breath went. "I guess not."

A door opened upstairs. Footsteps creaked in the hall and thumped on the landing. Aidan appeared at the crook of the stairs, his hair shiny from his shower. "Hey, Gabe. I have my book."

"Hi, sport. Let's see it, then."

Aidan danced from foot to foot. "It's upstairs."

Gabe looked at Jane in silent question.

She summoned a smile. "You go. I need to get these in water."

She lingered to watch them climb the stairs together, the tall man in jeans and work boots adjusting his stride to the little boy in pajamas and bare feet. The picture pierced her heart.

She and Aidan had each other, and that was essential. They had her father, and that was a blessing. Despite her recent worries about Aidan, he was a happy, healthy, well-adjusted child. Practically a miracle.

And yet . . .

She cut the tulips' stems over the kitchen sink, arranging them in a brown-glazed stoneware pitcher. The bright blooms glowed. Wistfully, she touched one, tracing its creamy texture with one finger.

She had never had a man bring her flowers before or climb the stairs at night to read to her son.

There was a danger Aidan could become too attached. They needed to talk about that. She had to protect her child.

But as she set out mugs for coffee and tidied the counter, she worried it was already too late for Aidan.

Too late for them both.

Sixteen

GABE FOUND HER in the kitchen, putting cups and cookies on a tray. Such a Jane thing to do, providing food and comfort. He paused a moment to appreciate the picture she made, her quick, neat hands, her smooth blond hair. Like Tess Fletcher, she had a knack, a need, for taking care of others.

He wanted to take care of her.

"Let me get that," he said. He felt the slight resistance in her grip before she released the tray.

She twisted her empty hands together, as if she wasn't sure what to do with them. "I thought we'd sit on the porch."

He smiled reassuringly. "Lead the way."

The screened back porch was shadowed and quiet, surrounded by overgrown shrubs. His contractor's eye noted a rip in the screen, a break in the lattice, rust on the chains of the old porch swing. The air smelled of sea and loam and faintly of citronella. A chorus of tree frogs swelled in the dusk. Through the skylight overhead, the stars were coming out, faint white points against a deep blue sky.

Jane gestured for him to put the tray down on a small table. "I need to . . ." Another nervous movement of those hands, smoothing the thighs of her jeans. "I should say good-night to Aidan."

"Take your time." Gabe eased his weight down on the swing. "I'll be right here."

The thought sank into him. *Right here on Dare Island.*

He was content here, happier than he could ever remember being. He had a job, friends, a dog, a truck. Like some cowboy in a country song instead of a punk from Detroit. Gabe grinned in the dark. Hell, he was sitting on a goddamn porch swing in the moonlight. All he needed to complete the cliché was the love of a good woman.

His breathing jammed. *Yeah.* All he needed . . .

"HE'S ALMOST OUT," Jane said, rejoining him.

"Kid worked hard today."

"You, too. Thank you."

He shrugged, uncomfortable with her praise.

She sat beside him on the slatted seat, propping her feet on the table, rocking the swing. Her position, bent knees, raised feet, exposed a strip of pale skin above her plain white sneakers. *Jesus.* He had it bad when even the sight of her ankles turned him on.

"You're good with him," she continued softly.

He cleared his throat, trying not to imagine her naked. "He read me a story. No big deal."

He liked the boy.

The swing creaked idly back and forth. He'd never sat with a girl on a porch swing in the dark. It was nice.

"He talked to you about his father," Jane said. "That's a very big deal. Lauren says it's important for Aidan to express his feelings, but he doesn't talk to me."

"It's a guy thing."

A smile played around her mouth. Her scent wrapped around him in the dark, sweet and edible. He'd probably never be able to eat chocolate again without tasting her. "Talking? I don't think so."

"Not making eye contact," he explained. "Uncle Chuck used to say I only opened my mouth when we were working together. Or driving in the car. Like I could only tell him stuff if he couldn't see my face." He grinned, remembering. "Some of the shit I told him, I'm surprised he didn't drive us off the road and into a tree."

She slid her hand along the seat, wrapping her small, scarred, capable fingers around his big, rough ones, giving them a little squeeze. "Aidan likes you."

Ah, Jesus. She might as well have squeezed his heart. Except that his heart was swelling too big for his body, pressing against his ribcage. He couldn't breathe, all of the room in his chest taken up by his rapidly expanding heart. "He's a good kid. You've done a good job with him."

"Thanks." She dropped her gaze to their joined hands. "But he's confused right now. Vulnerable. Especially where his father is concerned. I'm not sure it's a good idea for him to get attached to you."

Her words slid like a knife between his ribs, puncturing his heart. *Bang.*

He drew in a cautious breath, absorbing the pain.

The old Gabe would have argued. His instinct when wounded or threatened had always been to lash out. Fight back. But he'd known all along he didn't deserve her. He shouldn't be surprised she'd figured it out, too. What did he know about being a role model for a little boy?

"I'm all he has," Jane continued. "I don't want him hurt when you leave."

"You're worried I'll hurt Aidan," he said carefully.

She nodded, not quite meeting his eyes.

He choked down his churning panic. *This isn't about you, you bastard. Think about her.*

Something didn't fit.

He forced himself to consider what she was saying, to think before he spoke.

You don't scare me, she'd said.

This is what I want, she'd said.

I trust you.

Gabe frowned. Jane was a good mom. Maybe she was simply protecting her son. And maybe . . .

I don't want him hurt when you leave.

God. Maybe she was protecting herself.

"I'm not going anywhere," he said. "Unless you tell me to go."

Her gaze lifted. In the deep blue twilight, her eyes were searching. Serious. Her fingers clung to his.

Enough talking, he decided. He'd never been much good with words anyway. Jane needed reassurance.

Or that was his excuse.

He lifted the table, moving it farther away. She watched, her brow puckering.

Leaning forward, he dropped a kiss between her brows. His mouth drifted from her cheek to her jaw, finding the tender hollow of her neck, where her skin was silky and warm. Doing his best to reassure her, to show her with his body the things he could not say.

Let me take care of you. Don't tell me to go.

IT WASN'T ONLY sex this time.

The thought sank inside Jane, sending ripples of warmth that spread through her body to the tips of her fingers, the bottoms of her soles. He kissed her so sweetly.

Maybe it had never been only sex.

They played at kissing, brushing lips, teasing tongues, experimenting with depths and angles like teenagers exploring in the dark. His hands moved slowly up and down her sides. The heel of his palm brushed her breast, and her nipples contracted almost painfully. As if he knew, his hands slid under her shirt, texture dragging against her skin, closing over her breasts to claim them. The hard little points pressed against his palms. She whimpered against his mouth.

The sound shocked her back to awareness. She wasn't a teenager necking on the porch.

"Aidan . . ."

"He's out, you said."

"*Almost* out."

Gabe's eyes gleamed at her in the dark. His hands kept moving, stroking, playing. "That was fifteen minutes ago. You want to go check on him?"

She could feel herself softening, yielding. "N-no," she admitted.

He laughed low and kissed her. He tasted like coffee and chocolate, rich, addictive flavors. He pulled her to straddle his thighs, her arms around his neck, her knees resting on the old porch swing, rocking, swaying, moving together, jeans against jeans, male against female, delicious, grinding friction.

His hands tightened at her waist, lifting her away. She stumbled. He held her close between his legs, his arm a solid band at her back, his free hand popping open the button of her jeans. His knuckles brushed her stomach.

She sucked in. "I don't . . . I can't . . ."

He traced the seam of her zipper, his touch wandering, teasing, cupping her. "I think you do."

She swallowed. Could he feel how wet she was? "We're outside." *Exposed.* The risk made her heart pound.

"It's dark. Nobody can see." His voice soothed, but the devil was back in his eyes, as if the thought of the neighbors didn't bother him at all.

As if what other people saw or said didn't matter.

Her breath came faster. She glanced around at the shielding bushes as he coaxed her zipper down.

She squeezed her legs together, squirming, trying to relieve the tickle between her thighs "My dad will be home in an hour."

"That's okay." A glint through dark lashes, a smile tugging the corner of his mouth. "I won't take long."

She snorted with laughter. "Oh, that's seductive."

But it felt good to tease. And his playfulness relaxed her, releasing her muscles. He took instant advantage, easing her jeans off her hips, down her legs, taking her panties with them.

He tapped her ankle. "Step."

She stood awkwardly on one leg, grabbing his shoulder for balance, quivering as the breeze teased her butt and her damp sex. His belt clanked. His zipper rasped, the sound blending into the chorus of cicadas and crickets singing in the shrubbery.

She held up one finger in the universal sign for wait-a-minute. "Condom."

He raised up briefly and pulled a foil packet from his hip pocket.

Their eyes met. She shivered in anticipation.

"C'mere," he murmured after he had sheathed himself. "Let me warm you up."

He pulled her down again to straddle him, the swing lurching under their combined weight. Her breasts were practically in his face. He turned his head and bit her softly, suckled her hard, making her moan.

The heat moved everywhere as he tugged and adjusted, his fingers sliding against her. His body reared under her, smooth and thick and hot. She moved, trying to center him—*here, no, here*—and he scooted forward, bracing her weight, so that her dangling feet brushed the floor. With her legs spread wide over his, she couldn't get her balance. She toppled forward, falling into him, and he grabbed her, pulling her down, pushing inside her. *Oh, God, yes, there.*

He pulled her closer, spread her wider, rocked against her, and she bit her lip to keep from crying out, her entire body out of her control, shaking like the swing. She clutched his shoulders, the one sure thing in her swaying world, as he filled her, as the earth reeled and the stars swung wildly overhead and the tension spiraled inside her, concentric rings closing tighter and tighter with him at her center, hard inside her, sliding deeper, moving faster. *Nothing to do but hold on.* Her back arched. Her toes flexed, reaching, straining . . .

"Come on." His eyes were almost black. Fierce. "Let go. I've got you."

And she shattered and shuddered and came, the stars raining down softly behind her closed lids, showering sparks through her flesh.

His breath seared the side of her throat. His fingers dug into her butt as he jerked under her, as he thrust into her, and followed.

"ONE OF THESE days," Gabe said, his voice thick with satisfaction, "we're going to do it in a bed."

Jane's lips curved against his neck. "Sounds like a plan." *Sounds like a future.*

Her stomach tensed. She waited for the doubts to come, clustering thickly as the moths around the porch lamp outside. When they didn't, she sighed and relaxed, kissing his shoulder, inhaling the warm tang of his skin. He smelled so good.

"I could spend the night," he said.

There it was, the first qualm, a flutter low in her belly. She raised her head. "Not a good idea."

"Because of Aidan?" Gabe asked. "Or your dad?"

She shifted uneasily on his lap. This was not a discussion she wanted to have naked. "It's too soon." She tried to stand and wobbled. He steadied her with his hands on her waist. "*And* I have to get up at four in the morning," she added, inspired.

She bent and fumbled for her jeans, ignoring the draft playing around her backside.

"Jane."

She glanced over her shoulder.

"Nice butt."

Heat swept her face, incandescent in the dark.

He grinned, but his voice was serious when he said, "I get it. No sleepovers. But I'm not sneaking around. Not even for you."

She'd snuck around with Travis, hiding from Hank's disapproval, trying to avoid a confrontation between her father and her lover. But Gabe was not her ex-husband. And Jane was not nineteen anymore.

"I know," she said.

He nodded and stood, zipping his jeans. "Your father will just have to get used to the idea that we're together now." He regarded her thoughtfully, a twist to the corners of his mouth. "Guess you will, too."

She stared at him, wide-eyed.

He tucked in his shirt and approached her. Bending his head, he kissed her, a hard, brief kiss like punctuation, a period at the end of a sentence. "See you tomorrow."

Huh.

After he left, Jane brought the tray into the kitchen, still carrying the imprint of his body deep in her body, the echo of his words in her head.

We're together now. Flat. Possessive.

Like she didn't have something to say about that.

A vague disquiet brushed wings across the back of her neck, but it could not grip and sting. Not tonight, when she was warm and sated from their lovemaking. She let herself think about today, about Gabe painting her walls and reading to her son and making her shatter on the porch swing, how wonderful he made her feel, how right.

She put the mugs in the dishwasher. Maybe at some point, a couple months or years down the road when Aidan was older, when her business was more established, when she and Gabe had known each other longer and her father had time to accept him, she'd be ready to think about tomorrow, too.

She was packing Aidan's lunch for school when she heard tires on the drive outside and then keys at the door.

The back door eased open. Hank poked his head into the

kitchen, looking so much like a teenager sneaking in after curfew that she had to grin.

He frowned. "I thought you'd be in bed."

"Not yet. You're home late," she observed.

"I had something to see to."

Jane recalled Gabe's suggestion that her dad could have a lady friend. "Something?" she teased. "Or someone?"

A faint red stain appeared high on his cheekbones.

Jane lowered her knife. "Dad?"

"I, ah . . ." Hank cleared his throat. "You and Aidan weren't home for dinner. So I ate at Marta Lopez's house."

"Marta Lopez from work?"

He nodded.

Jane blinked. "I thought you two didn't get along."

"She's a very nice woman," Hank said. "Once you, er, get to know her. Nice sons."

Oh. A tiny pang, straight to the heart. Of course her father would like sons.

Jane gave herself a little shake. She was not even the tiniest bit upset by the idea that her father was dating. It wasn't like he was betraying her mother's memory. Mom had abandoned him. Abandoned them. Jane should take hope in the possibility that after all these years, her father was finally moving on. She should be delighted that he had a chance of finding happiness again. *Twenty years is a long time to go without sex*, Gabe had said.

Ew.

Jane shrugged. So maybe she wasn't ready to think about Dad and sex in the same sentence. She could still be happy for him.

"I'd like to," she said. "Get to know her, that is. Why don't you invite her to dinner here some night?"

Hank scowled. "I don't know. She might not feel right, leaving the boys to fend for themselves."

Jane ignored the implied criticism. "What are they, fifteen? Twenty?" When Aidan was grown, would she feel the same way? Like she still had to cook for him every night?

"I reckon."

"I see Tomás almost every day already. He's been working with Gabe on the addition. Maybe we should invite them all."

Hank's brows lowered. "You want to invite Tomás."

"Tomás and Miguel and . . ." Jane took a deep breath. If her father could get on with his life, then so could she. "And Gabe."

Your father will just have to get used to the idea that we're together now.

Gabe had a point. In a town the size of Dare Island, there was no way she could keep a relationship between them secret. And no way the two men could avoid each other forever. At least with Marta present, Hank would have to behave himself.

"Hell, no," Hank said.

Jane's stomach swooped. "Daddy . . ."

"No. I won't have that man in my house."

Probably not a good time to tell him Gabe had been inside a whole lot more than the house.

Jane folded her hands to hide their trembling. "Dad, I've always been grateful to you for giving me and Aidan a home. I know I made a mistake when I was nineteen. But I'm not nineteen anymore. You have to trust me."

"I trust you. It's Murphy I don't trust."

"I'm sorry I didn't listen to you about Travis. You were right about him. But you're wrong about Gabe."

"I don't give a damn about being right. I just want you to be . . ."

Her heart pounded. "Happy?"

Hank's gaze met hers. "Safe."

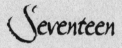

Seventeen

HANK CROSSED HIS arms and leaned against the side of his police cruiser, watching the crew install the roof on Jane's addition.

Working small-town law enforcement, you learned you couldn't depend on another jurisdiction to come pick up their bad guys, even with an outstanding warrant. You couldn't run somebody out of town or slap him in county jail for being a threat to public safety. You had to catch the son of a bitch actually breaking the law.

Or you could hang around, keeping an eye on things, making life uncomfortable enough that he moved on.

Gabe Murphy, damn his hide, showed no signs of moving on.

He was braced on the ladder between Jay Webber, on the ground, and Marta's boy, Tomás, crouching on the ridge line. As Hank watched, Murphy grabbed the top of a metal roofing panel from Webber and half hauled, half shoved it toward Tomás. Murphy took the weight as they wrestled the panel into place, the steel crackling like thunder. Murphy's ugly-ass dog flinched. Drills whirred.

"Watch your screws," Murphy called to Tomás. "You're flattening the washers."

"I think there's something wrong with my nut driver," Tomás said.

"Check the shaft," Murphy said.

Jay guffawed. "Boy can't screw if his tools don't work right."

Bunch of clowns.

"Don't you have someplace else to be?" Jane inquired at Hank's elbow.

Hank glanced down at his daughter, who had come out of the bakery to check on progress. Or to check on him. "Nope."

"I thought you were off duty today."

Hank shrugged. "Chief's off. Luke's tied up with a traffic complaint. I'm just keeping an eye on things."

Jane folded her arms, mirroring his pose. "On things? Or on me?"

Hank grunted. "Wanted to talk to you."

"Why don't you come in and have a cup of coffee?" Jane invited. "On the house."

"Marta says I drink too much coffee."

Jane raised an eyebrow, amused. "A brownie, then."

"You trying to fatten me up?"

Jane smiled. Her mother's smile, he thought with a pang. "Sweeten you up, more like."

"I'm not one of your old folks you can stick in the corner with a cookie and the crossword puzzle," he said. "You're not wrapping me around your finger."

Her dimple deepened. "Is that what you came to tell me?"

Bang bang bang. Murphy tapped the handle of his hammer against a metal seam as Webber wrestled another panel from the ground.

"Hold up," Murphy ordered. "Piece needs to be cut around the skylight." He started down the ladder.

Hank glared at them, distracted. "They better not be charging you by the hour."

"Gabe said they'll finish today," Jane said.

"Good. That's good." She deserved some good news today. Hank squinted up at the low roofline. He didn't want to watch her face as he delivered his news. "There's something you need to know, and you might as well hear it from me." He took a long breath. Released it. "Prison called the department this morning."

"I know."

He shot a look down at her. "What do you know?"

She tucked her fingers into the crook of his arm. "I got an automated call from Victim Assistance. Lauren got one, too. Travis is being released, it said. Within five days."

He scowled, relieved he didn't have to break the news to her after all. "It's nothing for you to worry about." He covered her fingers with his hand. "You've been taking care of yourself and Aidan a long time now. You'll be fine."

"Then why are you worried, Dad?"

He harrumphed. "Don't want this to get to you, that's all."

"It won't," she said. Sweet and simple and steadier than he thought she'd be. "I'm over this. Over him. I'm not a victim anymore. We're divorced. I got a restraining order. Isn't that a condition of his parole?"

Restraining order wouldn't do any damn good if her asshole ex took it in his head to ignore it. But Hank kept that thought to himself. "That's right. He comes sniffing around you, he's in violation of his parole and goes back to prison to serve out the rest of his sentence. Seven months." He patted her hand. "He's got no way to get here anyway. No call to—"

Metal rattled, clattered, and screeched. A cry. A curse. *Clang.*

Thud.

The ladder—and Tomás—sprawled on the ground.

"*Tomás?*" Jane covered her mouth with her hand.

Murphy dropped his tools, lunging to the boy's side. The dog darted in, danced back.

Hank started forward. "Don't move him."

Murphy ignored them both, dropping to his knees behind the boy's head. Tomás groaned.

Hank froze. He was no wuss, but, Jesus, that was Marta's boy lying there.

Murphy put a hand under Tomás's jaw—*checking his pulse?*—and then braced his head on either side. "Hey, pal. You fell. Try not to move, okay?"

"Ow. Ow."

"Can you tell me your name?"

Tomás groaned.

"Buddy, your name." Murphy's voice was calm. Insistent.

The boy opened his eyes. His bleary gaze fixed on Murphy's face. "You know my name. Tomás."

"Yeah. Good." Murphy slid a hand under Tomás's neck. "You remember what happened?"

"I fell. Fucking ladder. Oh God, my wrist."

"We'll get to that. Lie still." Murphy glanced up. His gaze speared Hank. "Call 911."

911. Shit. The call would go straight to Marta.

Hank grabbed his phone. "What should I tell her?"

"We need an ambulance," Murphy said.

There were people coming out of the bakery, customers alarmed by the noise or simply curious. Some damn fool pulled out a cell phone to take pictures. Jane hurried to intercept them.

Hank jolted into action. The scene needed to be secured. The victim needed medical attention and transport. He thumbed his phone. Took a deep breath. "Marta, there's been an accident."

TOMÁS WAS CONSCIOUS, breathing, not gushing blood.

He was bleeding, though, from the back of his skull. Gabe explored gently. No soft spots, no deformity, no grating of bone fragments. Good.

"Ow, my head. My head hurts," Tomás said.

"No shit," Gabe said. He braced his hands on either side of the boy's head, stabilizing his neck. "You allergic to anything? Any drugs?" Asking now would save the EMTs time later.

"I'm not on drugs, man." Tomás struggled to sit. "I frickin' fell."

"Stay down," Gabe commanded. "You're going to be fine. The paramedics are on their way, and they'll check you out and make sure you're okay."

"What can I do?" Jane asked.

Head wounds always bled like a son of a bitch. Gabe wasn't putting pressure on a possible skull fracture, but something to cover the wound, to staunch the bleeding, would be good. "Towels. Thanks."

She nodded, face pale, and ran into the bakery.

Tomás shifted his legs restlessly. Not paralyzed. More good news.

"Hold still," Gabe said. He looked up and found Hank. "Can you hold his head?" He was a cop, he should have some first aid training. "I need to check his spine."

"You sure you know what you're doing?" Hank asked.

"Combat lifesaver," Gabe said.

Hank nodded and kneeled down, placing his hands correctly over Gabe's.

Removing his hands, Gabe shifted to the left. "On three."

"Steady, now, son," Hank said. *To which one of them?*

Gabe positioned his grip at shoulder and hip, rotating the boy toward him to do a quick visual check of his back. No wounds, no bleeding, no protrusions. All good.

"Right. Let's roll him back."

Tomás moaned.

"You're doing great." Gabe pressed Tomás's shoulders and hips. Collarbone and pelvis, fine.

Sirens wailed faintly in the distance. Some moron started videotaping as Jane ran up with a pile of towels.

"Here." She set down the towels and took video dude's arm. "Let's move out of their way, okay?"

"Thanks," Gabe said. He made a pad, applying it to Tomás's bleeding skull.

"My wrist," Tomás said.

Gabe looked. His forearm was puffy, swelling, his wrist hidden by his work glove. "Let's take a look. You in pain?"

"*Mierda*, yeah." His voice slurred.

Gabe began to peel delicately at the glove. "What kind of pain?"

"I don't know, man. It— *Ow! Ow, shit.*"

"Hang in there, son," Hank said.

Broken wrist. No bones protruding through the flesh. "Can you squeeze my hand?" Gabe asked.

Tomás complied weakly. The sirens blared, closer now.

"I think I'm gonna be sick," Tomás moaned.

If he threw up lying on his back, he could aspirate chunks.

"Not a problem," Gabe said. "I'm going to rotate you on your side like I did before. Hank's going to hold your head." He looked at Hank. "Ready? On three."

Tomás puked on Gabe's knee as the ambulance pulled into the parking lot.

Two EMTs, one male, one female, came at a run.

"What do we have here?" the woman asked Hank.

Hank looked at Gabe, ceding control of the scene.

"Fall from this ladder, head wound, broken wrist," Gabe reported. "Patient alert and responsive. On a scale of one to ten, pain's at 'fucking hurts.'"

The guy grinned. "You an EMT?"

"Marine," Gabe said.

"Nice job," the woman said. "Okay, we're going to transport."

They went to get the cot and backboard while Gabe wiped puke.

The guy crouched beside Gabe, taking Tomás's hip and knee as the woman positioned the backboard. "Let's roll him. Hank, you've got the head."

The old cop nodded. "On my count. One, two, three."

Gabe helped the male EMT lift Tomás, now secured on the backboard, onto the cot.

"Thanks," the guy said. "We'll take it from here."

There was nothing else Gabe could do. He took a step back, shoving his hands in his pockets.

A late-model sedan bumped over the curb and into the lot.

The car door flung open and an attractive older woman got out. Gabe recognized her from the police station—Marta, Tomás's mom. She started forward, her high heels slipping on the gravel. "Tomás?"

"He's okay," Hank said.

She pressed her hand to her chest. "So much blood . . ."

Tomás raised his uninjured arm in a wavering salute. "Hi, Mami."

She burst into tears. Hank took her in his arms.

"We're ready to roll," the female EMT said. "Marta, we'll see you at the hospital."

"Can't I ride with him?"

"No room. You can ride up with me," the guy said. "In the cab."

"We'll take the squad car." Hank lifted Marta's chin, smiling reassuringly. "Lights and sirens all the way."

THE AMBULANCE AND the police car pulled out, orange and blue lights flashing.

Jane watched them go. Or more accurately, she watched Gabe watch them go, hands in his pockets, profile taut and strong against the sun-dappled trees.

This Gabe was a stranger to her. An attractive, competent stranger in a familiar fatigue jacket and ripped, filthy jeans.

She knew he was tough. She had admired his perseverance, his work ethic, his cocky humor. But his utter certainty in dealing with Tomás, his total command of himself and the situation . . . This was a side of him she hadn't seen before. Confident. Compelling.

And, she admitted, very, very hot.

Not that she should notice that now.

The sirens faded. The action over, his rigid stance relaxed, the tension slowly draining from his shoulders. She watched his certainty leach away and weariness take its place. Staring after the departed vehicles, his face was almost . . . lost.

A terrible tenderness seized her chest. He had so much heart. So much strength. So much pride. He didn't deserve to look that way, like something precious had been snatched from him.

Lucky crawled out from under the porch and slunk to Gabe's side, nudging his arm. Gabe glanced down, his expression lightening. He turned his hand out, petting the dog.

"Some Lassie you turned out to be," he said affectionately. "You're useless."

"You were wonderful," Jane said. "Thank God you were here."

Gabe shrugged. "Your dad could have handled it."

"But he didn't. You did. You knew exactly what to say. What to do."

He picked up the ladder without speaking and set it against the wall.

Jane pushed. "Have you considered becoming a paramedic? If . . . if you're staying."

"I'm staying." His voice was flat. Sure. "But I know my limits. I'd need training to do what you're talking about."

"You have training."

"I need the piece of paper."

She knew what it was to feel trapped by your circumstances. To have your faith in yourself eroded until you believed there was no way out. "So get it. Take classes or whatever."

His gaze met hers. For a moment, she saw hope flare, the possibilities kindle in his eyes, before their fire banked. He shook his head. "That's not for me."

"Why not?" she dared to ask.

"I missed my chance when I got out."

She was tempted to let it go, to leave him alone. But she knew exactly where that led. Nowhere.

"Is there a time limit to the GI Bill?"

"I meant I'm too old to go back to school."

"A friend of mine just got her associate's degree in dental hygiene. She's older than you are."

He threw her a smoldering look. She held her breath, fearing she had gone too far, nudged and nagged him and insulted his pride in the way that always drove Travis to drink. Or to rage.

And then the corner of his mouth lifted. "You're really something, Jane Clark."

Relief rushed over her. She released her breath. "Something good or something bad?"

"Something special."

She felt a flush work its way up her chest. "I didn't mean to badger you."

"Don't apologize. Having you believe in me . . ." He held her gaze, the smile deepening in his eyes. "Makes me think I've got a chance."

Her heart pounded. "At being a paramedic."

His smile spread. "That, too."

THE WAITING ROOM was alien and sterile, full of old folks struggling to breathe, bawling babies, listless children in their mothers' arms.

Hank hated it. Hated the smells and the bright lights that revealed the lines in Marta's face, hated the waiting and his own helplessness.

They had been at the hospital almost two hours. He prowled the aisle from the water fountain to Marta's chair, antsy as a drunk at a teetotalers' meeting.

Marta looked up at his approach, her complexion gray under the fluorescent lights, worry in her eyes. Her son was behind those doors, those doors where even Hank's badge could not win admittance, and there wasn't a damn thing Hank could do to affect the outcome.

"Want a cup of coffee?" he asked.

She shook her head.

"Magazine? There's a gift shop down the hall."

A smile touched her lips. "I'm fine, Hank."

His heart swelled with frustration. "What can I do?"

"You are here," she said simply. "That is the most important thing."

He sat down beside her and held her hand. Strong hands, with soft, lotioned skin and polished nails. She'd told him once that when she cleaned houses for a living, her hands were a point of pride. *I can take care of myself*, they said. *I am worthy of care.*

She was the most extraordinary woman he'd ever known.

He rubbed the back of her hand. "Guess this isn't the first time you've been to the emergency room."

Another smile. "No."

"Four boys."

She looked away. "Yes."

And a husband who died at the age of forty-one. Like she needed to be reminded of that.

Hell, Hank thought.

It was almost a relief when the sliding doors opened and Gabe walked in, scanning the room, and then strode toward them.

Hank stood, delighted to have a target for his frustration. "Can't believe your piece-of-shit truck got you this far."

Gabe bared his teeth in a grin. "I didn't drive my truck." He fished in the pocket of his fatigue jacket and pulled out a small, fuzzy pink bear attached to a key.

"What the hell is that?" Hank asked.

"My valet key!" Marta said.

Gabe handed it to her. "I found it in your glove box." He glanced at Hank. "Car was unlocked. Anyway, I figured you might want your own wheels in case Tomás was admitted and you were stuck here overnight."

"That was very thoughtful," Marta said.

It was, too. Hard to resent anybody who could put that smile on Marta's face.

"I haven't even thanked you yet for everything you did for my son," she said.

Gabe shrugged. "I didn't do anything special. Reached him first, that's all."

"That's not what Hank said. Tomás is lucky you were there, because of your medical combat training." She turned to Hank. "Isn't that what you said in the car?"

Gabe shot Hank a quick look.

Hank grunted. He'd been trying to reassure her, not compliment Gabe.

"How's he doing?" Gabe asked. "Tomás."

"His wrist is broken," Marta said. "But the doctor thinks he will not need surgery. She is more worried about his head injury."

"Probably broke his fall with his arm," Gabe said. "That's a good thing."

Marta gave him a grateful look.

"They took him back for a CT scan," Hank said.

"Mrs. Lopez?" The doctor, a fresh-faced redhead in a wilted white coat, was back.

Marta sat up straight. "How is Tomás?"

"He's doing great," the doctor said. "There's a little shadow on the scan caused by damage to the blood vessels between the brain and skull. This kind of bleed often stops on its own and then heals like any other cut. But to be on the safe side, we want to keep him overnight for observation."

"Can I see him?"

"We're moving him up to a room now," the doctor said. "As soon as he's settled, the nurse will come get you."

"I can spend the night?"

"Absolutely."

"Need me to bring you anything?" Hank asked when the doctor had gone. "A toothbrush?"

"I'm fine." Marta smiled at him, competent, calm, and

in control. "If I need anything, I will check out this hospital gift shop you are so fond of."

"I can swing by the house," he offered. "Check on Miguel."

"I called him already while you were parking the car. He is spending the night with his friend Ethan."

He admired her backbone. Made her a damn fine dispatcher. But it wouldn't kill her to lean on somebody else once in a while. To lean on him. He was willing to help. He just needed her to tell him what to do.

A nurse in blue scrubs came through the big doors. "Ready to take you up now, Mrs. Lopez."

"Well." Marta's gaze sought his.

"He'll be fine," Hank said, answering her unspoken need for reassurance.

"Of course. He has a hard head." She smiled and patted his cheek. "Like some other people I know." She glanced at Gabe. Lowered her voice. "Be nice."

"I'm always nice," he growled, and was rewarded when she laughed.

He watched her march after the nurse toward the elevator, indomitable in her straight black skirt and chunky heels. Nice legs.

He turned to find Gabe watching him, smirking.

Hank flushed. "I suppose you need a ride home now."

"Already called Luke. He's coming after his shift."

Be nice.

"Don't be a jackass," Hank said. "I'm here. You can ride with me."

Eighteen

AFTER FORTY-FIVE MINUTES in the car with Hank, Gabe wanted a shower, a run on the beach, and a beer. Not necessarily in that order.

Jane's dad may have been shamed into offering him a ride from the hospital. That didn't mean the two of them bonded during the drive home. They barely spoke.

At least this time Gabe sat in the front seat instead of being transported in the back like a criminal.

Gabe started his truck and followed Hank's squad car out of the bakery parking lot, careful to use his turn signal. When Hank turned into his driveway, Gabe was tempted to keep right on going.

Not that he would. Jane had volunteered to watch Lucky while Gabe delivered Marta's car. He couldn't leave the dog with her overnight.

He pulled in front of the faded blue frame house. Aidan and the dog were tussling in the yard. The dog was barking, the boy was giggling. Something loosened in Gabe's chest.

Aidan sent up a shout of welcome as he got out of the truck. "Hey, Gabe!"

"Hi, sport."

Lucky charged over, a ratty yellow tennis ball clutched firmly in his jaws, ears cocked, tail wagging.

"What do you want?" Gabe asked.

Lucky dropped the ball and danced back. Gabe stooped and winged the ball across the yard. The dog shot after it like a bullet, Aidan running in pursuit.

Gabe grinned.

Jane came out on the porch, and he felt the weight of the day slide from his shoulders like dropping his seabag after a long deployment.

"They haven't stopped since Aidan got home from school," she said.

"Good exercise."

"Yes." She smiled. "Guess they'll both sleep well tonight."

Their eyes met, and it hit him.

This. This must be what coming home felt like, the moment perfect as a postcard: the bushes around the porch struggling into flower, and the kid racing over the grass, and Jane smiling in welcome, so pretty she took his breath away.

Gabe cleared his throat. "Thanks for watching my dog."

"Anytime," Jane said.

The air trembled between them.

Hank came around the corner of the house. "Supper ready yet?" *Translation: don't let the door hit you on your way out.*

"Just about," Jane said.

Gabe shifted his feet. "We'll get out of your hair, then."

"But . . ." Jane glanced at her father.

"I already told her to set another place," Hank said gruffly. "You might as well stay for dinner."

So maybe they had bonded after all.

Dinner was excellent, meat loaf and mashed potatoes that tasted nothing like the MRE he remembered swimming in gelatinous brown onion gravy.

After dinner, Gabe figured it was only fair he help with the dishes. Or maybe he was seizing any excuse to stick around.

"You've done enough already today," Jane said, taking his plate from him. "You deserve to relax."

"You, too."

She smiled and shook her head, as if there was something funny in the idea that she could have a night off.

He intended to change that.

"I like doing things for you," he said.

"I don't need you to. I don't expect them."

He backed her against the sink. "Maybe you should." The scent of soap rose from the bubbles behind her, making him remember the last time they had done dishes together. "You smell so good."

Her lips curved. "Like meat loaf?"

"Dish soap." He nuzzled her throat. "Very sexy."

They were surrounded by counters. With no effort at all, he could boost her up, make a place for himself between her thighs and . . .

Aidan clomped down the stairs. Great kid, lousy timing. Although with her father in the next room, it was just as well the kid interrupted them before Gabe made a total fool of himself.

Lucky lurched from under the table, tail swaying hopefully.

"Down, boy," Gabe said, as much to himself as to the dog.

Just because they had been petted and played with before didn't mean anything more was happening tonight.

"Hey, boy. Hey, Lucky." Aidan fussed over the dog, then turned shyly to Gabe. "I brought you a book." He held it out.

Gabe turned the volume over in his hand to read the title. "'*Charlie and the Chocolate Factory*'?"

"It's a chapter book," Aidan said. "You might have to help me with some of the words."

"Sure," Gabe said before he remembered. Jane didn't want this. She was afraid of Aidan getting attached, afraid of being hurt.

You can trust me, he thought at her. *Let me prove it to you.*

She glanced from him to Aidan and then threw up her hands, clearly recognizing when she was outnumbered. "Go ahead. Fifteen minutes."

Maybe it was fifteen, maybe it was twenty, by the time Gabe finished the chapter and said good night.

Across the hall, the door opposite Aidan's stood open. Jane's room, Gabe guessed, from the lacy white curtains. The tulips he had given her stood on the dresser table, dropping yellow petals onto the wood.

He needed to bring her more flowers.

That's what it meant to be in a relationship, didn't it? More dinners, more stories, more evenings like this one. For both of them.

Hank looked up from his recliner as Gabe passed the living room. "You're leaving now." Not quite a question.

"Yes, sir."

"'Preciate what you did for Marta's boy today."

"Thanks."

"You starting something up with my daughter?"

Gabe put his hands in his pockets, starting to sweat. Pulled them out again. "That's between her and me."

"I'm her father."

There wasn't anything to say to that, so Gabe didn't try.

"That son of a bitch she married . . ." Hank paused, a frown gathering on his face. "He hurt her."

"I won't," Gabe said.

Hank's dark gaze speared him. "I'll come after you if you do. Doesn't matter how old she is, she's my little girl."

"I won't argue with you there. But she's tougher than you give her credit for."

Hank scowled and gripped the remote, flipping channels. "I don't recall asking for your opinion."

"Well, you're getting it. To go through what she's gone through and turn out the way she is . . ." Gabe shook his head. "Most people, they get beat up or pushed around, it breaks them. Or it makes them hard. Mean." Like his mother. Like

Gabe himself, that first year he joined the Corps, an angry, resentful kid desperate to prove himself, to do anything he could to survive. "But not Jane. She's an amazing woman. She does more than just feed people. She nurtures them. You should be proud of her."

"I am proud. But she took it hard when her mama left. And then to get mixed up with a no-account piece of shit like Tillett . . . Bound to leave scars."

Gabe had told himself the same thing. Jane had been through a lot. She deserved better.

But it was beginning to annoy him, the way people talked about her, the way they defined her as an abandoned eight-year-old or a deluded nineteen-year-old and seemed to ignore everything she had accomplished since.

"If you're telling me she's got a lot on her shoulders, I can see that for myself. If you're asking me if I plan on being a burden on your daughter, the answer is no. But I would like to lighten her load some."

Hank's face was as grooved and unreadable as a tractor tire. "Is that a fact."

"Actually, sir, it's a promise."

The grooves deepened suddenly. "Might be she'll have something to say about that."

He was grinning, the ornery old bastard.

Gabe rejoined Jane in the kitchen. She was bending over the contents of Aidan's backpack, which were strewed on the kitchen table. Her butt, in wash-worn denim, was firm and smooth, with a crease down the center like a ripe peach.

Gabe's mouth went dry. He ran his tongue over his teeth.

At his entrance, she glanced over her shoulder. "That took you a while."

"Yeah." The faint sounds of the television drifted from the living room. Hell. Had she heard him discussing her with her father behind her back? "It was a good book," he said, trying to distract her.

She straightened, putting one hand on the small of her back, the way she did when she was tired. The position did nice things for her breasts, which for once weren't shielded by her apron. "You never read it before?"

What? He shook his head, trying to focus. "I wasn't much into reading as a kid."

And he'd never seen a copy of *Charlie and the Chocolate Factory* in the library of the Williams County Jail.

"Mm." She tilted her head, studying him with those too-aware, too-amused eyes, all shining silver on the surface with depths a man could drown in. Like the sea at dawn.

He sighed, resigned. "How much did you hear?"

"Between you and my dad?" She smiled. "Enough."

He eyed her warily. "Enough to . . ." *Be embarrassed? Mad? What?*

"Enough to do this," she said, stepping in close.

Surprise rendered him motionless as she twined her arms around his neck, pressing her breasts against him. "And this."

She kissed him.

Her lips were soft and warm, all of her soft and warm and sweet, everything he craved, everything he cherished, right here in his arms. Lust surged through him, heavy and hard, and his brain shut down, his body taking over as he kissed her back, and she was with him all the way, opening her mouth, tightening her arms, her body straining against his.

"Don't mind me," Hank growled, and Gabe jolted as if he'd been tased.

He raised his head as Jane's father strolled in and opened the refrigerator door.

"I wanted some tea," Hank said, pulling out a plastic jug.

Jane folded her arms over the mighty rack. "Daddy, you never drink sweet tea."

Hank eyed her acerbically. "I do all kinds of things I don't tell you about. Same as you, I reckon. But there's a time and a place for everything."

Jane's face turned pink.

"No secrets here," Gabe said, coming to her rescue.

Hank shot him a shrewd look from under bushy brows.

Gabe grinned. "You've already done a background check on me."

Hank barked with laughter, which he covered with a cough.

Gabe kissed Jane briefly and firmly on the mouth—a gesture of support, a stamp of possession. "See you tomorrow," he said, and left, his dog at his heels.

TRUE TO HIS word, Gabe showed up at Jane's Sweet Tea House the next day to finish work on the roof.

Jane seized a break between customers to carry breakfast to the work crew—Gabe, Jay, and one other man.

Gabe met her gaze, a smile in his eyes. "Right on schedule."

Seeing him filled her with a dangerous heat, her insides rising light as a soufflé. She felt ridiculously happy just being near him. "The coffee?" she teased. "Or the project?"

"Can't be the project," he said wryly. "Between the rain and the accident, we're a week behind."

She had never known another man who pushed himself so hard or who downplayed his own efforts so much.

"You're not responsible for the weather," she said. "Or the accident. How's Tomás?"

He took the coffee she held out to him with a murmur of thanks. "His head looks fine, but he won't be back at work until his cast is off. Marta's springing him from the hospital as soon as the doctor signs off on the paperwork. I figured Hank would have told you."

"I haven't talked to Dad yet today. I left the house at four this morning."

"You don't get enough sleep."

She shrugged. "Baker's hours," she said lightly.

"Not just that." He tucked a loose strand of her hair behind her ear, his thumb lingering on her jaw. A tingle shivered down her spine. "You work too hard."

"I'm fine. I had a restless night," she confessed. Thinking

about him, warm and safe, holding her close. Dreaming about him, hot and dangerous, his hands hard on her hips as he pumped deep inside her.

"Me, too." His voice, sandpaper rough, scraped over her sensitized nerves.

The heat thickened. She swayed toward him, drew back, conscious of the sly grins and curious looks from the crew. The Lord only knew how many of her customers and neighbors were watching out the bakery windows. Speculating.

"Darn," she said, keeping her voice low so she couldn't be overheard. The gossip was bad enough without her feeding it.

"What?"

She'd never thought of herself as a particularly sexual person before. But now . . .

"I still want you," she whispered.

Gabe went very, very still. "You picked a hell of a time to mention it, cupcake." He raised his voice, never taking his gaze from hers. "Jay, Frank, take your breakfasts out front. You can eat at one of the tables."

And that, she was pretty sure, would give the gossips something to chew on for weeks.

Gabe watched them go and then turned back to her, his thumbs in his pockets. "So you want me," he said. "Damned if I can see why that's a bad thing."

"Not bad. Inconvenient, I guess. I reckoned that after we . . ." *Not slept together. No sleeping involved.* She blushed. "After we, you know, did it, that I wouldn't feel so needy. Greedy. Isn't having sex supposed to get it out of your system?"

His mouth quirked. "Not if you do it right."

She smiled ruefully. "We must be doing something right, then. I feel like I'm set to burst out of my skin. I want you all the time. Is it you? Is it me?"

He gave a short, strangled laugh. "Hell, I don't know. Maybe it's the tool belt."

An answering laugh bubbled deep within her. "It's not only the tool belt, trust me."

"Then it's got to be you." His gaze met hers. "I've never felt this way before."

Oh. She hugged his words to her heart the way she wanted to hug him.

But she could not linger. No matter what she dreamed or felt, she had work to do. Rudy came in at nine to help with the lunch prep, but Jane still needed to do the afternoon baking.

She clasped her hands together, keeping them to herself. "I have to go."

Gabe nodded, accepting that, but said, "I want to see you tonight. You and Aidan."

"I'm sorry. I have to do paperwork tonight. Pay bills. Place orders. My vendors only deliver to the island once a week. If I don't order my supplies on time, I'll wind up having to make a dozen trips to the mainland."

A long look, a slower nod. "Right."

Guilt and regret joined forces against her. "Maybe you could come by later," she suggested.

"Nine o'clock?"

She winced, thinking of the stack of things awaiting her attention.

"Ten?"

She bit her lip. "Maybe . . . ten thirty?"

He frowned. "I thought you had to be up at four."

Her throat tightened. She liked it so much that he remembered. More, that he cared.

I would like to lighten her load some, he had said to her father.

But it was *her* load, she thought stubbornly. Her weight to carry, her job and hers alone.

"I don't mind losing a little sleep," she said.

"I do. I won't come by tonight if it means you're exhausted in the morning."

"But I want to see you." *Great. Pouting. So attractive.*

"You'll see me tomorrow."

"Don't you have another job to go to?"

"We'll find time. I'll make time," he said.

She hoped so.

The truth was, there weren't enough hours in the day. She was already juggling as much as she could handle. She wasn't sure how to throw a relationship into the mix without everything crashing to the ground.

Nineteen

THE DAMN LETTER from the lawyer in Detroit burned a hole in Gabe's back pocket. The words were branded in his brain. *Sorry to inform you . . . Sole beneficiary . . . Contact us at your earliest convenience.*

The phrases swirled, a red cloud in his head, like the suffocating dust of Afghanistan stirred by chopper blades. Memories rose and choked him. Anger, grief, regret. His throat ached. His eyes burned. He dragged down his safety goggles and turned on the drill, focusing on the task at hand, burying his thoughts in action.

Metal filings flew. Two holes, ten feet up, one on either side of the pole.

Lucky barked from the back of the truck.

Gabe shut off the drill.

"Hey, Gabe."

He had an audience. Aidan stood with a couple of kids at the edge of the carport, gazing up at him on the ladder.

Gabe swallowed the dryness in his throat, dredged up a smile. "Hi, sport. Who are your pals?"

"This is Chris."

Right. Gabe recognized the smaller of the two boys who had walked home with Aidan a couple weeks ago.

"And this is Hannah," Aidan said, indicating the dark-skinned girl in purple-laced sneakers.

She cocked her head, regarding Gabe with big green eyes. "What are you doing?"

"You took down the basketball hoop," Chris said at the same time.

"Yep." He came down the ladder, went to his pickup.

Aidan tagged after him.

Gabe dropped the tailgate. Lucky bounded from the truck, running from child to child, throwing himself down at everybody's feet, leaping up to thrust his nose in hand after hand. Hannah giggled.

While the kids fussed over the dog, Gabe hefted his cargo from the back of the pickup.

"What's that?" the girl asked.

Gabe carried the box to the carport.

The kitchen door opened, and it was like the sun came out on the porch, because . . . Jane.

The howling sandstorm inside him eased. Not that the letter in his pocket went away. But he could breathe again.

She smiled at him, warm and a little shy. "I thought you were all done here."

"Got one more job to take care of." He set down the box, revealing the picture on the side.

"A new hoop!" Aidan shouted.

This time the smile came easier. "That's right."

"Gabe, you shouldn't—" Jane started.

"Cool," Chris said.

"Can anybody play on it?" Hannah asked.

"Once it's up," Gabe said.

"Awesome!" Aidan said. "Thanks, Gabe!"

"Don't thank me," Gabe said. "You still have to put it together."

"Me?"

The staggered delight on the boy's face caused a catch in Gabe's chest. He cleared his throat again. "If you're up for it. I need somebody to assemble the bracket before I attach the backboard. Think you can look at the directions, see how everything gets put together?"

"By myself?"

Gabe eyed the other two. "Wouldn't hurt to have some help." It might even do Aidan some good to get his friends involved.

Chris's face split in a grin, exposing a missing tooth.

"I can help," Hannah volunteered.

"Hannah's really smart," Aidan said.

"Great. Let's see what you got." He made them stand back as he slit open the carton, as he located the instructions and the bag of parts. "Keep everything on the cardboard now. Don't lose anything."

Three heads bent over the cardboard. Fingers poked through washers and bolts.

"You just made him really happy." Jane stood beside Gabe, their shoulders almost touching. "Thank you."

He looked down at her, warm and close and important. "My pleasure."

"It must have been awfully expensive. You need to let me pay you back."

His jaw set. "No."

"It's too much. You're too generous."

"Look, I wanted to give him something." Needed to give him something. Wanted to do anything to turn this crappy mood around. "He did help me paint."

"Gabe, I think we need tools," Aidan said.

"No, you don't."

"To tighten things up," Hannah explained.

"The bolts should just be finger-tight for now. We'll tighten everything down after it's all assembled." Gabe crouched beside them to check. "Yeah, like that. Good job."

He straightened, reaching automatically to make sure the letter didn't fall out of his pocket.

Hannah threaded a bolt through a hole.

"Not that one," Aidan said, grabbing. "Try this."

She snatched it back. "I've got it. Look."

He preferred their squabbling to the voices in his head.

"What's the matter?" Jane asked very quietly.

Gabe shook his head. He didn't know where to start.

"Bad day?" she probed softly.

"I got a letter," he heard himself say.

"Bad news?"

"My mother's dead."

Shit. He hadn't intended to tell her like that. He hadn't planned on telling her at all.

"Oh, Gabe." Jane turned toward him, her fingers squeezing his arm. "When?"

"Six weeks ago." About the time he got out of jail. It took the lawyers that long to find him.

"How?"

"Cancer." All the years he'd feared for her life, he'd never thought it would be a disease that finally finished her off. "I didn't even know she was sick."

What kind of son didn't know his own mother was dying?

Jane was silent. But for some reason, he wasn't afraid of her judgment. Maybe she was the one woman in the world who would understand.

"Stay right here," she commanded, with another squeeze.

Like he had someplace better to go.

He stood there numbly while the kids wrangled at his feet and Jane ran lightly up the porch steps and into the kitchen.

"Okay." She was back, holding a bottle of water. She put her free hand on his arm again. "Let's go sit down over here."

He let her lead him to one of the tables under the trees, within sight of the carport. She handed him the water.

Doing what she did best, providing food and drink. Not offering false reassurances, just her presence. Her acceptance. Her peace.

"Thanks." Unscrewing the top, he drank deeply. It was something to do, to avoid meeting the sympathy in her eyes. And it eased the ache in his throat, a little. "You should go back inside. You have work to do."

"Rudy and Lindsey can handle it. So, this letter . . ." Her fingers were cool and light on his arm. "Was it from your father?"

"No. He's dead, too. At least, I'm pretty sure he is."

"You don't know."

He shook his head once side to side. *No.* But he could guess. *Sole beneficiary,* the letter said. His mother would never have left him a dime if the old man was alive. She had made her choice between her husband and her son years ago. "The letter was from her lawyer. Some law firm in Detroit."

"I'm so sorry," Jane said.

"Don't be. I lost my mother ten years ago, when she kicked me out. My father . . ." He turned the bottle around and around in his hands. "He hit her all the time," he said suddenly. "When I tried to stop him, he hit me, too."

"Oh, Gabe."

He took a deep breath. "When I finally got big enough to beat the shit out of him for raising his hand to her, Mom threatened to call the police on me. She took his side. Even after he died"—*how long had he been dead?*—"she chose him over me."

"Because she was ashamed," Jane said. "It's hard to admit when you're wrong."

"I didn't need her to say she was sorry. I forgave her a long time ago," he said. It was true. Kind of a relief, that.

"Maybe she couldn't forgive herself."

"Yeah. Maybe." He exhaled. "Anyway, it doesn't matter now."

"Gabe." Jane stroked his arm. "You just found out that you lost both your parents. It's all right to grieve."

"I didn't lose anything. You can't grieve for something you never had."

"Yes, you can. You're mourning your family. Not the family

you had, but the one you wanted. The one you dreamed about."
Her voice was sad. "I still miss my mom sometimes. It's funny,
because I don't even remember her all that well. But I miss the
things mothers and daughters are supposed to do together,
getting our nails done or her coming to my high school graduation or shopping for my wedding dress. I told Travis I wanted
to elope because Dad didn't approve of our marriage. But I
think, deep down, I didn't want to get married without my
mother being there."

He didn't know what to say. Her mother had walked out
on her. Hard to get around—or over—that. He covered her
hand with his.

She sighed. "I guess maybe I just really miss the idea of
her, you know?"

"I know," he said, because he couldn't leave her hanging
out there all alone. "I sent Ma these postcards. So she could
reach me, if she wanted to. If she needed anything."

Like one day she would come around. *All is forgiven,
come home.* But she never had. And now it was too late.

Jane turned her hand over, lacing her fingers with his. "I
always wanted to hear my mother say it wasn't my fault."

"Yeah," he confessed. "Me, too."

Her eyes were shiny. Hell. Was she crying? He really
hoped she wasn't going to cry. He held her hand tighter.

She bit her lip. "I guess part of you never gets over wanting your mother's . . ."

He searched for a word to give her. "Acceptance."

"Love."

Ah, Jesus. Now *he* was going to cry.

He looked up, focusing on the distance, willing away the
burning in his eyes. There was the sea, bright and blurry, and
the neat roofs and snug houses of the town. There was the
addition he had built, square and strong against the weathered
oaks, and Jane, sitting across the table from him, the sunlight
shining on her smooth hair.

And there was Aidan, straightening carefully from the

cardboard mat, a smile on his face and the rickety bracket held aloft in his hands like a trophy. "Hey, Gabe. Gabe, we got it."

His heart swelled and filled. He cleared his throat. Tightened his grip on Jane's hand.

The family you dreamed about.

"Looks good," he said.

THAT NIGHT AFTER dinner, Gabe and Aidan built Legos and then went into the backyard to throw a Frisbee for Lucky. Their shouts and laughter as they tried to teach the dog to fetch made Jane's heart bloom.

The next morning at the bakery, Gabe brought her real blooms, a pot of fragrant pink hyacinth—"I can plant them for you. So you'll have flowers next spring," he explained—and made her sigh.

He reminded her they had a date that night, an adults-only Saturday-night date, and sent her into a mild panic.

"Sure, I can watch Aidan," Cynthie Lodge said when Jane called. "No problem. Max will be thrilled. Movie nights tend to get a little chick-heavy over here." Cynthie, the single mom of two daughters, had recently gotten engaged to Max Lewis from the mainland. "The real question is, what are you going to wear?"

"Oh, I didn't . . . I don't think it's that kind of date," Jane stammered.

"It's always that kind of date. Unless you plan on showing up naked."

A surge of memory, warm and low, temporarily robbed Jane of breath. And caution. "Not this time."

"Wait. Does that mean . . . You didn't. You did!" Cynthie said, delighted. "You had a naked date with Gabe Murphy!"

The warmth turned into a full-body flush. "How did you know?"

"I didn't. Not about the naked part. But everybody knows

he's stuck on you. I mean, he's there all the time, isn't he? Swinging his tools. About time you got some, if you ask me." Jane heard a rumble in the background—Max's voice—and Cynthie's muffled reply. "No, honey, not you. Jane."

She should have expected talk, Jane told herself, wavering between amusement and distress. Most of it would be kind. These were her friends, her neighbors. Nobody was going to throw stones at her simply for having sex with a man she was . . . well, that she was seeing.

Their speculation gave her pause, all the same.

Not that she should care what other people thought.

But she did. She wanted their acceptance. Their approval.

It hadn't mattered so much at nineteen. Then, it had all been about Travis, about how much he needed her. But things were different now. She was different. She had her son and her business to think about now.

"So, where are you two going?" Cynthie asked cheerfully.

I have no idea.

"He didn't say."

It was too early to say. Wasn't it?

"Honestly, men. All they have to do is put on a clean button-down and jeans, and they think they look fine. They think they're doing you a favor by not telling you what to wear, and don't realize they're setting you up for wardrobe disaster." Another rumble. "Of course I didn't mean you, babe," Cynthie said to Max. "You are the exception among men."

"I thought I'd wear jeans and a nice top," Jane said.

"If that's what makes you comfortable," Cynthie said kindly. Warmhearted Cynthie, whose nickname in high school was Body of Cyn, who never seemed to care what anybody thought and looked fabulous in everything.

Jane was competent in her own sphere. But just once, she would like to have her friend's brand of confidence. "What would you wear?"

"Sundress," Cynthie said. "With flats and a little wrap in case the restaurant's cold. You don't want to look like you're trying too hard."

Jane thought about her wardrobe, jeans and knit shirts and black-and-white catering outfits. "I have that dress I wore to Luke Fletcher's wedding."

"The blue one? You look great in that. Very boobalicious."

Jane laughed. "Um, thanks?"

She was twenty-nine years old, way past the age when she should be obsessing over her clothes or her boobs or dressing for a man's approval.

But Cynthie had the experience to know what she was talking about. Jane did not. Married at nineteen, pregnant three years later, changing diapers and living with her father the year after that. She couldn't remember the last time she got dressed up for a date.

Aidan sprawled sideways across her bed, his sneakers sticking out over the carpet. He'd never seen her getting ready for a date, either.

Jane was both relieved and dismayed that he seemed to be taking the change in routine in stride. He seemed more taken aback by the change in her appearance.

"You look weird, Mom."

She yanked at a drawer, hunting for a sweater to wear over the blue dress. "I'm wearing makeup."

"I mean, you look pretty and everything. But different. And your hair's down."

"Because I'm not going into the bakery." She shut the drawer and turned to look at him. "Are you sure you're okay going to Hannah's house tonight?"

Saturday nights had always been "their" time, the one night when Jane didn't have to open the bakery until nine the next day and Aidan didn't have to rush to school in the morning.

He nodded. "Mrs. Lodge is going to let us stay up really late. And she lets us drink soda," he added.

"Well, that will certainly help you stay awake," Jane said dryly. "But we won't be out that late, Aidan. I'm just going to dinner."

"That's okay. You and Gabe need time to be alone."

Jane turned from her closet. "Who told you that?"

"Grandpa."

"Oh." *Oh.*

"Because Gabe is like your boyfriend now," Aidan contin-ued conversationally. "Like Marta is Grandpa's girlfriend."

"Well, I . . . Well, um . . . Grandpa and Marta . . . I think you should call her Mrs. Lopez."

"She said I could call her Marta. When she came over the other day."

Jane's mouth opened. Closed. "Okay. Well. Obviously, when two people like each other, they want to spend time together. That doesn't always mean that you're boyfriend and girlfriend."

Aidan gave her a patient look. "But you like Gabe, right? Like, *like* like him."

"Ye-es," Jane agreed cautiously.

She had always tried to be honest with Aidan. She didn't expect to shield her little boy from the facts of life forever. But he was only seven. Too young for the discussion she was afraid they were about to have.

"Right," Aidan said. "And I figure he likes you because he brought you flowers. And you're always kissing and stuff. Like Hannah's mom and Mr. Lewis."

"Not exactly. Mrs. Lodge and Mr. Lewis are engaged."

"I know. Hannah says they have sleepovers. And Mr. Lewis takes Hannah and them out for ice cream. Probably he'll take me out for ice cream, too."

Ice cream and soda both in one night.

Well, one night's indulgence wouldn't hurt him, she reflected. Wouldn't hurt either of them. They could eat extra vegetables tomorrow.

"Good times," Jane said, opening her jewelry box.

Not much there. Some pretty dangly earrings that she wore at the bakery—no rings, no bracelets when you were working with dough, when your hands were in and out of hot water all day—and the pearl studs Dad had given her when she turned sixteen.

"If I had a dad, I would go out for ice cream all the time," Aidan said.

Her hand froze on the earrings.

He did have a dad.

A dad who had tried to abduct him. A dad with a restraining order. A dad she hoped fervently he never saw again.

"You don't need a dad for that. We can go out for ice cream tomorrow. You and me."

"Cool," Aidan said in a satisfied voice. "Maybe Gabe could come with us."

Oh. His words pierced her heart. To buy herself time, she inserted the hooks carefully in her ears with trembling hands.

She had worked hard her entire adult life to make certain that her son was healthy, happy, cared for, loved. To ensure that he never felt the lack of a father.

But she knew—she should know better than anyone—how the absence of a parent could sneak up and catch you.

The signs were there in Aidan, if she had wanted to see them. His readiness to get in the car with Travis last summer. His desire to write to his father in prison.

Her little boy was vulnerable.

She met her troubled gaze in the mirror, her heart pounding painfully with guilt and fear and hope. She had a right to risk her own heart again. But she had the responsibility to protect Aidan's.

Gabe said he wasn't going anywhere. But that alone was no guarantee for the future.

She tousled her son's fine, straight hair, pushing his bangs out of his eyes. "Let's not count our chickens before they're hatched, okay, Boo?"

He rolled his head to look at her. "What does that mean?"

"It means I don't want you to be disappointed." *Either of us to be disappointed.*

"Maybe we can have a sleepover, too," Aidan suggested. "You and me and Gabe."

Jane caught her breath. "Let's take things one step at a time."

Twenty

HE WORE JEANS with a button-down shirt and his dress shoes. Gabe figured as long as he didn't wear a feed cap inside the restaurant, he was good to go. But when Jane came to the door, he wished he'd borrowed a tie from Luke or something.

His tongue tangled. "You look beautiful."

Her eyes lifted to his, pleased but doubtful. Her hands smoothed her skirt. "You like the dress?"

"The dress. You. Everything."

The blue fabric flowed over her curves like water. He wanted to back her through the door and up the stairs and into that bedroom with the lacy white curtains.

Where her father could walk in on them at any moment. *Bad idea.*

She stepped back, and he realized too late that he should have kissed her hello, a hi-honey-how-was-your-day kind of kiss, like a boyfriend. Or a husband. He cleared his throat. "Where's your dad?"

"He has a date with Marta tonight."

Right. So . . . they were alone? The possibility sent a jolt straight to his groin.

Their dinner reservation was for seven o'clock.

But he could be quick. Or he could go slow. Whatever she wanted.

"Marta is Grandpa's girlfriend," Aidan said.

Hello. Not alone. Gabe looked down, regrouping. "Hey, sport. How's your jump shot coming?"

"Okay." A small smile. "I beat Hannah in Horse today."

"Good for you."

"Aidan is spending the evening at Hannah's house. I thought we could drop him off on our way to dinner," Jane said.

"Sure. No problem."

"We need to take my car. Because of the booster seat."

He'd never had to think about car seats before. Something else to add to his list, Gabe thought.

"Where's Lucky?" Aidan asked after he was buckled in.

Gabe turned, resting his elbow on the back of Jane's seat. His fingertips brushed her hair, loose on her shoulders, and another tingle traveled up his arm. "Lucky's spending time at a friend's house, too. I dropped him off at my buddy Luke's so he can run around in their yard with their dog."

Because if the evening went the way Gabe was hoping, he wouldn't be sharing his motel room with the dog.

AIDAN'S PAL HANNAH lived in Paradise Shoals. Jane walked Aidan up the rickety steps of the trailer, exchanging hugs and instructions with the very hot brunette standing on the porch.

When Jane returned, Gabe slid out of the car to open her door.

Maybe she was impressed by his officer-and-a-gentleman routine, because she stopped before getting into the driver's seat. "I don't know where we're going. Why don't you drive?"

"You trust me?"

Her eyes examined his face as if searching for some hidden meaning. His heart pounded. Because, yeah, that was the million-dollar question, wasn't it? The one she'd never answered directly.

Do you trust me? With your car. With your son. With your life. With your heart.

He grinned.

She made a sound between laughter and exasperation and got into the car. Giving up her keys. Giving up control, at least long enough for him to drive them to the restaurant.

The parking lot was full of Beemers and Mercedes. Gabe pulled Jane's Accord into an empty spot between a Lexus and a Land Rover. The aging sedan looked almost as out of place among the luxury cars as Gabe felt.

Jane blinked. "You brought me to the Brunswick."

The fanciest dinner spot on the island. Where she used to be a line cook. Where she still had a dessert contract.

"Too much like work?" he asked.

"No." Her smile warmed him all the way through. "No, this is perfect."

"It's not like you haven't eaten here before."

"Never for dinner." Her eyes sparkled. "And I've always used the service entrance."

He grinned, relieved. "Let's see if they'll let us in the front door."

They were barely inside when Jane excused herself and disappeared in the direction of the ladies' room.

Gabe approached the host station. "Hi. Murphy. Seven o'clock reservation."

The guy in charge—sleek blond hair, black shirt, black tie—sized him up and signaled an underling.

"Yes, Mr. Murphy," the underling said smoothly. "I'll see if your table is ready."

The dining room was quiet. Elegant. White tablecloths, exposed brick, and lots of shine. Candlelight flickered on clustered glasses and silverware. Wide windows showcased

views of the harbor and garden. Gabe shoved his hands in his pockets and prepared to wait.

Another couple came in and was seated. Regulars, he guessed, when the Man in Black greeted them by name.

"Everything is so pretty," Jane murmured behind him. "Look at that sunset."

The sunset was nice. Very orange. The water was silver and gold. And Jane . . . Her eyes were the color of the sea and almost as bright.

"Sweet Jane!" The Man in Black swooped in and hugged her. "I didn't know you were joining us tonight."

Jane emerged, blushing and smiling, from the Man in Black's embrace. "I didn't know myself."

The guy drew back to arm's length, directing another glance at Gabe. His eyebrows lifted. "And this is . . . ?"

"Oh, I'm sorry. Gabe, this is Shawn Prescott, the manager of the Brunswick. Shawn, this is—"

"Gabe Murphy. Her date," Gabe added, in case there was any doubt.

The underling returned. "Hey, Jane."

"Hi, Greg."

"Right this way, Mr. Murphy. Table—"

"Four," the manager said.

The underling hesitated. "I put them in Jesse's section."

"Table Four." Prescott smiled at Jane. "Enjoy."

Table Four was in the center of a long bank of windows, with an uninterrupted view of the changing waters of the Sound. A formation of pelicans skimmed the water, black against the brilliant sky.

"Thank you so much," Jane said after they were seated and the waiter draped her napkin across her lap and left. "This is such a nice surprise."

She was so pretty, her face pink in the golden light. She liked it here. She was happy, being here with him.

Gabe relaxed. "You got us the table," he pointed out.

"You made the reservation."

He asked Jane to choose the wine, ordered an Aviator IPA for himself. "I know the dessert will be good. But you're going to have to talk me through the rest of this menu."

She did. She was so enthusiastic, so into the whole food scene, that he found himself ordering things he'd never heard of before just to make her happy, to see her eyes shine and listen to her explanations. Duck confit with some kind of bitter lettuce and an egg. Braised short ribs with cheese grits. After talking with their server, Jane ordered mussels in a red curry and ginger sauce and the day's special, shrimp from the Sound and thyme risotto.

"You learned all that working here and reading cookbooks?"

Jane smiled. "Well, I took some classes. Business courses and cake decorating mostly. But you don't need a culinary school degree to get a job in a kitchen."

"It must help, though," Gabe said. "Having that piece of paper."

The busboy came around with bread and water. "Hey, Mr. Murphy. Jane."

The face—dark eyes, gold skin, solid jaw—was familiar.

"Hi, Miguel," Jane said.

Right. Tomás's younger brother. "How's it going?" Gabe asked.

"I'm good. We're all good." The kid used silver tongs to put a little hard roll on Gabe's plate. "Ma really appreciates what you did for Tomás."

"Glad I could help," Gabe said.

Jane looked at him after Miguel left, not saying anything. But her eyes spoke volumes.

It could have been annoying, that stubborn faith of hers, the expectation that he could make something of himself. But he wasn't annoyed. At all.

A corner of his mouth kicked up. "Five months."

"Five months, what?"

"To get my basic EMT certification. Classes start in August."

Her eyes widened. "You're going to take classes to become a paramedic."

"Paramedic's two pay grades up and another eighteen months of training after that," Gabe said. "But, yeah. The GI Bill covers tuition and fees. Even books."

Her beautiful smile lit her face, her gray eyes shining and soft, and his heart turned to mush. "Gabe, that's wonderful."

He nodded, trying to act like it was no big deal. Except that after three years of not believing in himself, her faith in him felt big and solid. Real. Right.

"The hours won't be great," he said. "Especially in the beginning, while I'm training and working for Sam. I'll be gone two nights a week from six to ten. And that's not counting the commute."

"But you'd be helping people. Like Tomás. Doing something that matters to you and to the community."

"It won't all be life-and-death stuff. But, yeah. Should be fun."

She smiled wryly. "You mean you'll get your adrenaline rush."

He reached across the tablecloth and took her hand. "I've pretty much got all the rush I need right here."

That flustered her. She looked down.

"There's a housing stipend, too," he added.

She looked up at that. "But wouldn't you have to live on campus?"

"No." He took a deep breath, stroking his thumb across her knuckles. "Actually, I've had my eye on—"

The server arrived with the smallest appetizers Gabe had ever seen. "Amuse-bouche. Chef's compliments," he said, setting the plate between them.

Gabe released Jane's hand.

She smiled up at the waiter. "Please tell Adam thank you."

"What is this?" Gabe asked when the waiter had gone.

"Amuse-bouche? It means 'to amuse the mouth.' A taste to tease your appetite." She sent him a shy look through her lashes. "It can also mean morning sex."

Gabe grinned. "Yeah? Then I'm really eager to try it. I meant . . . what *is* it?"

"Oh." She laughed. "I think this one is seared scallop with local pea puree and . . ." She dipped the tip of her finger into one of the green dots decorating the plate.

And . . . Hell, yeah. Watching her suck her finger into her mouth definitely teased his appetite.

"Cilantro gremolata," she proclaimed. She pressed her lips together. "Maybe a little lemon zest."

"I'll take your word for it."

He wasn't a big fan of green stuff generally, but he ate it out of respect for her.

Sweet Jane, who had turned around the lack of nurturing in her own life by making a career of feeding everybody else. He admired her more than he could say.

The pea puree tasted like fancy baby food, but the scallop was good. All the food was good.

As they ate, he told her about his phone call with the lawyer. "Turns out he's also the executor of my uncle's estate."

Jane lowered her fork. "But your uncle died years ago, you said. When you were seventeen."

"Yeah. Funny thing." Gabe stared into the amber lights cast by his beer, flickering like tiny candle flames on the white tablecloth. "Uncle Chuck, he never could convince Mom to leave my old man. He tried. I was just a kid, but I remember him talking to her when I wasn't supposed to hear. But he never gave up on her, either. When he died, he left all his money, from his house, his business, his life insurance, everything, in this trust. A discretionary trust, the lawyer called it. That way, my pop couldn't get his hands on the principal, and, if Ma ever did leave his ass, she would have a little income to get by."

"But she never did," Jane murmured.

"Nope. My . . ." His throat closed on the word *father*. "The old man died three years ago, and she kept living in that same rat-hole apartment. Like she was still trapped, even after he was gone."

Jane reached across the table, her touch, her voice, gentle. "At least your uncle gave her the choice."

"Not that she ever did anything with it, but . . . yeah." Gabe shook his head, dispelling the memories. The regrets. "The thing is, the lawyer said that when she died, that ended the trust. All the money goes to the residual beneficiary."

Jane didn't say anything, her eyes steady. Waiting.

"Me." He cleared his aching throat. "Uncle Chuck left everything to me."

"Because he loved you. Obviously, he wanted to take care of you. You must have still been a child when he wrote his will. Any money he left to you would have gone to your mother anyway. He loved you both. But he must have known that by the time you were an adult, you could take care of yourself."

Of course she would see Uncle Chuck's legacy that way, in terms of family ties and affection rather than money.

"There wasn't anybody else," Gabe said. "He never married. No kids. Just Ma and me."

"Even one person who's there for you can make all the difference," Jane quoted softly.

He stared at her, shaken. He'd said those words to Aidan. "Yes."

But who do you have now?

He wanted to show her that he could be worthy of her, that she could trust in him, that he had something to offer her and Aidan in return for everything she had given him. But he didn't want to make it about the money, either.

Money wouldn't buy her love.

He had to earn that.

Although, shit, who was he kidding? He'd use pretty much any argument that would convince her to give him—to give them—a chance.

The chef came to their table, a tall man built like a bear

in a white chef's jacket unbuttoned at the collar. "Jane. How was your dinner?"

"Wonderful." Jane smiled. "Which you know."

"I'm glad you approve." A bright blue, assessing glance at Gabe.

"Gabe Murphy." He introduced himself. "Great meal."

The chef nodded, accepting his due. "Adam Reeves."

They shook hands, a short, invisible contest that ended in a draw.

Jane glanced between them, her brow puckering slightly.

The server reappeared with miniature scoops of something that looked like ice cream and probably wasn't.

"Merlot and watermelon granitas." The chef bestowed a smile on Jane. "I took your suggestion about the cardamom."

"It's delicious."

"Your desserts will be out shortly. Also delicious. Jane is quite amazing," Reeves said to Gabe. "I would hate to lose her."

"I feel the same way," Gabe said evenly.

Dessert came, hummingbird cake with cream cheese frosting for Gabe, Tiramisu dusted with cocoa powder for Jane.

"You're a rock star," Gabe said when he and Jane were alone again.

She smiled, shaking her head. "Adam was just being polite. Plus, he would hate getting stuck making his own desserts. Pastry isn't really his thing."

"He was more than polite." There had been both professional respect and a subtle masculine challenge in the chef's visit. "You ever think about going back to work for him?"

"I do work for him. I mean, I sell my desserts to him. But the bakery is my dream. Mine. That's important to me." She poked at her dessert with a spoon, not quite meeting his eyes. "After Aidan was born, after Travis left us, I had to move home. It felt like such a big step back. I felt like a failure. I need to know I can stand on my own two feet, that I can provide for myself and my son."

"Seems to me you've proved you can do both," Gabe said quietly.

"Thanks." A quick glance. A brief smile. "I'm getting there. Maybe when Aidan is older . . . I don't want to live with Dad forever. I know I'm lucky to have his support, and I'm thankful for everything he's done. But I guess it's just natural for a woman my age to want her own space. There are nights I would love to turn off that TV. Or get a cat. Or let Aidan invite over as many friends as he wants for a sleepover one weekend."

He took her hand across the table, playing with her fingers, tracing the little nicks, the scar at the base of her thumb. There were so many things he wanted to ask her, so much he wanted to say, that he didn't know where to start. "You want a cat?"

"Maybe." She grinned suddenly. "Or a dog."

He raised his head and met her gaze. "I've got a dog. I need a yard to put him in."

Her eyes were soft and warm. "So you said."

He took a deep breath. "I'm thinking of buying a house. I was talking to Sam about a rent-to-own kind of deal, figuring I'd have the housing allowance from the GI Bill to help me save up. But now I can afford the down payment outright."

"You're buying a house." She made this sound sort of like a laugh. "Just like that?"

"If something's right, it's right."

"But you have money now. You don't have to stay on the island. You're free to go anywhere, do anything. Be anything."

Not exactly the response he was hoping for. "That's the plan."

"You have a plan."

He nodded. "There's this one house . . . cottage, I guess you'd call it. On the Sound side. Nice-sized yard, quiet street. Built back in the fifties, so it needs a lot of work, but that puts it in my price range."

"Well, you're good at work." Her hand squeezed his in

encouragement. "Maybe Aidan and I can help you paint. We have experience."

Hope opened like a pit beneath his feet, a chasm in his chest. Because, yeah, that sounded like . . . "I was thinking you could come look at it with me tomorrow. When you're done at the bakery."

"I'd like that."

"Don't expect too much," he warned. "The third bedroom's more like a closet. But I can build on later. Unless you need a home office now or something."

Her hand stilled in his. "No. No, I don't need a home office."

"Then we're set. One bedroom for Aidan, one for us."

"Gabe, are you . . . are you talking about me moving in with you?"

"That was the plan." Not the entire plan. Fuck it. He was going for it. *When something is right* . . . "First I was going to ask you to marry me."

JANE'S HEART SOARED. Her stomach plummeted. Like she was on some crazy carnival ride, the slow climb to the top, the breathless anticipation, and then . . . *Swoosh*. The bottom dropped out.

Somehow her no-strings hookup on the kitchen prep table had turned into this—this emotional roller coaster.

She should have known better. She wasn't any good at casual sex. There were *feelings* involved, hers and his, and now her stupid heart was careening off the tracks.

She stared across the table into Gabe's deep, warm hazel eyes. Tempted. Terrified. "I . . . I don't know what to say."

"How about 'yes'?"

She gave a little laugh, breathless and giddy and disbelieving. "It's not that simple. We've known each other *three weeks*."

"Four." His gaze held hers. "Long enough for me to figure out that I'm in love with you."

Oh. There it was again, that incredible high, that rattling, dizzying descent.

But marriage . . .

"I've been married," she blurted. "I don't want to be married again."

His lashes flickered. "So, we don't get married. You move in, we'll see how things go."

She was shaking. She wanted to shake him. She wanted to grab him and never let go.

Wasn't it just like a man, wasn't it just like Gabe, to think that action would solve everything?

Or anything.

"It's too soon," she said.

She wasn't nineteen anymore, free to throw her heart and her future away, ready to risk everything for love.

Oh, God. She loved him. And that was the most terrifying thing of all.

His grip tightened on her hand before he very gently, very carefully loosened his hold on her fingers. "I don't expect the two of you to pack up tomorrow. I haven't even made an offer on the house yet. Hell, it'll take a month to close. That will be *eight* weeks."

She opened her mouth. Shut it.

"You said yourself, you don't want to live with Hank forever," Gabe said.

She found her voice. "That doesn't mean I'm ready to move in with you."

He didn't move. She couldn't read his body language at all. But his eyes seared into hers.

Jane faltered. "I'm sorry. I have feelings for you, too. And they scare me. Because feeling isn't enough. I have to be sure. I have to do what's best for Aidan."

"Aidan and I are fine. I like Aidan. If you're worried about having somebody to watch him, I can do that. I don't mind getting him off to school. Whatever he needs."

It was the perfect answer. It was no answer at all.

"He needs stability," Jane said. "He needs security. He needs somebody who will always, always be there."

"He needs? Or you need?"

"It's the same thing. I'm responsible for his happiness. Please try to understand."

Their server hovered at Gabe's elbow. "Is everything all right here?"

Not all right. Not all right at all.

"Fine, thanks," Gabe said. "You can bring the check anytime."

"I'm sorry," Jane said again when their waiter was out of earshot. "I wish I had the courage to give you the answer you want. But I don't."

"Bullshit," he said, the first time he'd ever sworn at her, and she flinched. "You have plenty of courage. What you need is a little faith in yourself. In me."

"I need time." She hated the sound of her voice. Weak. Pleading. Like the echo of her years with Travis. *Please don't be angry. Please don't leave me. I'm sorry. Please. Please. Don't.*

Gabe drew an unsteady breath. "Okay. I get that you're not where I am. Not yet. Just tell me what I have to do to make you trust me."

Guilt flayed her. He was hurt. She was hurting him. She hated that. "You don't have to do anything. I trust you. I do. It's myself I don't trust."

"'It's not you, it's me'?" He shook his head. "That's the oldest cliché in the book."

"It's true. I have baggage. I need time to . . . to unpack."

"You've had six years. How much longer are you going to let that asshole control your life?"

She winced. Her first infatuation had gone down in defeat and humiliation, in bruises and heartache. She had worked hard to protect her heart, to strengthen her defenses, to rebuild her life since then. Maybe it wasn't a perfect life behind her fragile barriers, but it was safe.

"I'm not letting him control anything. Or you. I'm telling you I need time to think. We need to take a step back."

"I say we move forward. I love you."

Her heart ripped in two. She was so dangerously, so hopelessly, in love with him.

But once she told him so, once she admitted how much she wanted him, needed him, what then?

I love you wasn't simply a statement.

It was a demand. A call to action. And she was paralyzed by doubt.

Maybe he did love her—now. But how could she judge? He could leave, like her mother had left, like Travis had left, like her father had withdrawn into his recliner and the TV.

And then what would she have left? Not even her pride.

"I made the mistake of jumping into a relationship once before," she said painfully. "I can't do it again."

A muscle knotted in his jaw. "We are not a mistake. I am not that guy."

She threw up her hands, badgered, driven on the defensive. "How do I know that?"

Gabe went still. "I do not hit women," he said between his teeth.

Oh, God. Oh, God. She met his burning eyes. She might as well have thrown her wine in his face. "I know. I'm sorry. I didn't mean . . ."

Of course he wouldn't *hit* her. But he could hurt her in other ways. He could break her heart.

"Here we are, Mr. Murphy." Shawn Prescott presented the black check holder with a flourish. "You'll see that there is no charge this evening for your beverages or, of course, for your des—"

"Shawn," Jane said through her teeth. "Go away."

He threw her a startled look. "Excuse me?"

Gabe pulled some bills out of his wallet and handed the folder to the manager. "Thanks. It's been a . . . swell evening."

He was furious. Hurt. She couldn't blame him.

"I didn't mean that," she said as soon as the manager was gone. "I was upset."

She was terrified. Of loving him. Of losing him. Of making a mistake. *I'm sorry, I'm sorry. Please. Don't.*

"When people are upset, that's generally when they say what they do mean." Gabe stood. "Why don't you take the car and go on home."

Not a question.

She sat there, miserably aware that she had ruined everything. "But what about you?"

"I'll walk." His mouth set in a hard line. "I need some fresh air."

Twenty-one

THE MOON WAS a thin dime in a pocket of clouds, its edges corroded by soft gray shadows. The trees were black and solid.

No street lights.

Gabe trudged along the side of the road, his dress shoes slipping in the sand, making his way by the reflected light of the sky and the occasional beam of a porch light. The headlights of a passing car blinded him.

If he were in his truck, the darkness wouldn't be a problem, but . . .

Shit. His truck was at Jane's.

He almost turned around right there.

Except he really didn't want to see Jane again tonight. She'd made it pretty damn clear the date was over. He kept walking. Maybe he'd call Luke, ask his buddy to bring Lucky back to the motel. Gabe could pick up his truck in the morning, after Jane left for the bakery.

Of course, that would leave his truck parked outside her father's house all night. That would make the neighbors talk. *Hank* would know Gabe hadn't spent the night. As long as Jane's father wasn't coming after Gabe with a gun, who gave a shit about the neighbors?

Jane would care.

And Gabe cared about Jane.

He loved her. He'd never said those words to a woman before. He wanted her to move in with him. He'd asked her to marry him, for God's sake.

She needed time to think, she said.

She wanted to take a step back, she said.

He reminded her of her ex.

Jesus.

He raised his head. Breathed deep. But the wind off the sea didn't do a damn thing to ease the hot lump in his chest, to cool the burning sting of her rejection.

She accused him of being controlling when all he wanted was to take the next natural step forward in their relationship. To take care of her, to be there for Aidan. To let him be part of their lives.

After three weeks.

He shook his head. Okay, maybe that was a little . . . Not controlling. But quick. She had warned him she had baggage. He probably could have been a little more sensitive.

Or she could have been more trusting.

She might have trusted him if he hadn't pushed.

Hell.

He could at least have tried to see things from her point of view. Could have taken more time to listen, to reassure.

Maybe he was more like her ex than he wanted to admit. The admission didn't sit well with him at all.

The blue-and-white sign of the Fishermen's Motel stuttered over the parking lot. Most of the spaces were taken by SUVs and pickup trucks, weekend fishermen sleeping four and eight to a room. Gabe dug in his pocket for his room key.

A car door opened behind him.

He half turned, his instincts on alert. Even in this sleepy coastal town, a parking lot encounter could be anything. A belligerent local, a drunk Marine . . .

Jane.

His heart leaped, choking him. He cleared his throat. "What are you doing here?"

She stopped a few yards away, like she didn't want to get too close. "I wanted to talk with you. To explain."

He was still raw from their last discussion. "Cupcake, a woman shows up at a guy's motel room, it's usually not for conversation. Unless sex is your idea of an apology."

God, he was such an asshole.

Her chin came up. She looked him straight in the eye. "Not anymore."

Did that mean there was a time when she . . . ? Had her ex ever . . . ?

"Shit. Shit. I'm sorry."

Jane shrugged, as if she didn't count on any better from him. Which made him, of course, feel worse. "I suppose I expected that. You're angry."

He was. Or he had been—his usual knee-jerk response to rejection.

It was hard as hell to figure out what he was feeling now. Harder still to put those feelings into words.

But by some miracle, Jane was giving him another chance. All he had to do was not screw up.

He took a deep breath. Exhaled hard. And tried, really tried this time, to think before he opened his big mouth. "I'm disappointed you don't feel the way I do, sure. I'm mad at myself for pushing you before you were ready." He attempted a smile. "Mostly I'm trying to figure out what to do next. Just like you."

Those big gray eyes regarded him steadily. He forced himself to hold her gaze.

"I know what I want to happen next," Jane said softly. "And it doesn't involve us standing out here in the parking lot where anyone can see."

NOT AN APOLOGY, Jane thought. Her heart beat like crazy.

It was important he understand that she wasn't offering

sex as a sort of amends, a way to make things right between them.

It was vital that she did.

Because with Travis, sex had too often been a matter of obligation. *You owe me. For my dead-end job and this crappy apartment, for getting pregnant, for leaving for work. For forgetting to buy beer or buying the wrong mustard.*

After a while the reasons all blended together in a dreary chorus of coercion and compliance.

"Whatever you want," Gabe said.

His hoarse admission was somehow louder than all the voices in her head.

"I want you."

Those eyes, those beautiful hazel eyes, widened. He looked stunned. Confused. "Now?"

She smiled. "Unless you don't want to."

"Oh, I want to. I mean, I want more than sex in a cheap motel room. But we both know I'll take whatever I can get. Whatever you're willing to give me."

That was just so . . . hot. Him wanting her. On her terms. On any terms at all.

I'll take whatever I can get.

She melted all over. "Then maybe you should invite me in."

His gaze burned into hers. "Right."

He unlocked the door.

Inside the cramped, low-ceilinged room, she was struck all over again by Gabe's height, by the discrepancy reflected in the mirror. She was so much smaller than he was. Rounder, softer, defenseless.

But his eyes, meeting hers, were deep and vulnerable. He leaned against the bureau. Despite the casual pose, there was no relaxation in him at all. His body was taut with tension, his strength tightly leashed and controlled. For her.

Arousal flooded her. Arousal and tenderness. She wanted to touch him, to communicate without words the things she couldn't trust herself to say: *I love you. I care about you. You are important to me.*

She reached for the buttons on his shirt. One by one, she undid them, her fingers brushing his skin. His breath lifted his chest and shuddered out of him, but he did not reach for her. Not yet. She smoothed his shirt from his shoulders, revealing his hard, lean body, the hair that was darker than the hair on his head, his velvet skin, his sobering tattoo. Her arms weren't long enough to push his shirt all the way off. For a moment they stood trapped, tangled, his arms at his sides, her breasts brushing his chest, before he helped her, shrugging and tugging at the constrictive fabric, leaving himself open to her, exposing his heart. She kissed his chest, licked his nipple. His groan reverberated through them both.

She loved it. How beautiful he was, how powerful she felt.

She undid his buckle with shaking fingers, tugged down his jeans and his dark briefs with them, kneeling with the movement. His erection sprang free, warm against her cheek.

He sucked in a ragged breath. "Jane . . . you don't need to . . ."

"I want to," she said fiercely. She gripped him firmly, owning her desire, owning him, taking control.

She kissed him, tasting, exploring, a conqueror mapping new territory, taking it for her own. His hands moved to the dresser behind him, curled around the edge with white-knuckled strength as she nuzzled him. She lapped at him like a cat before fitting her lips around him, taking as much of him as she could into her mouth, into herself. Trying to swallow him, to possess him, the heat and the hardness, the pulse, the life, the sweet-salty taste of him. *Mine. All mine.*

She was drunk with power, dizzy with arousal, her lower body clenching on nothing, wet with wanting him.

His hands moved to her hair. "My God. Jane."

She laughed, smug and joyful, and stood, yanking her dress over her head. He ran his rough hands all over her.

Together they turned and stumbled to the bed. She pushed him down and crawled over his naked body, delighting in his warm, dense skin, the delicious abrasion of his body hair.

He stretched out one arm, reaching for the bedside table, and almost knocked over a lamp. She lunged to steady it.

"Condom," he said. "In the drawer."

She fumbled and grabbed, straddling his thighs as she rolled the condom in place. And then—*oh, yes*—she took him hard inside her, rocking on him, sliding with him, slow and steady. Riding to her own rhythm, absorbed in her own pleasure, until the vibrations started deep inside her, until the tremors spread, lengthened and strengthened and quaked through them both. His grip tightened as he moved her up and down, driving deeply inside her, taking his own release.

She collapsed, both of them breathing hard, dissolved in bone-deep pleasure.

She turned her head and kissed his shoulder. "Thank you," she whispered.

His puff of laughter stirred her hair. "Honey, after the best sex of my life, I should be thanking you."

She raised her head, seeking . . . What? "Was it really?" *The best sex of his life?*

He stroked her hair from her face, his eyes deep, his touch gentle, that tiny groove at the corner of his mouth. "You destroyed me," he assured her solemnly.

She snuggled back against him, but her mind refused to settle.

It wasn't only sex, she thought. What they shared was raw and real, tender and more honest than any words she had said to him tonight.

She just didn't know if it was enough.

For either of them.

"THANKS FOR WATCHING my dog," Gabe said.

"No problem," Luke said. His blue eyes narrowed in the porch light. "Beer?"

Gabe hesitated. It was ten thirty when Jane left the motel, almost eleven o'clock now. "I should let you get to bed."

Luke was a family man now. Lucky bastard.

"I wish." Luke grinned. "Taylor's having a sleepover tonight. I go in there now, I'll be watching *Pitch Perfect* for the fourteenth time. Anna Kendrick's hot, but a man can only hear 'Titanium' so many times before his balls drop off."

Gabe dragged up a smile. "Sure. Thanks."

Luke returned with two long-necked bottles and Lucky, who jumped all over Gabe and then rolled over, begging for a belly rub. Gabe obliged.

Luke sat on the steps beside him. "How was dinner?"

Gabe stared out at the darkened yard. "I don't want to talk about it."

"Well, that's good," Luke said. "Otherwise, we'll be braiding our hair and painting our nails in no time. I might as well go back inside."

Gabe managed another smile. They drank beer in male solidarity.

"Sam says you're looking at a house tomorrow," Luke said after a pause.

Gabe frowned down at the bottle in his hands. Jane hadn't said "no" to looking at the house with him. Just to living in it. "That's the plan."

"Kind of rushing into things, aren't you," Luke observed.

"Don't you start. I know what I'm doing." Even if things didn't work out with Jane, he was here. He was home. He was staying.

There was some comfort in that.

"Easy, pal. I'm just saying, you won't be seeing any money from the GI Bill until you start classes. August, right?"

"Yeah. But I've got the down payment now. I'm making good money working for Sam. I don't need the housing allowance."

"You did six tours," Luke said. "You earned it."

"Yeah."

There was satisfaction in that, too, in knowing that even

without Uncle Chuck's money, he could have, he would have, gotten into the house eventually. *Improvise, adapt, overcome.*

Luke took another pull on his beer. "So, what's your long-term strategy?"

"I'm working on it."

A sidelong look. "Winning hearts and minds?"

"Yeah," Gabe said dryly. "Because that worked so well for us in Sangin."

Luke chuckled. "So we're better at fighting than talking."

Gabe flinched. *That's what Jane's worried about.*

But he couldn't say that, even to his oldest friend. He turned the bottle around in his hands. "She doesn't want to move in with me."

"Jane?"

Gabe nodded.

"Big surprise," Luke said. "You've known each other, what, three weeks?"

"Four."

"No time at all."

Gabe frowned. "How long did you know Kate before you proposed?"

"That's different. You want another beer? I can drive you back to the motel."

Gabe shook his head. "I'm good." Luke hadn't answered the question. "How long?"

"Three weeks." Hard to tell in the dark, but it was possible the Staff Sergeant was blushing. "But it took another four months to convince Kate to say yes."

"How come?"

"Family stuff."

"No shit. She had a problem with your family?"

Gabe couldn't imagine anybody not jumping at the chance to belong to the Fletcher family. Hell, if he'd been a little younger the first time Luke brought him home to meet the parents, he would have begged them to adopt him. On the other hand, their tight-knit family bond could be overwhelming to outsiders. And Luke had a daughter from a previous relationship.

"Nope. Hers. Her old man was a Colonel, a real hard-ass. Kind of guy makes Hank look like Mr. Rogers. When we first met, Kate didn't want anything to do with another Marine."

"Jane's fine with Marines," Gabe said. "It's me she doesn't trust."

Luke shook his head pityingly. "This isn't about you, stud. The lady's got baggage."

"Yeah. She said."

"So maybe you should listen. She's bound to be a little freaked right now anyway."

The short hairs lifted on the back of Gabe's neck. "Why 'right now'?"

"Because of her ex. Tillett."

"Why," Gabe repeated, "now?"

"Because he got out of prison yesterday." Luke's expression changed comically. Maybe because Gabe's had, too. "Oh, fuck. She didn't tell you?"

"No," Gabe said evenly. "She never said a word."

Twenty-two

JANE TIPPED HER head back to steal another look at the house. "It's perfect."

Gabe gave her a sardonic look.

Because, okay, "perfect" was a tiny bit of an overstatement. The gray shingled house had clearly suffered from a botched upgrade in the 80s and at least a decade of uncaring tenants since. The carpeting was funky, the awful acoustic tile installed over the original ceilings was stained, and the dirty turquoise-and-purple walls belonged in a run-down Florida motel.

But the house had—as Shelley from Grady Real Estate pointed out numerous times during their tour—*potential*. With very little imagination, Jane could see how the house could be, how she wanted it to be. The cozy kitchen outfitted with new appliances, a wood-burning stove in the open front room, the hardwood floors stripped and shining.

"Needs work," Gabe said.

"It needs paint," Jane acknowledged. *Lots and lots of paint.* "But it has . . ."

Falling-down gutters. Peeling windows.

"Potential?" he finished dryly.

So he'd been listening to the real estate agent, too.

"A wonderful view," Jane said.

Two honest-to-goodness maple trees in the front yard and a long private drive going down to the Sound. A yard for the dog. There was even a concrete pad at the side of the house where you could put a basketball hoop. She pulled her thoughts back. This was not her house. Not her decision. She was along merely for support.

"Are you having second thoughts?" Jane asked. *Please don't have second thoughts.* Not that she was planning on moving in with him; it was way too soon for that. "Is it the bathroom?"

He jammed his hands into his pockets. "The bathroom's fine."

Something was wrong.

He'd been terse, almost tense, all afternoon. Jane had chalked up his silence in front of the real estate agent to home-buyer caution.

Her instinct was to smooth things over, to appease him, the way she'd learned to do with Travis. But Gabe wasn't Travis. She didn't need to fear him. Or coddle him, either, when he had the sulks.

If he was going to act as if he were Aidan's age, she would simply treat him like Aidan. "What's the matter?"

"Heard your ex is out of prison."

The words, the look, thumped into her like stones. "Oh."

"Yeah. 'Oh.'" His tone was flat, his face grim. "Why didn't you tell me?"

"Well, I . . ." Her mind raced, but she couldn't seem to assemble her thoughts, let alone form them into a complete sentence. So much had happened since that phone call. "It didn't come up."

"You could have brought it up."

"I could have," she acknowledged cautiously. "If I thought about it. I'm not used to dumping my problems on everybody else."

"It's not dumping to tell me your abusive ex could be coming around." Something—hurt? temper?—flashed in Gabe's eyes, but his voice was tightly restrained. "And I am not everybody. I'm the man who's in love with you. I don't want anything to happen to you."

His concern just *melted* her. *I'm the man who's in love with you.* What was she supposed to do, what was she supposed to say, when he said things like that?

"I don't want anything to happen to you, either," she said.

He shot her an edgy look. "I can take care of myself."

"So can I."

"Until that son of a bitch comes after you. You're no match for a grown man in a fight."

Her heart bumped. "No fighting," she said. "I won't stand for fighting."

Their eyes met. His were dark with frustration. "That's why you didn't tell me," he said. "You think there will be trouble."

"No." *Not really.* "I don't reckon Travis will be coming around anymore. Before last summer, I hadn't seen him for six whole years. I don't have anything he wants."

"You're kidding."

"Well, money," she admitted. "But he's not getting another penny from me."

Another straight look. "I'm talking about you. You and Aidan."

She shook her head. "He never wanted us."

"Then he's a fool."

Gabe wanted her. The thought wrapped warmly around her heart. Wanted them both.

She blushed and looked away. "Anyway, I got a restraining order. It's a condition of his probation. According to my dad, if Travis violates the protective order, he goes back to prison for the rest of his sentence—seven months."

"You talked about this with Hank." *And not me.*

He didn't say the words. He didn't have to.

Jane winced at the hurt in his tone. So, yes, all right, she probably could have, should have, told him about Travis's release. "Dad already knew. Marta got a call at the police station."

"Good," Gabe said, surprising her. "The more people who know, the more people you've got looking out for you."

Her throat caught. He was trying so hard. They both were. She laid a hand on his arm. "I appreciate your concern. But Aidan and I are fine. I had an alarm system installed at the bakery. And Daddy has a gun."

Not that she wanted her father to actually *shoot* Travis. But Travis knew Hank was armed. He wouldn't risk coming to the house.

Gabe's face set in stubborn lines. "Hank can't be with you all the time."

"This is Dare Island. People look out for each other here. I don't need a bodyguard."

"Yeah, you do. At least for a while."

"How long? A week? Six weeks?" She shook her head. "I can't live my life based on what Travis Tillett might do or not do next. I won't let him control my life. I did that often enough when we were married. I'm trying to be . . ." Better. Braver. "Stronger now."

"You're one of the strongest women I know," Gabe said. "The way you run your business, the way you're raising your kid alone, the way you take care of everybody all the time . . . You're amazing. But part of being strong is being able to admit when you need help. It doesn't make you any less competent if you'd lean on me a little every now and then. You thinking otherwise underestimates us both."

The way he said it—two words, flat and close—made them sound like a thing, a couple, a unit, a heartbeat. *Us both.*

She drew a shaky breath, more tempted than she would have believed possible.

It's not like she was ever truly alone. She lived with her father, for crying out loud. She had her son. Her days were filled with neighbors and customers, the warm, close-knit island community she hugged to herself like a security blanket, all of them wanting something. Needing her.

She had remade her life so that she could never be abandoned again. She fed people. She had value. She was strong.

But what Gabe was offering was different.

Lean on me.

Could she?

Did she dare?

"That's hard for me. Needing someone," she confessed. "Lauren says I have work to do before I'm ready for a long-term relationship. It takes time. Trust."

"I can give you time. Trust . . . I figure you'll have to find that for yourself."

Their eyes met. Her heart beat like crazy.

"What if I can't be what you want?" she whispered. "What if I can't give you what you need?"

"I need you."

As if that was enough. As if she could ever be enough.

"Why?"

"I love you."

A little shock ran through her at the words. They were still so new. New and precious.

Gabe paused, as if he were waiting for her to say something back. When she didn't, he continued. "My uncle Chuck used to say, when you frame a house, choose hardwood, not pine. Maybe it takes more time, more investment, but hardwood stands. Hardwood lasts." He cupped her face in his large, warm hands, the texture of his calluses scraping all her nerve endings to life. "I'm rebuilding my life here. I figure you're hardwood."

He kissed her gently and then not gently at all, and the heat and the glow rose inside her, radiating deep inside her, until she broke and giggled.

"What?" he asked, mystified.

His body was solid against her. She blushed. "Hardwood?"

It took him a second before he laughed. They were holding

each other and kissing and laughing, and for that moment everything felt perfect.

"WHAT IS THAT?" Jane said from around Gabe's knees.

Gabe looked down from the ladder he'd dragged to the back corner of the carport. *Busted.* "It's a deer camera."

"A what?"

He tightened the strap around the post. "A heat and motion activated camera. Hunters use them to take digital pictures of wildlife trails."

"You do a lot of hunting in Detroit?"

He grinned, enjoying the spark in her eyes, the sass in her voice. "Nope. I had buddies who were hunters, though."

"So you're taking pictures of what? The cats?"

"The cats or . . ." He adjusted the time setting. "Anybody else who comes sniffing around."

She tilted her head. "Leaving aside for a minute how I feel about you installing a security camera without asking me, I don't see how it helps to have pictures of something after it's already happened."

"I can set up the camera to send photos to an e-mail address. Or my phone. This model has a one-second trigger speed and takes about a minute to send a compressed image by text message to my phone. So I'll be able to see almost right away if somebody comes in or out that door."

She crossed her arms over her apron. "You don't find that a little creepy stalker-ish, to get a message alert every time I take out the garbage?"

"Look, inside, you're safe. Either the bakery is closed and locked up, or you've got customers coming in and out. But going to and from your car at four in the morning or at the end of the day, that's when you're most vulnerable."

"I'm not the only one who uses this door, you know."

"But you use it most often." He adjusted the camera angle.

"Does that thing take pictures of the basketball hoop, too?"

Shit.

He started to sweat. He knew how important it was for her to feel in control, to be independent, to take care of herself and her son.

If she thought it was creepy that he was keeping an eye on her, how would she react to his taking pictures of Aidan?

He took a deep breath. Confessed all. "Yeah."

She turned her head and held his gaze for a long moment, a small smile playing around her mouth. "Good," she said, and went back into the bakery.

GABE WHISTLED AS he hammered the last piece of baseboard in Ashley Ingram's coffee shop. In two more hours, he'd be off work and taking Jane and Aidan to dinner. But for now, a brick propped open the front door, admitting a fresh breeze from the harbor, welcome in this afternoon heat. On an April Monday, the waterfront was almost empty of traffic. A few wannabe fishermen eyed the catch of the returning charter boats. A couple on a bench ate ice cream. Once in a while, a local strolled by to check on the progress of the upfit.

A shadow wavered in the dirty plate glass window. Wavered and stuck. Lucky woofed, tail stirring the sawdust.

Gabe glanced up. *Aidan.* Shoulders hunched, lower lip sticking out about a mile.

Rising, Gabe set down his hammer and crossed to the door. "Hey, sport. What are you doing here?"

The boy stooped, opening his arms to the dog. Lucky wriggled and leaped, trying to lick his face, both of them acting as if they'd been cruelly separated for years instead of less than a day. "Hey, Lucky. Hi, boy."

"Aidan?"

Aidan buried his face in the dog's neck. "I'm walking home from school."

The harbor was at least half a mile out of the boy's way. And even on the island, where the kids ran free as the colonies of feral cats, Gabe didn't see Jane allowing Aidan to roam unsupervised. Especially not with Tillett getting out on parole. "You walk home by yourself?"

"I did today," Aidan mumbled into Lucky's fur.

"Your mom's going to be worried about you."

"No, she won't. She thinks I'm with Grandpa."

Gabe studied Aidan's down-bent head, the defensive set of his shoulders. Something going on there. It was still new, and revealing, how the boy's problems had somehow become his problems. How the boy had begun to feel like his.

"How about we get my truck and I give you a lift?" he suggested. "We can grab a snack and let your mom know there's been a change of plan."

A quick, bright glance upward through the fringe. "I can't ride without a booster seat."

Gale smiled. "I've got you covered. Jay, I'm taking a break," he called to the other workman. "You finish before I'm back, go ahead and lock up."

"Sure thing, Gabe."

Gabe clipped the leash to Lucky's collar before handing the other end to Aidan. They ambled around the curve of the harbor toward the Fishermen's Motel, the dog pausing to pee on every telephone pole and stop sign along the way.

Aidan kept his head sunk between his shoulders, his eyes on the ground. "You said I could come talk to you."

"Anytime," Gabe said. "Me, or your mom."

"I can't talk to her. Not about this."

"Okay," Gabe said.

He really hoped the kid wasn't going to ask about sex. Given that Gabe wanted to marry Aidan's mother, he figured that task might fall to him sooner or later. But later would be better, when Aidan was more ready. Or he was.

Lucky stopped to sniff the grass at the side of the road.

Aidan tugged on the leash. "I don't want her to feel bad. She feels bad enough about stuff already."

Gabe cleared his throat. "Generally, I'm against making your mom feel bad. Of course, she might feel worse if she thought you were keeping secrets from her."

"It's not a secret. It's just . . ." Aidan kicked at an invisible stone in his path. "Do people make fun of you for going to jail?"

Shit.

Gabe looked down at the top of Aidan's head. "Kids at school giving you a hard time about your father?"

No answer. Which was all the answer he needed.

"They don't make fun of me," Gabe said. "Not to my face. But they have plenty to say behind my back. I figure that if people want to talk, that says more about them than it does about me."

"When Ryan says something, I want to punch him right in his fat face," Aidan said.

"That's probably what he wants," Gabe said.

Aidan shot him a startled look.

"Some reaction, anyway," Gabe said. "You want to give him what he wants?"

"N-no," Aidan said.

"Right. So, what else could you do?"

"He said my dad is a criminal. A bad guy. And that means I'm a bad guy, too."

"Do you believe him?" Gabe asked gently.

"No." Aidan's gaze flicked up and away again. "I don't know."

Little boy, you are not your father.

But Gabe knew where the kid was coming from. It ate at you, when you had your old man's blood. His eyes. His hands. His temperament.

But when Gabe looked at Aidan, he saw Jane's smile. And Hank's shrug. He saw . . . Aidan.

"Listen." Gabe stopped and dropped down on his haunches so that he and Aidan were eye to eye. "You are a great kid. This Ryan guy, he can call you names. But you don't have to let them stick. You don't have to let him define you. You can define yourself."

"But how do I stop him?"

"Probably not by punching him," Gabe said. "You've got

to be the person you know you are inside, the best person you can be. You have to act like that person."

"He's still gonna tease me. He's a big jerk."

"So, what else could you do?"

"I don't know. He just makes me so mad."

Gabe smothered a grin. He could have been listening to a younger version of himself. Could he be grown-up enough to give this kid advice? "That's not a good enough reason to fight. When you're a Marine, you need what we call a desired objective. Like, what do you want?"

"I want him to shut up."

"That's a good objective. You think if you hit him, he'll leave you alone?"

Aidan kicked at the ground again. "Maybe."

Gabe decided to let that one go for now. "Okay. So, then you have to ask, what's it going to cost me to fight? That means, what do you lose? And then you ask, can I win this fight? Say you punch Ryan. What happens?"

"He beats me up."

"He beats you up, and you get in trouble, right?"

"Yeah."

"So who wins?"

"He does. But he wins anyway. The other kids listen to him."

"Not all of them. You're a great kid. You've got other friends, right? People who aren't jerks. Like that girl, Hannah, and, what's-his-name, Chris."

"Chris Poole."

"Right. The thing about jerks is they can't stand up to a crowd. So the next time this Ryan gets in your face, you walk away. You find your people. Your friends, the people who know you and like you the way you are. And you'll be okay."

Another sidelong look. "You're my people," Aidan said, testing.

A blow, straight to the heart. It knocked Gabe flat. "Yeah," he said unsteadily. "I am."

They resumed walking. Gabe's pocket buzzed. He pulled

out his phone and checked his incoming messages. There was a picture of Jane, taking out the garbage.

"Hannah says when her mom gets married, Mr. Lewis is going to be her dad."

Gabe smiled and slipped the phone away. "How does Hannah feel about that?"

"She's okay with it. Mr. Lewis is cool."

They stopped again while Lucky investigated a particularly intriguing mailbox.

"If you asked Mom to marry you, then you would be like my dad," Aidan said, as relentless on the scent as the dog.

Another sucker punch.

Gabe took a careful breath. "That's how it would work, yeah." His cell phone buzzed again. "If she said yes and you were okay with it."

"What if she says no?"

Gabe exhaled. "I'd be really sorry. Because I love your mom. But that wouldn't change things between you and me. I'm buying a house. I'm sticking. I'm here. Your mom . . . You know she'll always be there for you. But if you ever need me, I'm here for you, too."

Aidan's lips curved in a smile. "Cool."

He put his hand in Gabe's.

Together, they walked the rest of the way.

Twenty-three

ALL THE COOKIES were mixed, scooped onto trays, and resting in the refrigerator, ready to be baked off in the morning.

Jane carried out the garbage, stopping to fill the pans of food for the cats. Spring meant kittens on the island, fuzzy kitty tails and wide kitten eyes hiding in the bushes, waiting to sneak up on her and pounce like joy.

She left the back door open as she did a final run-through, making sure the bakery was prepped for the coming week, pausing to arrange the lines of organic juices in the refrigerated case. She caught a glimpse of her reflection in the glass. Smiling.

And why not? Maybe the season was trying to tell her something. New life. New beginnings.

Gabe was taking her and Aidan out to dinner tonight.

A noise from the kitchen scraped at her attention. Jane straightened as the door swung open.

"Hello, Janey." He stood in the kitchen doorway, a rictus of a grin stretching his stubbled face. Jack Nicholson in *The Shining.* "I'm back."

Her skin shrank. Adrenaline dried her mouth, flat and metallic as a penny on her tongue. "Travis."

She glanced instinctively toward the entrance. Locked. Even if she got a head start, he would catch her at the door. So. No escape there.

At the end of the day, that's when you're most vulnerable, Gabe had said.

Oh, God. Gabe.

"We're closed," she said. "I'd like you to go."

Travis sneered. "Or what?"

I won't live in fear, she had boasted. But her stomach clenched just the same.

"Or I'll call the police." Assuming she could reach a phone. Her cell phone was in her purse on top of the filing cabinet, the landline in the kitchen. The security alarm was by the back door.

She looked past Travis at the swinging door into the kitchen, calculating her chances.

His eyes followed her gaze, calculating, too. He smiled, and something went cold inside her, cold and numb.

She forced herself to think. He must have come in the back way, in range of Gabe's security camera.

So Gabe would get an alert, a text message.

Oh, no.

She didn't want trouble.

Travis strolled forward a step. "What are you going to tell the cops, Janey? I haven't touched you. I haven't threatened you. I'm rehabilitated. A changed man."

He looked the same, tall and rangy, with lank blond hair and faded jeans, a battered gym bag in one hand. Prison had not changed him. But something was different. Maybe the way she looked at him had changed.

He was . . . smaller somehow.

"My father will come."

Or Gabe. Her heart pounded. Even now, Gabe could be on his way. She had to get rid of Travis before Gabe came.

"Janey, Janey." Travis shook his head, as if her answer disappointed him. "Always with the drama. Every time I had a few, every time I didn't toe your line, you'd start squawking and crying and carrying on. You used to whine I didn't pay you any attention. Now you gonna freak out and holler for Daddy because I decided to pay you a little visit? I thought you'd be happy to see me."

"Not really," she said, so dryly that his forehead wrinkled. "You need to leave."

"You haven't even heard what I want."

His wheedling tone. This was how he operated, this was how it started. Charm, manipulation, threats, then violence. Whatever it took to get his way.

Her palms were damp. She was not letting him control her again.

This time he didn't have Aidan in the car. This time he couldn't threaten her with taking their son away.

"I don't care what you want. We're divorced now. I got a restraining order."

He slammed the counter. "Fuck that!"

She flinched, body memory taking over at the sudden violence in his voice, her muscles tensing, her shoulders rounding.

"You owe me. I went to prison because of you. You and your bitch friend. You think your stupid piece of paper from your fancy lawyer gets you off the hook?"

His voice battered her. Her gaze darted over the counter. No frying pan, no rolling pin, no knives, nothing she could use as a weapon. Nothing but her own determination.

You're no match for a grown man in a fight.

She had to stay safe. She had to be smart. For Aidan's sake. For Gabe's. The thought of them steadied her.

"I'm sorry," she said. Using her fear, using the quaver in her voice to assuage him. She offered a trembling smile. "You must be hungry. Can I make you a sandwich?"

Get to the kitchen. Get to the alarm.

His eyes narrowed.

Her heartbeat quickened. *Crap.* She shouldn't have capitulated so quickly. Now he was suspicious.

But he was used to her placating him. Doing as she was told. *Jane, the good girl, the obedient wife.*

He smirked, appeased. He'd always been able to do that, turn his moods on and off like a switch. Like a toddler converting tantrums to smiles as soon as he got his cookie.

"I can't stay. I got a little job down in Elizabeth City. I need to leave something with you. I'll be back in a few days to pick it up."

Back? She shuddered in rejection. *You can't come back.* Why would he need to leave something with her, anyway? Unless it was a ruse. An excuse.

She inched closer, edging toward the kitchen. "What is it?"

"Just a bag. Nothing much." His mouth twisted, his eyes stabbed. "They don't leave you with much in prison."

Guilt seeped from an old wound like rusty blood. Travis had always known how to get to her.

"Do you want to go get it? Your package?" she asked, trying to keep her voice steady. If he left, she could lock him out, lock the door behind him.

"Right here." He held up the gym bag.

The back door squeaked open. Light, quick footsteps crossed the kitchen floor, followed by a long, assured stride.

"Hey, Mom!" Aidan burst from the kitchen, the swinging door almost catching Travis in the back. "We—" He faltered. Stopped. His face was white. "Dad?"

Cold fear sliced her to the bone.

Travis jerked his chin in greeting. "Hey, kid. How's it going?"

Gabe appeared behind Aidan, one hand dropping easily to the boy's shoulder. He took in the situation with one swift, assessing glance before moving Aidan slightly to one side.

"Jane," he murmured.

The sound of his voice melted the paralysis of her limbs, the ice around her heart.

Travis scowled.

Seeing the two men side by side for the first time, she was struck by the differences between them. Oh, there was a superficial resemblance. Both were tall and lean with sun-streaked hair. But Gabe was harder, more muscled, more solid in every way. Beside him, Travis appeared paler, softer. Under-baked.

Gabe's gaze switched to Travis. "What are you doing here?"

"Paying a little visit to the family. Who the hell are you? The nanny?"

"Yeah." Gabe's voice was flat, his eyes as hard as stones. A different kind of fear moved in Jane's bones. "Now get the hell out."

Travis took a step back before he recovered. "I was going anyway," he sneered. "Nothing to keep me in this shit hole."

Aidan's white face flushed red. His eyes were round and stricken. Jane held out her arms, but he stayed where he was, under the protection of Gabe's hand.

Travis sauntered past them toward the kitchen, hefting the gym bag. "On second thought"—he glanced at Gabe—"I don't think I'll give this to Janey after all. But I got a little something for the kid." He reached for his pocket. Gabe went very still.

Travis grinned. "Relax, nanny." He pulled out a roll of bills and peeled one off. Smirking at Gabe, he tucked the bill into the collar of Aidan's T-shirt. "Here you go, kid. Buy yourself a birthday present from your old man."

The steel utility door swung shut behind him.

"Are you all right?" Gabe asked Jane.

She swallowed. Nodded.

"My birthday's in October," Aidan said in a small voice.

Jane's eyes stung. "Boo . . ."

"Don't call me that."

"Okay."

His mouth trembled. "I'm too old for baby names."

She put one arm around his bony shoulders, gathering him as close as his stiff body would allow. Her boy. She rubbed his back, the tiny bumps of his vertebrae sliding under her palm. "All right."

He hid his face against her throat. His hot tears seared her heart.

Lucky barked in the backyard.

"Call Hank," Gabe ordered. He strode toward the door.

Panic seized her. Panic and doubt. "Gabe, *don't* . . ."

He turned with a bleak and bitter look.

And whatever had been in her mouth dried up. "Be careful," she begged instead.

His lips thinned. His face was flint. "Don't worry."

LUCKY BARKED AND snarled, lunging against the window of Gabe's truck. Tillett was crossing the carport. From the wrong direction. He paused beside the cracked-open window. Taunting the dog, or . . . ?

Gabe made a noise in his throat not unlike the dog's. "You touch my truck, I'll kick your ass. Get out."

Tillett turned and rounded the hood of the other vehicle, an old gray Dodge Neon. "I'm going." He shot Gabe a sly smile. "Did what I had to anyway."

He'd seen Jane. Aidan, too.

"Don't come back."

"What do you care? She's not your wife. She's not even a good fuck."

Gabe had him by his shirtfront and up against the side of the car before he was aware of even moving.

Tillett's eyes—brown, like Aidan's—stared into his. His breath wheezed in his throat. He smelled rank, like prison and flop sweat.

"Go away. I see you around either one of them again, I'll kill you," Gabe said and dropped him.

Tillett fumbled for his door handle, scrambled into his car.

Gabe watched him peel out of the parking lot in a spray of gravel and oyster shells.

Maybe Hank would pick him up for speeding. Gabe hoped so.

He turned and saw Jane standing in the door, holding the phone, her free hand pressed to her mouth. He didn't meet her eyes, afraid of what he would see there.

Her choked cry had followed him out the door. *Don't . . .* she had said.

No fighting, she had said. *I won't stand for fighting.*

So he hadn't fought. Hadn't roughed the guy up or bashed his face in or done any of the things he'd been tempted to do.

But if he'd walked in and found Tillett with his hands on her, he would have.

And now she knew it.

He'd told Aidan he needed a reason to fight. *What do you want? What do you have to lose?*

Sure, he'd won. Jane and Aidan were safe for now.

But what had his victory cost him in Jane's eyes?

POLICE CHIEF JACK ROSSI had his notebook out on the corner table of the bakery's dining room. Late thirties, Gabe judged, dark, cool, and quiet. The kind of guy who shaved three times a day and never broke a sweat.

Jane sat on the long bench opposite the chief, Aidan in the crook of her arm. Hank scowled from a nearby chair.

Gabe watched from the other side of the room, arms crossed against his chest, trying to hold in the fear and rage still pumping inside him. He didn't belong here. Not in the family tableau or the police investigation. But so far nobody had sent him away.

"So he didn't hurt you?" Rossi asked Jane, reviewing her statement. "Threaten you in any way?"

Jane had been murmuring to Aidan, but she raised her head to answer the chief's questions. "No. He wanted to leave a bag here. Like a gym bag?"

Rossi glanced at his notes. "But he didn't."

"No, he . . . he changed his mind."

"He's in violation of a protective order and his parole," Hank said. "That's enough to sling his ass back in jail."

"I shouldn't have left the back door open," Jane said. "It was just for a minute, while I closed, but—"

"You handled yourself," Rossi said. "You handled the situation."

"I couldn't make him leave."

Why was she beating herself up? She was a baker, not a Marine. What was she supposed to do? Smother him in fondant? Mace him with whipped cream?

"You kept your head," Rossi said with calm reassurance. "You called 911, you didn't try to be a hero and escalate the situation. Anytime we get a domestic disturbance that doesn't end in violence, we call it a good outcome."

"Because of Gabe," Aidan piped up. "He made my . . . He made him leave."

Jane's eyes met Gabe's. She swallowed, her throat moving, before she looked away. "Aidan has had enough excitement for today," she said to Rossi. "Could he wait somewhere else?"

The chief nodded. "Hank, you want to take Aidan outside?"

Aidan clung to Jane. "I want to stay with Mom."

"You come with me," Hank said. "We'll wait in the police car. You can talk to Marta on the radio."

Jane whispered to Aidan. He slipped from the shelter of her arm and hopped from the bench, his shoulders hunched, his thin face pinched.

Gabe gave him a wink as they walked by. And was staggered when the boy launched at him, wrapping his arms around Gabe's waist, holding on for dear life.

Gabe's throat tightened. His hands closed protectively on Aidan's shoulders. "It's all right," he said, his voice hoarse. "You're okay. Everything's going to be all right now. You go on with your grandfather."

"I don't want to."

"Lucky's still out in the truck. Think you could check on him for me?"

Aidan raised his head and nodded jerkily, releasing Gabe's waist. Hank patted his shoulder, steering him toward the door.

Gabe watched them go.

"You'll need to go to the magistrate and swear out an affidavit warrant that Tillett was actually here," Rossi was saying to Jane. "You can also file for civil contempt at the clerk's office, but—"

"You're wasting time," Gabe interrupted. "Why does she need to see a magistrate? Just arrest the son of a bitch."

"We only have Jane's statement that Tillett violated the protective order," the chief said coolly. "Fortunately, that's usually enough for the judge to find probable cause."

Gabe's blood went from a simmer to a boil. "You think she—we—made this up?"

Rossi's face was impassive. "We want to go after this guy, we have to follow procedure."

"It's all right," Jane said. "I don't mind."

"You need proof he was here, I can give you proof," Gabe said. "I've got pictures."

Rossi's eyes narrowed. "Show me."

"They're in the security camera out back."

"Nice," Rossi said, inspecting the setup a few minutes later. "When did you put this up?"

"Yesterday."

Rossi's brows rose. "Convenient."

"I just found out about Tillett's release the other day." Gabe removed the SIM card from the camera and handed it to the chief. "There are pics on my phone, too, but the resolution's not so good. These should be better."

"Do you know what they are?"

"I saw the first few," Gabe said. "After that, I was too busy to check my phone."

The chief opened his laptop on the bakery table and

inserted the card. And there they were, in thumbnail, with a date and time stamp in the corner of every frame.

Jane, taking out the garbage.

Jane, scooping cat food from a plastic tub in a corner of the carport.

"The camera's triggered by heat and motion," Gabe explained. "It takes a full minute for it to send a photo to a cell phone and recover before it can be triggered again. So the pictures are going to be at least one minute apart. Longer, if nothing's happening."

A front view of a car parked under the basketball hoop.

"That's Tillett," Gabe said.

Rossi zoomed the shot. No license plate from this angle. He clicked the next image.

Gabe scowled. "Son of a bitch. He got inside before the camera reset."

Jane leaned over Rossi's shoulder. "That's your truck," she said to Gabe. "You and Aidan."

Another click.

"There's Travis," Jane said. "Leaving."

"Good shot of his face," Rossi said.

Click.

"There he is again," Gabe said.

Rossi frowned. "From another direction."

Click.

Shit.

"Tell me about this one," Rossi invited dryly.

Gabe suppressed a groan. Of course the camera *would* go off at the exact moment he had Tillett up against the side of his crappy car. "Doesn't need much explanation."

"You followed him out."

"I wanted to make sure he didn't come back."

"You exchanged words," Rossi said.

"Yeah."

"What did you say?"

Gabe bared his teeth in a grin. "Don't come back."

"Is that all?"

Gabe locked eyes with the police chief. Rossi knew his record. He couldn't hide the truth of who he was, from the police or himself. "I think my exact words were, 'Come back, and I'll kill you.'"

"Where's his bag?" Jane asked suddenly, breaking the tension.

Rossi turned his head. "Excuse me?" He was a polite fucker.

"In the picture. Travis doesn't have his bag."

"So he dropped it," Gabe said. *When I throttled him.*

Rossi frowned and scrolled backward, forward, and backward again, slowly.

"He has it when he comes out," Gabe said.

"But not here." Rossi tapped the image of Tillett crossing the carport. "What's that behind him?"

"A storage bin. For the cats' food," Jane said.

Gabe's heart kicked into gear, his body reacting before his brain had analyzed the threat. Car bombs, roadside bombs, suspect packages. The memories detonated in flashes and pops.

Tillett's gloating smile. *Did what I had to anyway.*

He drew a quick, shallow breath. Rossi was saying something, a wordless rumble.

Jane touched his arm. "Gabe?"

He shook his head. "I have to . . ." *Go.* "Get out of here," he ordered. "Go out front."

Dear God, don't let her get hurt. Don't let me be too late.

He ran through the kitchen and burst out the back door, aware of Rossi's footsteps thumping behind him. Of Aidan, somewhere out front in the patrol car with Hank. Of Jane.

Mostly, though, he thought about the bag with the bomb in it.

He should wait. Evacuate the area and wait. For what? There was no bomb squad on this island, no explosives expert at the front of the column with a mine detector. He didn't know how much time he had.

He reached the plastic storage bin. Threw open the lid.

Yep, there it was, a scuffed-up black gym bag with . . . He eased open the zipper. The way Tillett had handled the bag, he didn't expect it to blow.

Clothes. He tossed them aside.

And stared, bewildered, at the tightly wrapped brick inside. Plastic explosives? But no timer, no wires, no detonator, no tape.

Rossi came up behind him, saw the shrink-wrapped brick, and grunted in satisfaction. "We've got the bastard now. There's enough there to put him away for a long, long time."

"What is it? C4? Semtex?" Gabe asked.

"I need to do a field test to be sure." Rossi smiled. "But my money's on cocaine."

Twenty-four

"YOU WANT A brownie to take home today, Leroy?" Jane asked.

Leroy smiled shyly, tucking his paper under his arm. "Not tonight, thanks, Janey. I got some pals coming over. Going to have some beers, play some cards, and tell some lies."

"Is that right?" She was pleased that the widower was making friends, making changes in his routine. Moving on. There was a lesson there somewhere. She picked up his empty cup. "Well, you all have a good time."

"Will do." Leroy hesitated. "You and your little boy doing all right?"

The island grapevine at work again.

She smiled, touched by his concern. "We're fine," she assured him. "Thanks for asking."

They would be fine, she told herself firmly. If she repeated the words often enough, maybe they'd come true.

She had said them over and over. To Lauren and Meg when they called last night. To Cynthie Lodge, who dropped off fried chicken, and Tess Fletcher, who delivered lasagna.

To Marta Lopez, who brought enchiladas for dinner. It was unexpectedly nice to have her friends and neighbors turn the tables, to realize that even when she wasn't feeding them, they cared enough to provide for her.

Before she left, Marta enveloped Jane in a long, warm, perfume-scented hug. *Her father's girlfriend.* Cradled against Marta's soft, solid body, Jane felt the shell holding her together start to crack. Tears pricked her eyes. When was the last time she'd been hugged by an adult woman like that? Like a mother.

"Sorry," she apologized, pulling away. "I don't know what's wrong with me."

Marta patted her cheek. "You've had quite a day. You can stand a little coddling."

Jane nodded. Aidan needed coddling, too.

That night, she sat for a long time on the side of his bed. rubbing his back, breathing in his salty-sweet little-boy smell.

Aidan turned his head restlessly on the pillow. "Where's Gabe? I wanted him to read me a story."

Jane swallowed the lump in her throat. "He had to take care of Lucky," she answered, smoothing the fine, straight hair from her son's forehead. "We'll see him tomorrow."

She hoped.

Something was bothering Gabe. She could see it in the shadow of his eyes, in the flatness of his mouth. Last night, focused on Aidan, she hadn't had time to get to the bottom of whatever it was.

But she would find the time and the courage today.

If he ever came in.

He walked into the bakery right before close, and her heart lurched, the surge of love and lust and relief almost making her dizzy.

"Hi," she said. *Not a great opening.* She should have kissed him. "I missed you last night."

His face stayed somber. "I thought you and Aidan could use some time alone."

Oh. Well, that was considerate. Wasn't that what she kept telling him? She needed more space. More time.

Was that what was bothering him?

"Aidan missed you, too," she said.

"I brought him something. I thought maybe he could use . . ."

Love, she thought. *Security. Therapy. A father.*

"A distraction," Gabe finished. He held up a bag from the Treasure Chest, the island gift shop. "It's the new Lego Avengers set."

That would work, too. "He'll love it," Jane said. "But you don't need to buy him things."

He glanced toward the corner, looking for Aidan the way Aidan had watched for him last night, the gesture so natural, so automatic, it stopped her heart. "Where is he?"

"I made an appointment for him with Lauren Patterson after school today. The counselor?"

"Good idea."

"I wondered . . ." She wiped sweaty palms on her apron. *You have plenty of courage*, Gabe had told her. *What you need is a little faith in yourself. In me.* "Do you want to go outside? To talk?"

Another of those unreadable looks. "I don't want to bother you."

She blinked. "Not *bother* me?" After everything he'd done? She thought they were past that.

Or maybe not.

Her fault. She was the one constantly setting limits on their relationship. She couldn't blame Gabe if he'd finally decided to listen to her.

"Lindsey, I'll be out front," she called to the girl behind the counter. She grabbed two bottles of water and a cupcake and carried them to one of the picnic tables.

"This looks new," Gabe said, eyeing the cupcake.

"Mocha with espresso buttercream." She waited while he tasted it. "Do you like it?"

"Mm." He swallowed, that deep appreciation in his eyes, the smile that made her feel so good about her baking and herself. "I'd have to try it five or six more times to be sure."

Her face eased. She smiled back.

"I talked to Luke last night," he said abruptly. "He said the Elizabeth City cops are looking for Tillett."

She took a deep breath. "Dad told me. He said between the likely drug charges and violating the protective order, Travis will be back in jail for a long time."

"How's Aidan?" Gabe asked.

He'll be fine.

She pleated her fingers together. "He's upset," she heard herself say. "I thought it was a good thing that Travis wasn't part of his life. I thought I was doing the right thing, shielding him."

"You're doing great. You're a great mom."

She threw him a grateful look. "Thanks. But I let him build up this picture in his head of who his father was. Seeing Travis yesterday . . . it shook him."

"A father is supposed to love you. To look out for you," Gabe murmured. "It's hard to let that go."

Understanding cracked her heart in two—for her son, for Gabe—and both halves ached. Because whatever Aidan was feeling, Gabe had lived through worse.

She reached across the table and took his hand. "Would you talk to him?"

He hesitated. "I thought you set him up with that counselor's appointment."

"I did."

"Then he doesn't need me."

But he did. They both did.

She squeezed Gabe's fingers. "You understand him. He looks up to you."

Gabe looked down at her hand covering his. "I'm not used to that."

She frowned. But whatever she might have said was

crushed by the crunch of gravel and oyster shells. Sunlight flashed off the windshield of a car turning into the bakery lot.

Her father's patrol car, with another marked vehicle behind him.

The black-and-white parked on the edge of the grass. The door swung open, and Hank got out. "We need to talk," her father said.

GABE GLANCED FROM the two patrol vehicles to Hank, in rumpled uniform and mirrored sunglasses, and Luke, pressed and serious.

There was a third guy with them, wearing a cheap suit like a cut-rate lawyer.

"This can't be good," Jane said to her father. "You never want to talk."

Hank didn't smile.

Uh-oh.

Gabe forced down his misgivings and looked at Luke. "You bringing reinforcements to buy doughnuts now?"

"This is Detective Pete Chadwick of the Elizabeth City Police Department," said his oldest friend in the world. "He'd like to talk to you."

Gabe's lungs tightened. It was as though the past ten months, the last five weeks, had never happened. It was his worst nightmare.

It was worse.

Because now he had more to lose.

He'd been waiting for this moment, for something like this, since he left the Williams County Jail, since he came to Dare Island, since Jane had looked at him yesterday with fear and doubt in her eyes. Like he was a dog that might bite. He didn't know yet what was going on. But he was pretty sure who was going to get the blame.

Jane stood. "What is it? Is it Travis?"

"In a way," Luke said.

"He's dead," Hank said. "Found shot in a burned-out car in Elizabeth City this morning."

Aw, shit.

Jane swayed slightly on her feet, locking her hands together in front of her. He moved closer, willing her his support.

"Are they sure?" she asked.

"You're not asking her to look at the body," Gabe said to Luke.

"No need," Hank said. "Whoever torched the car did a piss-poor job. Or maybe they got scared off." He shrugged. "Anyway, there was enough left to ID."

Jane sucked in a distressed breath.

Gabe's muscles bunched to defend her. But the enemy was dead.

And he could hardly slug her dad for breaking the news like an insensitive asshole.

Detective Chadwick cleared his throat. "I'm sorry for your loss. Maybe we could continue this talk at the station. Mr. Murphy?"

Gabe shoved his hands in his pockets. Out of trouble. "You bringing me in?"

"To help with the investigation," Luke said. "You want to ride in the squad car, that's your choice. Or you can drive your truck."

Gabe bared his teeth in a battle grin. "Sure I'm not a flight risk?"

"You're a moron," Hank said.

"This isn't right," Jane said.

"Easy, girl," Hank said. "You don't have to defend him. Though if you did, 'he needed killing' used to work fine with most juries around here."

Jane whirled on her father, crossing her arms. "You are not helping."

"It's okay," Gabe said.

One lesson he'd learned in the Marines was that things could blow up in your face at any time. Just when you thought you were safe—*Mission accomplished*—the situation could always go to hell.

The only thing he could do was make it easier on her. Easier on them both.

"It is not okay." Jane glared at Luke. "And you. You're his friend. You know Gabe had nothing to do with this."

Not like ten months ago, Gabe realized, his chest expanding. Or even five weeks ago.

Because Jane had his back. Because she trusted him. Believed in him.

He grinned at her.

"Nobody's saying he did," Hank said.

"Then why the police escort?" Gabe asked.

Luke threw him an amused, exasperated glance. "Why do you think? I came to hold your hand, pal."

"So I'm not a suspect," Gabe said, testing.

"Nope," Hank said. "Tillett got killed over the cocaine in his gym bag."

Chadwick shot him an annoyed look. "Any other details you want to disclose to compromise the investigation? We're still ascertaining the facts," he said to Gabe. "But given Tillett's known associates in prison . . ."

"Got mixed up with a biker gang," Hank said cheerfully.

"We're treating his murder as a gang-related crime," Chadwick finished.

Because, yeah, Gabe bet the bikers didn't appreciate being ripped off by a new member.

"I've already read your statements from yesterday," Chadwick said. "I'd like to talk to you, too, ma'am. I just have a few follow-up questions. Your testimony could be extremely helpful."

Gabe looked at Jane, standing pale and straight. She was holding it all together, dealing with it the way she dealt with everything, but the combination of a dead ex with a crime investigation was a lot for anybody to handle. "Can you give us a minute?"

Chadwick pursed his lips. "It's already been twenty-four hours since the incident. The less time that elapses, the better."

He talked like a dick.

Gabe stuck his thumbs in his belt loops. "What, are you afraid we'll get our stories mixed up? Or are you in a hurry to get home to dinner?"

The detective flushed red.

So, yeah. One—maybe both—of those things.

"I can talk with you now," Jane said clearly. "If you can pick up Aidan, Dad. Whatever will help."

God, she was something. So brave in her quiet way, so determined to do the right thing, to bear witness to her ex-husband's crime and seek justice for his killer.

He couldn't protect her from what had happened, couldn't shield her from reliving the events of yesterday afternoon with the stiff-necked detective.

But he could be there for her, as much as they would let him. And he would be there for Aidan.

"Let's go," he said. "I'll follow you in my truck."

JANE COULD FEEL the coiled tension in Gabe as he sat beside her in the outer office of the police department, waiting for Marta to finish typing their statements so they could sign them and go home. Hank had left to pick up Aidan from his counseling appointment.

Gabe's knee jiggled and was ruthlessly stilled. "I hate police stations," he muttered.

To Jane, the station was simply where her father worked. *Daddy's office.* But she understood why Gabe felt differently. She covered his rough hand with hers, stretching her fingers as wide as she could to make them fit. "It's no worse than the doctor's office."

He slanted a look at her. "Bend over, this won't hurt a bit?"

She laughed and squeezed his hand. "I meant the waiting."

"Right." He rubbed his thumb over her knuckles. "Thanks for having my six today."

"Your what?"

"My back."

"Oh. You're welcome."

"You didn't even ask me where I was last night."

She narrowed her eyes slightly. "I didn't have to. You're a good man, Gabe Murphy. You don't need an alibi."

"I threatened to kill him. You heard me."

"It's okay," she assured him. "I know you didn't mean it."

He raised his gaze from their joined hands. His eyes were dark. Opaque. Her heart jolted. "Yeah. I did."

And the threat had been eating at him ever since, she realized.

"You didn't start the trouble," she reminded him gently.

"But I was ready to finish it."

"To defend me. To protect Aidan." Tears sprang to her eyes, shocking them both. "I like to believe that I can handle things myself. That I can take care of myself. But the truth is, I couldn't make him leave. You did. I was glad you did."

He shrugged his wide shoulders. "I'm trained to fight. That doesn't make me a hero."

"It makes you mine," she said. "You're a protector. That's why you went into the Marines, I reckon. How can I love you, and not love that about you?"

His eyes met hers, stunned. Hopeful. Filled with love. His grip tightened to the point of pain. "You picked a hell of a time to mention it."

A laugh like a sob escaped her. "You might have gotten a clue. I've been throwing myself at you naked since you got here. I love you. When you walked into the bakery, I was so glad to see you. I was still scared, and worried about Aidan, but when I saw you, I wasn't alone anymore."

"You're not alone. You never have to be alone again."

She swallowed. "Neither do you."

He pulled her out of her chair and kissed her. Right in the middle of the police station, in front of Marta and whoever might happen to walk in. Not a quick punctuation peck, either, but a full-bodied, urgent, "as soon as we're out of here, I want to get naked with you" kiss. She kissed him back the same way, as if she were starving for his taste, clinging tight.

"Ask me," he said when they came up for air.

Her mind spun. Did he want her to propose? "Ask you what?"

"What I was doing last night."

"Oh." Okay. "What were you doing last night?"

He smiled down at her. "I bought the house."

"What house?" Marta asked. "Here, sign these."

"Three bedrooms. Lots of potential." Gabe looked at Jane. "I hope you like it."

She smiled back, happiness bubbling inside her. "Are you living there?"

"I will be."

"Then I love it," she said and kissed him again.

"Mom? Hey, Mom." Aidan came through the door, her father behind him. "Hey, Gabe. What are you doing?"

"Kissing," Marta said.

Jane blushed, turning in the circle of Gabe's arms.

"Are you okay with that?" Gabe asked seriously. Like it was a real question, like what Aidan felt mattered.

If Jane hadn't realized she loved him before, she would have known it then.

"Yeah. Whatever." Aidan's shrug could not disguise his pleasure. "Cool."

"Nobody asked what I think," Hank said.

Jane smiled. "I don't have to ask, Dad."

He grinned back at her. "Hell, I know that. It's about time you realized it."

"So, what happens now?" Marta asked.

Gabe looked at Jane. "That's up to Jane," he said.

Her heart swelled and soared.

After Travis, she had thought of being with someone in

terms of what she would be giving up, all the ways she could be less instead of the ways she could be more. More trusting. More loving. More loved.

She looked around at her family and took Gabe's hand. "Let's go home."

Epilogue

MEG FLETCHER'S WEDDING to Sam Grady had all the ingredients of a perfect ceremony. Like a good cake, rich and sweet, seasoned with tears and tenderness, leavened with laughter.

Jane, sitting with Gabe and Aidan at a pew in the back, reckoned Meg had never looked more beautiful. Her shimmering mermaid gown skimmed over the gentle curve of her pregnancy. She floated down the aisle on her father's arm toward Sam, white-faced with emotion at the front of the church. The Fletchers stood with him, shoulder to shoulder, in an impressive display of male solidarity: her brothers, steady Matt and warrior Luke, and teenage Josh with his lightning grin.

Tom kissed his daughter and clasped Sam's hand. The congregation rustled and sighed. Clearing his throat noisily, Tom joined Tess in the front row. Forty years, they'd been married. A long time. Forever, it seemed.

Jane had to swallow a lump in her own throat. The certainty on Meg's face, the stunned joy on Sam's, the way their parents leaned into each other . . .

She blinked hard, gripping the seat in front of her.

A large, warm hand covered hers. *Gabe.*

She turned her palm, linking her fingers with his. Lifting their joined hands to his lips, he pressed a kiss to her knuckles.

Her eyes filled. Her heart swelled, full of love and hope.

But all too soon, it was time for her to slip away and direct the caterers.

Usually Jane closed the bakery on Sunday afternoons. But the change in wedding date had left Meg and Sam without a venue. With a suddenly smaller guest list, Meg had declared that the bakery's intimate setting would be perfect for their reception.

Jane was happy to be useful. She honestly didn't even mind leaving the ceremony a few minutes early. It was what she was good at, what she enjoyed, feeding and taking care of people. Somebody needed to be on hand to check and re-check every detail before the guests arrived from church. So many little things could go wrong with a wedding.

Jane smiled. But sometimes everything went exactly right.

With the right person.

When she arrived at the bakery, she did a slow survey of the dining room. The tabletops were transformed with linens and flowers. Rows of stemware, borrowed from the Fish House for the occasion, gleamed behind the makeshift bar.

She popped her head into the kitchen for a word with Rudy, checking on the progress of the hot hors d'oeuvres, before she stepped through the sliding doors to the screened enclosure.

The patio floor had been cleared for dancing. Strands of white firefly lights wrapped the supports and twinkled from the rafters. High-top tables in the corners were decorated with glass hurricane lamps filled with candles and calla lilies.

There had been some anxious moments in the past few days, when an early summer storm threatened travel and knocked out power to the island. But at the last moment, the storm had veered north and east and out to sea.

Jane looked up at the sky, where high clouds billowed

before the wind like fresh laundry, and drew a deep breath of salt air and satisfaction.

"Looking good," Gabe drawled behind her.

Her heart gave a little hop.

He stood in the open sliding door, his white collar in starched contrast to his freshly shaved jaw, his broad shoulders stretching the seams of a navy blazer. A rush of love for him swept over her in a wave, making it hard to breathe.

"Thanks." She smoothed a hand over the cake table, displacing a scattering of pale rose petals. "The cake is the most photographed part of any wedding. After the bride, of course."

Gabe grinned. "I meant you."

"Oh." Happiness rose inside her in giddy bubbles, as if she'd been into the champagne already. She stepped forward to kiss him lightly, conscious of the caterers in the other room, the guests expected any minute. "Where is everybody?"

He released her slowly, thrusting his hands into his pockets. "Stuck taking pictures."

She glanced over his shoulder. "Aidan?"

Her son was usually found at Gabe's heels these days. Jane had been determined to take things slowly, to respect Aidan's loyalties, like the books said. She had braced herself to deal with all kinds of adjustment problems that Aidan didn't seem to be having.

Maybe her son hadn't read the same books. Maybe, as Lauren suggested, Aidan's age made him more open to change.

And maybe it was simply that her son loved Gabe and knew Gabe loved him in return.

The thought curled snugly around Jane's heart, warming her from the inside out.

"Your dad's bringing him with Marta," Gabe said. "I came ahead to see if you needed anything."

Because he was looking out for her. The way he always did. The way he always would. The glow in her chest grew heavy and golden.

"I'm fine," she said. "I've got everything I need already."

"Enough ice?"

She grinned, twining her arms around his neck, giving his words back to him. "I meant you."

That earned her another, longer kiss.

"Jane." He drew back, his gaze searching.

"Mm?" He felt so good, so warm and strong against her.

He opened his mouth as if he were about to say something. Shook his head as if he'd changed his mind. "Nice wedding."

She tilted her head. "Yes. Yes, it was."

"The thing is . . . It got me thinking. Maybe this isn't the right time." He expelled his breath. "Hell, I know it isn't. This is Meg's day, Meg and Sam's. And I promised you I wouldn't rush things. I was going to keep my mouth shut. But seeing everybody together like that—Luke with his family, you know, and you with yours—"

She took his face in her hands. "Yes," she interrupted.

A smile touched his lips, at odds with the dark, intent expression of his eyes. "You don't know what I'm going to say."

She smiled back, loving him. "It doesn't matter. The answer's the same."

"This matters. What the Fletchers have . . . What we've got, you and me . . . I don't have the right words, but that's what I want. What I've wanted all my life, feels like."

"Someone to be there for you," she said softly.

"Yeah. Somebody to count on. Something to believe in. Not just you giving that to me, but me being that for you and Aidan."

Her heart thumped. She met his gaze, finding her courage in his eyes. "That's what I want, too." With confidence in herself, with faith in him, she could say the words. "I love you, Gabe."

"I love you, Jane. I can't tell you how much. You make me be a better man, the man I want to be. Luke and his folks . . . They're the reason I came here. But you are why I stayed."

She laid her head against his chest, against his heart. "Stay always," she whispered.

His arms tightened around her. "That's the plan."

It was everything she'd ever dreamed of and more.

Someone to care for who would care for her right back. Someone she could trust with her fears and her dreams, her life and her son.

Someone to believe in.

Forever.